HOPE *makes* LOVE

HOPE *makes* LOVE

TREVOR COLE

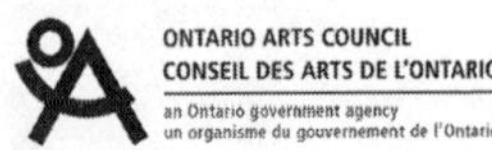

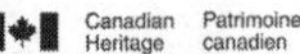

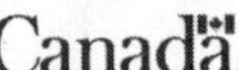

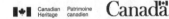

The publisher gratefully acknowledges the support of the Canada Council for the Arts and the Ontario Arts Council for its publishing program. We acknowledge the financial support of the Government of Canada through the Canada Book Fund (CBF) for our publishing activities, and the Government of Ontario through the Ontario Media Development Corporation, an agency of the Ontario Ministry of Culture, and the Ontario Book Publishing Tax Credit Program.

LIBRARY AND ARCHIVES CANADA CATALOGUING IN PUBLICATION

Cole, Trevor, 1960–, author
Hope makes love / Trevor Cole.

Issued in print and electronic formats.
ISBN 978-1-77086-456-6 (bound). — ISBN 978-1-77086-457-3 (html)

I. Title.

PS8605.O44H66 2015 C813'.6 C2015-904657-2
C2015-904658-0

Cover art and design: Alessandra Ferreri & angeljohnguerra.com
Interior text design: Tannice Goddard, Soul Oasis Networking
Printer: Friesens

Printed and bound in Canada.

The interior of this book is printed on 100% post-consumer waste recycled paper.

CORMORANT BOOKS INC.
10 ST. MARY STREET, SUITE 615, TORONTO, ONTARIO, M4Y 1P9
www.cormorantbooks.com

For S.

Monday, April 13

THERE ARE THREE STAGES to a decision. As far as the brain is concerned.

In Stage 1 you examine the available options, set them out before you like an array of apples, evaluate their hue, the waxy shine of their skin, press them to see which of the apples are fresh, and choose the one you prefer.

In Stage 2 you select and execute an action. You might pick up the chosen apple and bite into it. But Stage 2 is also about how this will be done. Motivation comes into play here, the intensity of your emotional response to that option, your anticipation of the outcome. How hungry are you? What have you heard about apples like this? How much do you crave the taste of this particular apple? What fears about the apple play at the back of your mind? Perhaps someone has put a pin in the apple you chose. Or maybe it's poisoned. Maybe you'll die.

And as you reach for the apple, as you lift it to your mouth, you must work to suppress any actions that conflict. Any hesitation, any tremble of limb, any urge to throw the apple away before you taste it. Before it's too late.

Finally, in Stage 3 you evaluate the outcome of the action. The brain wants to learn. The brain needs to know what comes of this choice. Were you right to select this apple? Was its taste all you'd hoped for, or everything you'd feared? Should you risk eating such an apple again?

And what if the apple is a man?

At each stage, various parts of the brain have jobs to do. The parietal cortex weighs the probabilities; the anterior cingulate cortex processes your uncertainties. The left middle and inferior frontal gyri bring reasoning to bear on the matter of which apple to bite, or whether to bite it at all. Maybe one of the apples reminds you of someone. Maybe, a few weeks ago, he picked up an apple just like this one, and pared away its bright skin, and sliced it and baked it in a blanket of pastry for you, as an act of love. The two tiny nuclei accumbens, deep in the brain's limbic system, will work to determine what the memory means to you. Whether it pleases you to select this apple over any other. Whether it pleases you to bring it to your mouth to taste. Whether it pleases you to think of this man.

This is what you have to decide now, Hope. This first thing, first. And then each new thing after that.

I TRY TO IMAGINE what someone else might do, someone much better equipped. Someone whose brain has at least one or two useful experiences to draw upon for comparison's sake. The woman across from me now on the subway, in skinny jeans and a lace jacket that displays a small, pale fillet of belly. I want to go close to her, tell her about Adnan, describe what he is, what he said, what he did, and ask what she would do.

She would probably ask me what I'm feeling, and I would have to tell her, No, let me describe it to you again. Let me take you to the moment. Let me make it live for you, here, and let me borrow what you feel. I trust that more.

There are certainties in my life, things already determined, and I am better with those. The route I take to work. The diplomas on my wall. The number of times each week I eat fish.

My mother is a certainty. I can count on the watercolour pain in her voice when she calls to say she hasn't heard from me in months.

The precarious laughter as she comes from the kitchen, when I finally do appear on her doorstep, the laughter that says I might be a chickadee that's alighted unexpectedly on her thumb.

Lesley is a certainty. She is always there, my friend and housemate, my guard dog at the door. After one of those nights when a cavity of sleeplessness has opened in the middle darkness and pushed oblivion to the edges so that I don't go under until the sun has nearly started to rise, I can count on her. She will wake me when I miss my alarm, gently but firmly. Ruthlessly. She will be undeterred by my whimpered pleas.

"You can't miss work, Hope. You can't give in."

And my memories are certainties. I can count on them most of all. And when I imagine something, or someone, new entering my life, I think that what I dread most is the possibility of creating more memories. More images that will not leave me. I already have plenty of those.

ZB Transcript 1

OKAY, HERE WE GO, Marcie. Here we go, here we go, here we go!

What the hell?

Sorry, Marcie, I'm driving while I'm doing this. You know how I hate planes! So, yeah. That was a groundhog or some stupid thing. Important word being *was*.

Anyway! Thanks for setting up this recorder-thing for me. I guess I'll just start with my name. Make this official. Here I am, Zep Baker. And it's April something, I dunno ... It's Tuesday, I know that! And I'm driving through ... Fuck, where am I? ... Orangeburg, yeah ... driving through Orangeburg on the 26 on my way up to Toronto of all places *what the hell*?

Jesus Christ there's a lot of groundhogs around here. Is that a South Carolina thing or what? Better not be any cops watching me or they'll think I'm drunk the way I'm swerving all over the goddamn place.

Hah! At 10:25 a.m., not likely. Right?

Anyway, you just keep transcribing, Marcie. Like we agreed. I'll keep talking and you keep typing and maybe we'll have something, okay? I dunno what, but you can sell anything these days, right? Stay positive!

Maybe I'll just start over. Here we go!

OKAY THIS IS ME, Zep Baker. Horrace Zep Baker. Called Zep all my life, since I was fifteen anyway, 'cause Horrace is a shit name and I love Led Zeppelin. Jimmy Page! Anyway, uh, former third baseman for the Cleveland Indians and the Montreal Expos and the Minnesota Twins and the Toronto Blue Jays and sundry — that's a word, right, Marcie? Sundry? — uh, sundry minor league affiliates. Former 1998 minor league all-star of the International League. Former husband of Emily Baker, now going by her single name, Emily Good. Current father of Patricia Baker — I call her "Pebbles" — thirteen-year-old piece of pure sunshine.

So, I was thinking ... you know, about Emily, my ex-wife? I mean, that's what this is all about. Can't stop thinking about her. Not since she left me a year and a half ago. And it doesn't matter how many girls I've been with since then *and there have been a lot*. Sorry, Marcie! You know me too well, baby.

Anyway, uh, keeping this professional, I was thinking about Emily, and thinking about how nothing's been the same since she left me. And I was thinking about what I needed, you know, to be happy and ... and how a man isn't complete without a woman in his life, a woman he loves, who loves him and ... Hold up.

What the fuck is going on here?

Sorry, Marcie. Got some goddamn construction going on or something. They want me to — Jesus Christ. No, sir! *No, sir*! I am not driving this — Excuse me! You see this car? It's a Maserati Ghibli, my friend. You are not making me drive a fucking Maserati Ghibli on some *goddamn dirt road in the* [unintelligible]

SORRY, MARCIE. HAD A SLIGHT detour there. I am now on Route 601 heading toward Camden and if I get lost just look for the buzzards, I guess. That's what my father used to say. "If you don't hear from me just look for the buzzards." Like we were ever gonna look for that son of a bitch. Anyway. That's not what this is all about that's a whole other story!

This is about me and my wife, my ex-wife Emily, and I had this idea and that's a cop ... just gonna check here ... yeah we're safe, sixty's okay, right? Sixty is a-okay. Nobody's gonna pull over a Maserati Ghibli doing sixty unless they got a real bug up their ass about something. Though anything's possible, I suppose.

I dunno, fuck, I'm startin' to have second thoughts about this whole driving-north thing. Canada seems like a long ways away.

Emily! Emily is what I'm talking about.

Okay, so, I had this idea. See, life is fine right now, right? Nothing wrong with it. Got the nice house in Tampa, got that ace pool, decent neighbours who don't swim in it when I'm gone. Got my car wash chain. Got my body wash project. Hey, Marcie! Did I tell you I got a call from Lino? Yeah, he called me yesterday. He said he's got a guy in for a million-two, maybe even a million-five. The guy totally bought the whole Stay Clean concept. You know, like how car wax helps keep the dirt off, but for skin.

We just have to get the formula right. 'Cause on skin, you don't want it to be, like, waxy. So anyway, Lino's just gotta work out the details, but that's a go. That's a Golden Go, baby!

So, yeah, everything's good ... but, I dunno. Shit still feels empty or something. It's hard to ... see, I look back on when

Emily and I were together, and we had Pebbles, and we were a family, and ... I mean, my career wasn't going so hot then. Got suspended and all that bullshit. But still, we were a family. And I look back on that time, and from where I sit it just seems, you know ... better. Just seems way better. More complete in some way.

Kind of like a picture in my mind, how it's meant to be.

So, I figured, what I needed for my life to get back on the right track — you know, the "Good track" ... uh, that's a stupid pun just skip that, Marcie. Just skip all — anyway, whatever whatever. *Stay positive*!

Take a sip of water.

What I need is to, just, get back with Emily. That's what I need. Okay? Bam. That's it.

So, how does that happen? Right? That's the question you're asking, isn't it, Marcie? I know it! You're saying, uh, Zep, she kicked you out. You did some stupid shit. You think she's going to take you back? I can see you with your hands on your hips. Your stern face on. I see you, Marcie!

So, you're right. She's not going to just take me back like everything's normal. No way! But what I'm thinking is, what if ... okay? Ready?

What if ... she falls in love with me again?

Right?

And so ... how does that happen? That's the question. How does Emily Good fall back in love with Zep Baker? Like, the husband she got rid of, and yelled at, and called a scumbag, a year and a half ago? 'Cause, right now, she kinda fucking hates me. So how does love come into it? I'll tell you how.

Mind control.

Don't laugh now, Marcie. I know you think I'm full of shit. But this is science. This is science just as much as my body wash is science. Totally. Hitler did it. Okay? All those Third Reich fuckers. And we know a lot more about the brain now than they — Look, I'm not saying they were right to do it. Don't get me wrong, those guys were ass-wipes. I'm not saying I'm going to do any Nazi shit. Fuck. Marcie, maybe just cut this whole Hitler Nazi part. This is totally going to give people the wrong idea. I'm not some goddamn Nazi! I'm just saying —

Mother*fucker*!

Okay, look. Let's get this straight. Nazis are bad. Okay? Hitler was bad. Goebles or Gerbles or whatever his name was — bad, bad, bad. I'm not doing any of that crap. Mind control is not a, you know, *per se* Nazi thing.

The CIA! They're American and they did it. All right? Brain-controlled Marilyn Monroe or something.

And anyway, all that stuff was done for evil reasons, by bad people. So automatically it's not the same, because I'm doing this for love, Marcie. All right? I'm a good father, and I can be a good husband. And I love Emily. And she's going to love me. And I'm going to Make. It. Happen. That is a Golden Go, my friend.

And I'm not doing it alone, by the way. I know someone who's going to help me. Her name is Hope something. Hope ... last name starts with an R. She's at the university up in Toronto. That's why I'm driving up there. Hey, Marcie, maybe you could find her name for me. And let her know I'm coming. Okay, sweetheart? I figured I'd surprise her but maybe that's stupid. Like, who knows, maybe university people travel or something. Go on sabbaticals. And it's been a few years. Maybe she's not even there and here I am driving up the goddamn 601 in the middle of ...

What the fuck is *this*? Fucking detour on the detour?

Hey! No! You can't — Excuse me! *Excuse me*!

[Unintelligible]

Tuesday, April 14

SOMEONE NAMED MARCIE HERNÁNDEZ called me this afternoon. She seemed a little harried and said she'd had a difficult time finding me. She'd phoned around several universities and departments and I gather the problem was that I'm not registered as faculty here yet. Post-doc fellows are well down the list of administrative priorities.

She said Zep Baker is driving up to see me and mentioned something about "mind control." I have no idea what she's talking about.

I remember Zep Baker, though. He's a baseball player I interviewed eight years ago, during my first year of graduate work, for a study on the effects of performance enhancing drugs on brain chemistry. Zep had been suspended in 2006 for using the anabolic steroid Methyldienolone, and then a year later he was traded to the Blue Jays for their minor leagues and he ended up in Toronto for about six weeks. I suppose as an injury fill-in.

Zep was thirty-four then, I think. His career was almost over. The Players Association didn't want me to talk to him, and the team wasn't very helpful, so I contacted him through his agent. And when I met him in the underground parking lot after the game he seemed like a golden retriever. Eager and rambunctious and utterly unselfconscious. A bit out of control.

Immediately after meeting me he tried to pick me up. He said he thought I was "hot" and we should go out, but when I didn't react well to that he was very apologetic, almost ashamed. It seemed sincere. For the rest of the time we were together, two interviews over the next two days, things were a little easier. Perhaps he could tell I was skittish. He became quite subdued. Which was good because there was so much of him, just so much Zep Baker, when we were in the same room, I couldn't have handled it otherwise.

The Hernández woman asked for directions she could pass on to Zep, to let him find me. When I didn't answer right away she asked again, as if I hadn't heard. It was necessary to say something. I could sense her fingers poised above her keyboard, and my silence was not definitive. I had to make a sound that declared who I was now. If I gave her what she wanted, I was someone who could face uncertainty. If I said no, I was still the paling coward I was before. Whatever the truth, I had to declare. Silence was an abdication of accountability.

I told her she could give Zep my phone number. I would talk to him, and then I would see. So, not a total failure of resolve. Not quite.

Later, when I told Lesley about Zep, she naturally began establishing parameters. If there is to be a meeting it has to be in a public place. And in the daytime. And she wants to be there at the start, she said, so that he knows I have a posse behind me. The truth, of course, is that she wants me to know.

I feel guilty that I haven't told her everything that happened with Adnan. But I think I can't bear her amazement on top of my own.

ZB Transcript 2

CHANGE OF PLANS, MARCIE. Fuck this whole driving thing, it was a stupid idea. There's construction everywhere! The way it was going I figured out it was gonna take me like two days to get up to Canada and that's too long. I wanna get on this. Good ideas don't wait! So what I'm doing is I'm flying out of Charlotte. Yeah, fuck it. Flying, whatever. I can fly. What am I, a pussy?

I'm at the airport now, just walking to the check-in. It's not ideal. I'm gonna have to leave the car here a couple of weeks. Probably cost me an arm with the parking here and the ticket and the car rental up there, but I figure it's all worth it. Investment in happiness or, I dunno ... yeah. That's what it is. Investment in happiness! Sometimes I say the right thing and I don't even know it. Or I question it or something. What the hell is that? Fucking doubting myself. Probably why I never hit .300 in the majors. So stupid!

Investment in happiness. Bam. Done.

Hey, Marcie, could you look into that for me? The car rental, I mean. Get me something nicer this time, would you? Nothing too small. And no Chevys, okay? Jesus, I hate Chevys. I'm trying to live a first-class life here!

I got your email, by the way. Thanks for finding Hope for me. Hope Royple? Is that how you pronounce it? Reo-pe-lay? Jesus Christ, I should remember. But maybe I should just be happy she didn't get married, huh? Never would've found her then. So anyway, thanks for finding her and calling her. I probably don't say thanks enough to you, Marcie. Emily used to say I wasn't appreciative enough. I ever tell you that? I was too critical, she said. Always picking everything apart, making it out worse than it was. Which, maybe she was right.

I think about that ... about how, you know, if I was a bit less critical of stuff like her cooking or the way she dressed Pebbles, or maybe if I'd said thank you a bit more, maybe we'd still be together. I know it wasn't the biggest thing but everything helps, right? Positive energy.

It's not like I'm perfect. That's what she'd say to me. "It's not like you're perfect."

I know I'm not.

Mind control, right? Gotta practise it on myself, heh. *Zzzzzt!*

— *Stop being so critical.* Heh. Maybe I can get Hope Royo — Jeez I should figure out ... Hey, sir? Excuse me. *Sir?* Shit.

Ma'am? Sorry, excuse me. Okay, see this name here? How would you say that? Not Hope. Right here. R-I-O-P-E-L-L-E. Is that French? How do you ...

[Woman's voice. Unintelligible.]

Okay, it's Ree-yo-pell, Marcie. REE-yo-pell.

I hope that lady knows what she's talking about.

Wednesday, April 15 (morning)

IT WAS CHILLY THIS MORNING, steam clouding out of the subway grates, smokers standing tight, arms pressed to their sides. I like it when it stays cold in the spring. It means delaying that time when others start looking at my clothes with questions in their eyes. July and August are the worst, the months when I most wish I was living somewhere Nordic, and empty. The frowns, the shakes of the head, the little coughs of exasperation when it's thirty-four degrees and they can't see my skin. "Aren't you hot?" I tell them I've had melanoma. Of course, it isn't true, but shame is an effective silencer.

Walking along Bloor this morning, on my way to the subway, a cold breeze rode up the back of my neck, and then a hand of wind began to push on my shoulder blades. I like that hand. It makes me think of my father, hurrying me home from kindergarten. I was a dawdler, finding fascination in every sidewalk crack, and he wanted to get home. To get me to move along he'd set his huge hand in the middle of my back and tell me to imagine a big wind pushing me. I'd lean back into his hand and ride it, a laughing leaf, almost running down the sidewalk. We'd get home in no time.

There are times when I look back at that rushing home and think, maybe he sensed something. Maybe he knew there was danger lurking and simply didn't realize he was pushing me toward it.

But I know he was just impatient.

When the breeze picked up for a moment this morning I heard an "Oh!" from behind and a small hat, an infant's floppy cap, came past like a tumbleweed, filled with air and rolling on its rim. Before I could react a woman rushed past me and snatched it up, then took it back to set it on the head of a little boy, perhaps a year or two old.

The boy was riding in a carrier on the back of the father. They were nine or ten paces behind me and I stopped to watch them. The mother adjusted the cap on the boy and then the boy in his seat, giving him a tug by the shoulders. She kissed his head and they started forward again. I pulled out my phone to appear preoccupied and let them come. The adults split around me and then reformed like a droplet of oil, the mother's hand sliding into the father's, the child riding his father's back and clutching at the collar of his sweater with little grub fingers, trying to pull it into his mouth. With her other hand, the one not being gripped, the woman swung a cloth purse, let it play in the folds of her long skirt. If she hadn't been held by her husband, she might have skipped, she looked that happy.

I almost followed, to see where this happiness took them. I get an urge sometimes that is so powerful.

Zep Baker called my university number last night. He left a message that I picked up when I got in this morning. Sort of breathless, saying he'd just landed and something about me being the smartest girl he'd ever met and he had this idea and he knew I could help him. It was all kind of a jumble.

And then around ten this morning he called and said, "Hi, hi, it's Zep Baker, remember me?" He told me where he was staying and said he wanted to meet right away. I said no. I told him he couldn't just call and expect me to drop everything. I have a schedule. I have a full day.

He stumbled for a moment, hesitated, then said he'd flown up to see me. And I felt cruel. I felt like a horrible person. He sounded so hurt.

So I agreed to meet him for coffee at four this afternoon.

ZB Transcript 3

HEY, MARCIE. I'M IN TORONTO. Flight got in last night around eight. Jesus, I thought we'd never land. I had to fly coach 'cause there were no business class seats. Guy beside me couldn't stop burping the whole way. Could not. Stop. Burping. Like, what the fuck is that?

Anyway, I wanna say, look, I'm sorry you can't take off with Ramone next week like you wanted, but Vegas'll wait, you know? It's not like it's gonna dry up and blow away or something. Fuck, I used to wish it would. But, like, the point is, I really need you to stay there and keep things going. Keep all those assholes in line. Julio especially. And I'm gonna be sending you these voice-file things like every day, so you're gonna be busy typing. And what am I paying you, like, double for this? So, you know, you're gonna get your week, and you're gonna have a lot of extra cash to put on number 23 or whatever. So.

By the way, good call on the car. Acuras are all right. I mean, it's no Maserati but, you know, in the plus column it's no Chevy. And it's blue too — like Gators blue! I swear I saw that and I said like, Shit, where's the orange seats, dude? Go Gators! Orange and Blue! … Guy looked at me like I had fish eyes. Then I remembered I'm a long way from Tampa.

Anyway, I'm not using it right now, I'm walking. Talked to Hope this morning and she was gonna blow me off or make me wait till, like, Friday. Did you tell her what this was all about? I shoulda maybe said don't say anything. 'Cause I was thinking maybe I should ease into it or just talk science with her for a bit. You know, like molecules and frontal-cortal-whatever. She doesn't know me that well, right? And it's been like, what, eight years? Nine? Maybe it's a freaky thing to hear right away, like, bam, mind control! Let's go!

I don't wanna scare her off. This whole thing, I mean, I'm fucked without her. Nobody else is gonna …

But I guess, I dunno, she changed her mind so we're meeting, like, soon. I'm walking there now. It's a coffee place. I think … I'm not exactly sure where it is but I think I'm on the right … I should use that map thing on the phone but I hate those little appy things. My thumbs are too fuckin' big!

Wednesday, April 15 (evening)

ZEP WAS TWENTY MINUTES LATE. Which I anticipated — it's been my experience that professional athletes, even retired ones, are like someone else's small children, unpredictable and uncontrollable and you count yourself lucky if they don't swallow something they're not supposed to.

He came through the door dressed in a tight-fitting charcoal suit and found me with one glance. It was crowded at the entrance, a logjam of people waiting in line, and he moved someone out of the way — literally took a man by the shoulders and gently but firmly shifted him, smiling, in order to clear a path to come to me. His eyes were on me the whole time, as if I were a ball he was following to catch. The first words out of his mouth as he shook my hand were, "Shit, I forgot you'd be older."

Then he added, "You've totally still got it, though."

We sat. He moved around on his chair for a while as if he were uncomfortable. For one minute we chatted — "So, are you a doctor now or what? Paging Dr. Riopelle! Ha!" — then he jumped up and asked if I wanted anything. He seemed so desperate to buy me something — "Anything you want, no problem!" — I agreed to a green tea latte. He grinned as if I'd made a joke. His tanned skin crinkled around his eyes. Then he realized I was serious and got into line.

It was odd to see him there, surrounded by students, mothers, a writer or two. And what was odd wasn't just his difference, the fact that he so clearly belonged in another context — Florida, the seat of a muscle car, a field of cut grass. Of all of the people there, his presence seemed the most complete. He was not only fully a man — taller, thicker and yet better proportioned than most men you see — he seemed fully himself. Everyone else looked in some way partial. Distracted, uncaring, casually dressed, they were people who you could imagine looking much better, giving more attention, being more present, at a wedding, say, or a funeral. But the Zep Baker waiting in line for my latte seemed the entire, best Zep Baker. From this version of him, you could only imagine taking things away.

He did not stand in line long. After what might have been thirty seconds, he stepped forward and nudged the arm of someone ahead of him — it was the same man he'd shifted, as if they now had a connection. He handed the man a twenty dollar bill and, talking and smiling the whole time, pointed over to where I was sitting. Then he grinned and slapped the man on the back and returned to me.

"He's gonna bring it," Zep said. "I hate standing in lines."

At some point around then, when the conversation paused, I looked at my watch. Not because I was late for anything. I'd cleared my schedule, because I suspected that one way or another I was going to need time in the aftermath of whatever this was going to be. But it was already worse. Or just, *more* than I'd imagined. Already I was beginning to wilt under the intensity of this man's expectation. He hadn't even articulated yet what he wanted from me, but somehow I knew that it would test me. Even if it was bizarre. Even if "mind control" turned out to be as loony as it sounded. It was already testing me, just sitting there.

And I admit that perhaps I was allowing this expectation to stand in for everything else in my life that seemed about to press in on me. Maybe it was convenient. I looked at my watch.

"You don't have to go, do you?"

I hesitated. The distress in his eyes. I said, "Do you mind if we walk? I just need some —"

Immediately he was up and handing me the bag I'd draped over my chair.

As we walked out the door I said, "Your money."

He shrugged. "Whatever. I figure that guy can use it."

WE WALKED ALONG COLLEGE. It had warmed only a little since the morning. The sky was mostly grey, streaked here and there with blue as if the cloud cover had been rubbed away. I wore my usual long skirt and a jacket, but Zep seemed cold. He stuffed his hands in his pockets and looked at restaurants we passed as if he wished he could take shelter. I thought he deserved some kind of explanation.

"Are you cold?" I asked him.

"In Tampa this is bad February weather."

"I'm sorry. It's hard to explain, but sometimes I just can't be where I am."

"Hey, no problem!" he said. "I get it! Sometimes I didn't want to be in the box when it was oh and two." He looked sideways at me then with a small grin, and I thought it was because he wondered whether I'd understood what he'd said. But that wasn't it.

"I remember," he said, "back the first time we met, you didn't want to be in that parking garage."

"That was because you hit on me."

For a moment, as we walked, Zep said nothing but simply looked down at his alligator shoes, shiny black lizards, as they met the concrete. "Yeah," he said finally. "That's probably it. We got past that, though. Right?"

I was looking ahead, along the sidewalk. Two men in T-shirts were coming toward us, smoking. Because it was chilly, the T-shirts made the men anomalous.

"And then today I said ..."

It is important, always, to know who is near, who is approaching and who is leaving. And what danger they may pose. Anomalies increase the chances of danger. This is why watchful dogs will bark at people acting against the norm. *You*, the dogs say. *You do not belong.*

"And now you're a doctor, and I'm still an idiot."

"I'm not a doctor," I said. "I'm a Ph.D."

Zep seemed to consider this. The two men were only a few paces away now, and I was calculating whether it was better to move toward Zep as they passed, or toward the sidewalk's edge.

"You're still doing brain stuff, though, right?"

"Brain stuff, yes."

I moved to the edge, along the parked cars, and stopped. Made myself thin. But it seemed the men weren't focused on me. The older, more gut-endowed one, perhaps in his late fifties, his grey hair combed into strings, was looking at Zep. His eyes lingered on him for three or four seconds. It wasn't a threatening look, just inquisitive. There was nothing dangerous about these men. There usually isn't.

Finally they were gone.

Zep came over to me and watched them go. He stood close enough that I could smell the grooming product on his skin. "That happens in a few cities," he said. "I look familiar to him, but he doesn't know why. I wasn't here long enough. That's a brain thing, right?"

I stepped back, felt the breeze on my cheeks and took the opportunity to breathe. "You're probably filed in his long-term memory, but specific to a context. In a suit, you don't match the image he's stored."

Zep arched backward and a huge grin commandeered his face. "Y'see? This is why I'm here."

I WANT TO SAY THAT, when Zep Baker finally told me why he flew north to see me, I laughed or screamed and ran toward the open door of a streetcar. I want to say that I went home and told Lesley, and we drank ourselves giggly with gin. And there is no doubt that when Zep told me what he wanted to do — and, yes, when he mentioned Nazis and the CIA — my first reaction was a cinch of alarm and the mental flash of my hand on a phone.

But the more I listened to him on the College Street sidewalk, beside the little Academy of Music storefront, near Palmerston Boulevard's inviting brick mouth, the more I was able to hear past what he was saying to what he really meant. What he wanted.

He is an ex-athlete, that's the first thing. Athletes define themselves by how much of the impossible they are able to make possible. In that way, they're a little like victims, the wounded and invalid, for whom much of the possible has been taken away.

And, something I understand, they perform best outside of emotion. They learn how to detach from it in order to be productive. Like a concert pianist. Or a war veteran. For someone like that, "mind control" is nothing sinister. It's a way of life. And if you are a high performer who has lost whatever effectiveness you once had, there is no shame in saying that your problems are "all mental." That you have lost control of your mind.

As for wanting to control someone else's mind, how is what Zep wants to do any different from a coach, or a counsellor, or a hospital psychiatrist helping someone to think or feel a particular way for their own good? It's no different at all. If you are a teenager who wishes to kill herself, who has already tried, you will be counselled to think differently. You will be given drugs to make you feel differently. The person in control will have no ethical qualms because these actions will be to your benefit. And eventually, when you emerge from the stupor of self-loathing, you will be thankful. You will be grateful that, for a while, someone who knew better took control of your mind.

Zep was just trying to find a way to express that. He wants his ex-wife to feel something she doesn't feel anymore, because it will be better for him. And he believes it will be better for her, too, because he's convinced of the goodness of his heart and the rightness of his purpose. He wants me to create, in Emily's mind, the sensation of love. He worried that I wouldn't understand or want to help him. But he didn't realize how much he and I have in common.

Or why I would see this as an opportunity.

ZB Transcript 4

HEY THERE, MARCIE. It's, uh … Jesus … 10:23 in the morning and I'm in my hotel room and my head feels like a goddamn speed bag because I'm a … I'm a fucking idiot. I met up with Duke Lorden last night. 'Cause the Twins are in town playing the Jays. There's this Italian place he always goes to when he's here and he had them serving me fucking grappa. All night! That stuff's like, I dunno, really nice paint thinner. Really nice fucking solvent … I'm pretty sure I puked at some point, I'm just not sure where.

I've got the hotel sending me up some Advil with my coffee.

Uh …

Sorry, just digging some crap out of my eye there. Uh, so … got some good news. That meeting with Hope went pretty well, I think. She's gonna help me, which, you know, I wasn't sure she was going to at first. She's kind of jittery or something.

She was like that the first time we met too. I don't know if it's me or what but … probably doesn't help that I always come on to her right away. Like I said, I'm an idiot. But, what it is … I think I'm like one of those cats that like people that don't like cats, you know? Like "Stay away from me" so they're all up on your lap. She gives off this vibe … it's not an I-like-women vibe, though — that's a whole different thing. It's more of an I-don't-trust-men vibe. Like, she thinks men are maybe, whaddaya call 'em, like, shape-shifters! Right? Like that blue chick in

X-Men. Like, watch out. Be careful! Something might happen! That seems to be her general attitude. And that's more, I dunno, interesting in some way.

Maybe I'm full of shit. But the way she dresses, all these rings on her fingers, everything covered up from her neck to her ankles. And she's not even Muslim! It's like she's got armour on. Like she's going into battle or some goddamn thing. And her back is like, straight. Just like a fuckin' brick wall. And she's serious as anything. It's like I gotta pull a tuba outta my ass to get her to smile.

She's nice, though. She's cool. And fucking smart, like I remembered. And she's going to help me, so, she's ace in my book.

Hold on, that's the door.

HA! ALMOST FORGOT TO PUT on pants. Room service guy wouldn't've liked that too much. Or maybe he would've. Never know these days.

Shit, these are not the right Advil. I wanted the gel kind.

Coffee's okay, though ... Not bad. Not as good as yours, though, Marcie. You're still the queen. The South Florida Car Wash Queen of Coffee, that's you.

Oh, and it was the bathroom, apparently. That I puked in. So it could've been worse. They're gonna have to deal with it though, I'm not touching it.

Oh, man, Duke had me goin' last night. Holy shit. He started getting on me about that time we were playing in Vegas. This was like twelve years ago, after the Padres cut me and Emily was not happy. Oh, man, she did not want to be in Vegas again. Or she did not want *me* to be in Vegas, 'cause she knew what it was like the first time. And this time she had Pebbles.

Pebbles was just ... I think a year and a half old. So Emily was stuck at home with her and, I dunno, a few months before, back in spring training, Pebs had got that damn Japanese disease — you know, that Kawasaki disease. Who knows how the fuck she got it. And it would've been nothing if we'd got on it fast. But, you know, they were trimming rosters and I was tryin' not to get cut, right?

So, Emily kept saying, Zep, she's sick! and I'm like, What is it? and she's saying she's got a fever and her feet are red and her tongue's swollen. And I'm like, fuck, I dunno! I'm no doctor. Her feet are red, is that bad? I'm hitting a buck-ninety here! I'm trying to not to get my ass sent down. Call your mom! Right?

I mean, she shoulda just taken her to the doctor. I'm not blaming her, but that's what should've happened. I blame myself for not being focused and saying, you know, Em! Take her to the goddamn hospital. Take a cab and I'll meet you there! But I didn't. So, I wear that. You know? I wear that.

We did take her, but not till a few days later when she got this bad rash. And then the doctors were saying she might have heart trouble. From now on. Like the rest of her life. 'Cause of the delay, right? 'Cause of the delay ...

Wouldn't have been a problem if we'd got her in there sooner.

But, so, Duke. So, Duke's on me about my three-error game. This is a few months later and we're in Vegas now. And I mean, that Vegas field was shit. It was already so fucking dry the grounds crew just gave up practically. Anything hit on the ground to me, I didn't know where the fuck it was going. And he knew it. Everyone knew it. I mean, I had like nineteen errors that season. But this one game. This one game.

Duke's on me. Last night, he's on me. "Kryptonite!" he says. "You were Superman, and that ball was Kryptonite, and it just fucking zapped you. Every ball comin' to you just zapped you! Drained all your superpowers." Not that I had any to begin with. "You could see the fear in your eyes!" he says. He's laughing so much he's choking. "Bring another grappa for Superman!" he says.

And, you know, I never told him that Em and I had been up all night and into that morning with Pebbles, and Em was in this crazy state. Like, eagle-eyed. 'Cause now we're watching, right? And Pebbles was sweating, she'd been sweating all night and it was weird. So we called the hospital and they said monitor her. Right? Monitor her. If her lips get turning blue, bring her in. 'Cause it means her heart's not working.

So we're just watching. All night. And you kind of go crazy, right? You forget what a kid's lips are supposed to look like. So you're like, fuck, shine a light on her! Get a light! And she's crying, and you're just, are they blue? Is that blue? Are they fucking blue enough?

And we did take her in, even though her lips never really got too blue. But Em was just like, that's it. She said she'd take her and I should've let her go, because I really needed some kind of sleep. But I went too. And we were there till ten in the morning, and then I went, you know, to the stadium ... and that was my three-error game.

"Bring another grappa for Superman," he says. Yeah, I lapped that shit up.

So, here's the plan, Marcie. Hope and I are gonna meet later and talk about strategy. Probably go to dinner someplace. I have to be careful. I don't want to, like, piss her off. So, it's like, wherever she wants to go. You always say I push too hard and I don't! I just get pumped. But this time, I know, I have to be cool. It's not a problem. I sure as hell know I'm not gonna be drinking.

And Hope and I have to talk more about Emily. I haven't said too much about her living in Buffalo now with her folks and I'm hoping I can get Hope to go with me. I don't want to count on that. But I'm thinking everything's going to work better if she's with me, or at least around somewhere. Might be hard with her job, but I'm hoping. Gotta stay positive, right?

Thursday, April 16

LESLEY WANTS TO KNOW what I'm doing.

Adnan called while I was out this evening. I gave him only our landline number so Lesley could be a filter. When she answered he told her that he hadn't heard from me in two weeks. Actually, it's been longer — nearly three weeks, in fact. Was this a mistake on his part, or denial? Would admitting that it was three weeks have been too great an indignity? Can he block this fact from his awareness?

That would be something to admire.

"What are you doing, Hope?" she asked. I would like to know as well.

She understands that Adnan and I have been together. I revealed this to her two mornings after the event, when she was making us oatmeal. It's not a mystery to me why I chose this moment. Lesley was standing at the stove, and therefore facing away from me. I have no interest in seeing someone's pupils dilate when I tell them something that stimulates a flood of norepinephrine. It's enough that I have to listen to them struggle to maintain their composure and keep the surprise or delight or alarm out of their voice. All of that unbridled concern.

Lesley was very good. She didn't throw herself splat against the wall with the shock. The hand stirring the oatmeal paused only the tiniest degree.

But I have not told her everything. Because I do not know what I am doing.

I asked if he'd sounded angry.

"No, not angry. I would say concerned." She had tea in her hands, and she took a judicious sip. A conversation with Lesley can be an almost musical experience. She understands about pacing. She lets in air between the words. And even so, I rarely feel managed when I talk to her, or *helped.* Most conversations with Lesley don't feel like so many I've had, the ones like doctors' examinations, with words used like palpating hands, pressing here or there to locate the discomfort.

"He seems to really care about you."

Lesley has met Adnan twice. Like me. The first time was at a dinner party hosted by our friends John and Holly Ballinger, which Adnan catered. We both met him that night, although I suspect if Adnan were asked he would not remember Lesley was there. He seemed focused on me the entire night. And I was surprised that it didn't bother me. At one point, Holly began telling her story about interviewing the one-armed Afghani activist, and while everyone was distracted, Adnan approached my seat at the corner of the table closest to the kitchen. I noticed him just before he arrived, his black hair tied back, his face so serious. He laid an amuse-bouche in front of me and bent to my ear. "That is scallop tartar topped with candied bacon and some dust of pepper and rosemary." Before I could respond he slipped back into the kitchen, wiping his hands on a cloth draped from his shoulder.

For the main course, my plate had a design of herb-oil swirls around the rim that was far more elaborate than any other. "Oh, that's pretty," Barb Fitler said, looking at my plate. For dessert, I got two extra chocolate straws.

The second time Lesley, and I, met Adnan, we were at an outdoor market. She noticed him loading a van with crates of red onions and lettuce. At the time I was somewhere else, probably among the jars of extra-sweet and expensive maple syrup I have never had the gall to buy. When we met at the coffee stall she mentioned she'd seen him. “That caterer,” she called him. I shrugged. And I meant that shrug. And then, when I was looking at a display of butter tarts, he was there, his arm against my shoulder.

“Do not buy those,” he said. Quietly, so the vendor wouldn’t hear. “The pastry is no good, the wrong texture. And the filling is too runny.”

“Isn’t it supposed to be runny?”

“I can make you some better.” His mouth showed no trace of a smile.

“That’s all right, thank you.”

“Look, I show you.” He paid $3.50 for a tart as I started to move away, into the flow of people, and he caught up to me between the rows. He had the tart pinned to its white napkin with his thumb and motioned for me to come to the side.

“Please.”

He broke the tart in two. The filling, released, oozed over the napkin and his hand toward the floor.

“Look how it tears,” he said, pulling at the crust like a tailor examining fabric. “This is *puff* pastry.” He dabbed a calloused finger in the filling. “And this is soup. It’s an insult.” He crumpled the works, tart and napkin, into a ball and tossed it into a metal bin, then licked his fingers clean.

“Does it at least taste good?”

“No.” He wiped his hand on the side of his workman’s pants, that an electrician might wear, and looked from my eyes to the floor. He seemed almost in pain.

I did not, in that moment, know where to move. We were moored next to a display of artisanal soaps. My hand knocked over a pyramid of oatmeal bars, and this was all that allowed me to breathe. When I had restored the pyramid, he was two tables away, staring at milk-glass jewellery that could not possibly have interested him. For some reason, I found this heartbreaking.

Lesley came up to me then. She was going to show off the loaf of nut bread she'd bought, but she saw where I was looking.

"Oh."

OUTSIDE, WE STOOD SQUINTING in sunshine. Lesley had gone. A handful of shouting children raced around a sandy play area near us as their mothers attempted conversation. Adnan kept rubbing his large hand against his hip. When I reached out he let me take it. Patches of stickiness discoloured his fingers and palm. I pressed my thumb to a spot and it held.

He said, looking at our hands, "I am afraid my lettuce is wilting." Then he lifted his eyes at me, for just a few seconds, and turned toward his van in a way that took me with him.

Nine hours later, I left in a cab. And I have not spoken to him since. And I do not know what I am doing.

But I do know I am the wrong person to help Zep Baker with his problem. He should not travel where I lead him, because I am a guide who has never been there. He should not trust me with his prayer, because I am a priest who cannot believe in God. Worse, I'm a priest who wants to use his prayer to prove God doesn't exist. Zep wants me to make his ex-wife fall in love with him again, and I will try. I will do everything I can think of. I will make his Emily's love my work. And when I succeed, if I succeed, then I will know. Love is just a story. A mix of chemicals. A delusion. Zep will have everything he hopes for, and nothing he should want.

And I will know what to do.

Friday, April 17

ZEP SHOWED ME A PICTURE of Emily. He searched for it on his phone, shaking his head at himself the whole time as his wide, roughened hands worked the precision interface with vague swipes and jabs. It was like watching a jackhammer operator try to write with a fountain pen.

"There," he said finally. "That's her."

It was an image from a gathering of some sort, perhaps a cocktail party or an awards ceremony, framed at the edges by the sleek shoulders and arms of other guests. Half of Zep, in a dark suit, filled the left third of the image. Only a portion of his face could be seen, but he looked to be eight or ten years younger.

The main focus of the image was Emily, shown from the waist up in an ocean-green dress, apparently in conversation with someone just beyond the frame on the right. She had short hair the pale yellow of chickpea flour that curled behind her ears, and a wide mouth set in a broad jaw, V-shaped like the prow of a yacht. Her teeth were perfect, the teeth of a TV personality or a flight attendant. Her eyes were big and bright and outlined in delicate, frosty makeup. She was very pretty, probably even beautiful. In the image, it looked as if someone had just said something funny. The camera had flashed in the midst of Emily's delight.

Were I able to place the Emily of that precise moment in either an fMRI or a PET machine, I would expect to see portions of her amygdala showing signs of heightened neural activity and her accumbens and dorsal striatum flooding with dopamine. With that information, supported by an interview to determine the factors contributing to her emotional state, I would conclude with high probability that Emily "enjoyed" whatever she was feeling and wanted it to continue. That's how science usually works. The limbs we walk out on are thick and short. Usually.

"What's significant to you about this picture?" I asked Zep.

He took the phone back and studied the image. "That's what she looked like when she loved me."

I ASKED LESLEY, while she was reading, whether she had ever been in love. She took a breath, as if collecting her thoughts, set down her book, and asked why I wanted to know.

"Research," I said.

I knew she wouldn't push the issue. She wouldn't couch her answers or try to steer me to a safer subject. She would simply answer honestly.

"Three times," she said.

The first came when she was eleven. In her class there was a boy whose name she could no longer remember. He had long blond hair, which hung very straight and just past his shoulders. It was the same hair as a doll she had, and she remembered that his face was doll-like too. Pretty and somewhat blank.

"I pretended I had shrunk him and kept him under the covers in bed," she said. "He was very good about doing whatever I made him do."

A few years later, when she was sixteen, there was a boy named Gregory. "He was never 'Greg,'" she said. "He often wore a vest, with pinstripes, and he had a way of shifting his bangs with a flick of his head, which I found intensely attractive." One day a school trip took her geography class to explore caves in eastern Ontario. When the group of students were leaving a certain cave, Gregory secretly held Lesley's hand and made her wait until everyone had shuffled out. Then he pressed her against the cold cave wall and French kissed her.

"I let him," she said, looking at me. "It wasn't anything forced."

"I can tell by the way you remember it."

Lesley closed her eyes. "It was the most thrilling thing." She took a deep breath and pressed a hand to her chest. "My heart's racing a little now just thinking about it. Anyway, that lasted about two weeks."

"And the third time was Philip?"

Lesley's eyes held the book in her lap. "No," she said finally. "I loved Phil. More each day until he died. But love and in-love are two different things. That obsession, and that … heart-skip. I never had those with Phil." She smiled at me, and her eyes were glistening. "I pray he never knew that."

Her third, in fact, was a man named Samuel Cuthbert, who operated a whale-watching boat off the coast of Nova Scotia. She worked for him the summer she turned twenty-three.

"He was not tall, and his beard was shaggy," she said. "But he had quite incredible thumbs. He could lift me off the ground with them." She laughed, with a girlish flip in her voice. "To this day, the smell of hair wet with seawater makes me horny. Before Phil got sick he used to love going to PEI with me, and one of the reasons was I became so voracious!"

She looked up at me then, as if checking for my reaction.

"Did you say the word to each other?" I asked.

She smiled and nodded.

I think I must collect more stories. It's possible that two or three of the women I work with won't mind if I ask them, if it's for a project. I need, somehow, to get inside of this feeling, to understand the mechanisms.

My mother cannot be a candidate, of course, although I'm sure at one time she was in love with my father. Any conversation that ventures there would become fraught, because talk of my father would lead her to the memory of him leaving. And from there the linkages would be swift, from the absence of my father, to the need to make up for his lost income, to the decision to take in tenants, to one tenant in particular. She would have no control, shuttled down the synaptic path like a child down a waterslide. This is how it happens.

In fact, by now, the path has probably become so set, ingrained by compulsive repetition, that merely the mention of my father's name might be enough to conjure the face of the man who rented our basement in the spring of 1999. Warren Ghil. And from this sour nugget lodged in her neocortex, her brain's co-conspirators, the hippocampus and amygdala, maestros of emotional memory, would conspire to pull up the face of his friend, Cory Nickroe.

And then she would go cold.

And she would hate me for making her think of them, and what they did. And she would hate herself for hating the victim. And then the vodka would flow and flow.

All this because I asked her about love.

So my mother cannot help me with this question, this need to know how "in-love" feels. And I cannot go to books, to poetry or songs, because there is no scientific foundation for "I need you so that I could die." Artists exaggerate. There are no measurement standards that I can apply to "At last, the skies above are blue. / My heart was wrapped up in clover / the night I looked at you." I cannot ask Sylvia Plath about her neurotransmitter activity in the hour she wrote "I dreamed that you bewitched me into bed / And sung me moonstruck, kissed me quite insane."

I cannot work with art.

To do this properly requires my own peer-reviewed study. A minimum of twenty "in-love" subjects, with a control of at least ten participants without any current emotional connections. I should be doing fMRI scans and monitoring their autonomic nervous systems. But Zep is impatient. There's no time. So I will have to glean insights from the work of other researchers. I will speak to my friends. And when they ask why they must tell me about falling in love, and why I cannot draw from my own experience, I will remind them of the need for objectivity. I will say my own experience is not relevant to the specific parameters of this investigation.

There will be no need to lie.

THIS MORNING ADNAN CALLED and, without speaking or giving any signal, Lesley handed the phone to me. It was strangely unsettling to hear his voice. His first words came slowly, a respectful procession. There was a question about my health, another about the tarts he had sent home with me, four large tomato, onion and ricotta tarts and one apple, fig and rhubarb galette. They would not have kept long. Had I enjoyed them? Had I shared them?

I assured him that I had. He didn't need to know the truth.

A number of his words then came all at once, a splash of them, as if he had been holding them back and they suddenly broke free. Why hadn't I called? Why couldn't he speak to me? Did I know that he had been worried? Did I understand that I was important to him? Did I realize he wanted to be with me?

And if I knew, he said, then what had he done wrong? What could he do differently? And when? He asked this twice. When could we be together again?

I wanted to ask him, in that moment, if he could describe what he was feeling. Could he articulate the sensations, and if so, how would he label them? I wanted to know if he considered what he felt to be pleasurable or painful. This surely wasn't joy. It sounded nothing like that. Was it anguish he was experiencing? Was it agony? Was it love?

But I knew it would have seemed unkind to ask him any of this. He would have thought I was mocking him, which is so far from the truth. A scientist has no feelings about the rat confined to its maze. The animal under the glass elicits no pity. Neither delight nor contempt nor ridicule nor concern has any place in the relationship between the observer and the observed. At all cost the distance must be maintained.

The last words Adnan spoke, before I hung up the phone, were that he would find me. He would come to me. He would accept nothing less than a meeting, face to face. I could tell him then, he said, whether the hours we had spent together had meant anything to me at all. And I could tell him what I wanted, what I felt.

ZB Transcript 5

LOOKS LIKE WE'RE GOOD, Marcie!

Don't know what the fuck I said that was so convincing, but who cares? I took Hope out to Enzo's last night, that place Duke and I went. We were there for a while, talking — and we didn't drink, by the way. Not one drop. Had the same waiter and he was all over me with his goddamn Stravecchias and Invecchiatas and — those are grappas, by the way — and I was like, "Dude, if you want me to puke my guts out right here, keep talking." So he backed off.

But anyway, bottom line, Hope seems okay about going to Buffalo. When I mentioned it she kinda perked up. Said she could take time off work, like, right away. I said, "Really?" and she said, "Yes." I said, "You're sure?" and she said, "Yes." Just straight. No bullshit.

So, that's good, right? I mean, sometimes, I mean with Emily, it was like "Yes" one day and "Talk to my lawyer you fucking asshole" the next. Shit can change, right? Shit can always change.

Jesus, how many times did I have a roster spot and then, Bam! Your ass is in Triple-A, motherfucker! Goddamn rug's never nailed down under Zep's feet.

But whatever. Whole new situation, I guess. I'm just gonna fucking go with it.

She asked me some questions. This was before we talked about Buffalo or made any plans, but it was like she was working already. I mean, I was into ordering some food but she was like, into her pages. It was almost like she didn't realize we were in a fancy restaurant. The menu was *buried*! Which was cool. It was like, hey, she's a pro, so I gotta step up! I mean, this is why I'm here, right? She's the one who's gonna make this happen.

She wanted to know what it felt like to me when Em and I were in love. And I said, well, it felt awesome! Best feeling ever! Right? And, man, she was not impressed by that at all.

She was like, "Zep, this isn't going to work if you can't be specific with me. You need to be very specific." Her eyes were all serious. Dark and sharp, like black diamond drills or something. Fuck, she was hot! Holy shit. But anyway, never mind that. That's not the point.

Fuck. Stay focused! Jesus.

So, anyway, I turned it right back on her. I said, "Okay, ask me a specific question." And she liked that. She didn't smile but, you know ... almost.

She said, "When you first knew there was something special to you about Emily, what did you feel in your body?"

At first I was thinking, like, fuck, is she asking if I got a hard-on or something? I mean, she's sort of a doctor so maybe that's okay, you know, to talk about. But then I thought about when I saw Em that one game.

It was June of '97, middle of June, I think we were playing Louisville, or maybe Iowa, and she was sitting near the dugout, third row up. And I'd seen her before, sitting there, and I remembered her, because whenever I looked over she wasn't watching the game. She was reading! Right? Fucking reading a book. She had her Bisons cap on, and she's at the game, so she's a fan. But she's fucking reading. Like her book is more interesting than the game!

I remember it pissed me off.

'Cause we had a good team that year. We had Richie Sexson, and Sean Casey. We had Bartolo Colon before he got fat! Jesus, we ended up winning the championship that year. What's she doing reading a book? So this one day I shouted at her. "Hey!" I said, "Why don't you watch the game?"

But when I did that she looked up and said, "Why don't you do something worth watching?" And she smiled at me.

And, you know, it wasn't a big, wide, "fuck you" smile. It was one of those small, shy smiles. Like maybe she'd secretly hoped I'd shout at her. I mean, that's what it seemed like. She was beautiful. And that smile ... in one second I went from pissed off to totally whacked out on this chick. It was like, *Vooom*! Like an injection. Right in my chest. Almost couldn't breathe for a second.

So that's what I told Hope.

She nodded and said a long goddamn word and made a note. I said, "What?" She said it again. I wish I could remember what it was, Marcie. Honest to God it was like she'd suddenly turned Chinese or some damn thing.

Anyway that's how we went, for like an hour. "What'd you feel here? What'd you feel here?" Just questions and notes and pages. Jesus Christ, it was like doing infield drills combined with taxes or something. I never worked so hard in my life. By the end of it I was ready to order some grappa.

But that's what I wanted, right? That's why I came to her.

It wasn't much different the first time, back in '06, except that wasn't so long. And she was more nervous then. Didn't seem as sure of herself. She was way younger and, you know, whatever was going on then. This time she was all "Dr. Riopelle in charge."

I almost asked her, though. After we were done and they brought us some food — she had the fish, of course. I could tell right off she'd do the fish. It's like this sixth sense I have with chicks and food. Except now with all that gluten-vegan stuff it makes it harder.

Marcie, did I tell you Em's maybe going gluten-free? She's thinking about it. Pebbles told me. Fuck, I hope she doesn't. 'Cause that's a total pain in the ass.

But anyway, Hope and I were eating. And I almost said, "Hey, remember when you interviewed me that time? Like, what was going on then? I know I came on to you and that wasn't cool, but it was more than that. 'Cause the whole time, you seemed ready to bolt. Like you did *not* want to be there. So, what was that about?"

And I don't want to say it stood out because most chicks I meet are happy to be talking to me. But, you know, it did kind of stand out for that reason.

But anyway. I didn't ask her. Didn't seem like a good time.

Maybe in Buffalo, right?

Oh, yeah, so get me a room somewhere, okay Marcie? I guess two of 'em. I dunno, there's gotta be someplace good to stay in Buffalo, right? And you gotta rent me another car. The Acura's pissing me off. But nothing too sportsy. Em always hated anything that looked fast. Probably a good thing I ditched the Ghibli. A Caddy maybe? A Buick? I dunno. Just no goddamn Chevys!

And start thinking about body wash. Like what kinda scents you like. I'm thinking we gotta do something new, something nobody's ever done before, so there's two things that'll make us stand out, the whole Stay Clean concept, and new scents. Like cinnamon maybe. Or no, wait, wait ... what about tastes? Tastes! Holy shit. 'Cause soap tastes like crap, right? What if we had body wash that tastes good? Fuck, that could be killer. Why'd I just think about that? *I shoulda had my formula guy on that the whole time*!

So think about it, Marcie. Tastes. Fuck the scents. And book two rooms, and a car, and I'll talk to you in a coupla days from Buffalo.

Say hi to Ramone for me.

Saturday, April 18

HIS FACE COMES TO ME. Adnan's, I mean, and it's nice to have a new visitor that way, I admit. The others had a good fifteen-year run of exclusive rights in my orbitofrontal theatre. A little repertory couldn't hurt.

But I wish the image were different. I only have myself to blame for that, of course. You make your memories by what you allow your eyes to see, your ears to hear, your nose to inhale. There was surely another, better moment to stare at his dark and solemn face. But I picked the one when he was crying.

He is above me, in my image. Propped up by his arms, looking down at what's beneath him. He has chosen to look, and so he is mostly responsible for the image now smeared over the walls of his own memory. But he has not expected this, I can tell. Nothing like this. And in the moment of my image it is surprising to me that I have allowed him to see. I can feel that surprise still. It's as if I've chosen to punish him for a crime I haven't yet imagined. Or perhaps I hope to avert it.

At any rate, he cries. Angry, remorseful, hopeless tears. They river and plop from eyes that he seems to strain to keep open, as if he means to honour me by seeing what I have unfairly chosen to show him.

And it's this face that comes to me. Again and again. Of all the memories I could be seeing.

THIS MORNING, PROFESSOR SING suggested I looked unwell. I'd been wondering how to broach the subject of needing two weeks, immediately, and he brought it up himself.

For several hours I'd been meeting with two of my fellow fellows, Eve Harier and Xia Jai Ying, interviewing them as I had Zep. We had arranged to come in early and set up in the cafeteria, at a round table next to the emergency exit. I'd worried about their ability to discuss emotional memories amid all that hard plastic, stainless steel and lemon-lime Jell-O, and even about the willingness of these particular women to admit to something as commonplace and banal as love, but I needn't have. They seemed to enjoy it. And because they know nothing about my history, their confessions and intimations became inclusive. They assumed I knew, just as well as they did, how their bodies would respond to someone they wanted, how their lips felt fuller, how their throat constricted and their breathing became shallow. They took as a given that I'd experienced "hamster pulse," as Jai Ying put it, that I too had lost sleep and found it impossible to concentrate on work because of an infatuation. That I had, in some strange, intoxicated haze, committed a momentous indiscretion — as when, at a gathering, Eve spied the new assistant dean and blurted, "I want to suck that earlobe," not realizing the wife of the earlobe was standing next to her.

And they were certain, just as certain as they were that I had experienced every one of these embarrassing, bewildering events, that I had enjoyed them. Because there is no one who doesn't. Love is the syrup that makes everyone sticky.

I let them believe whatever they wanted. If it helped them to speak openly, then I was one of them, a fellow happy sufferer.

When Professor Sing came to the door of my tiny office later, I was turned away from my desk, facing the far wall. For a few minutes nearly every morning, unless it's cloudy, a sliver of light blooms there as the sun passes between two wings of the research centre. In spring, the sliver extends downward from a spot about fifteen centimetres below the ceiling, touching the edge of the frame holding my graduate degree, to the top of the lateral cabinet. It glows for a few minutes, like a crack in a doorway to some brighter time and place, then vanishes. There's no meaning to it, an accident of architecture and geography, as random as a raindrop hitting a bird's wing or the wrong man taking up residence in your basement. But there are occasions when I find myself anticipating it, waiting for it. Relieved by it some days, dreading it others. For no reason other than I know it's coming.

Sing cleared his throat and, when I turned to face him, he studied me for a second. "You look pale," he said. He gripped a green folder, having come to discuss the serotonin receptor data from our memory reconsolidation study. He'd been concerned we weren't properly picking up abnormalities in serotonergic function. Since the point of the study was to find new ways to treat anxiety in PTSD sufferers, it was important to capture fluctuations in the receptors implicated in emesis and gastrointestinal contraction.

"I'm not feeling all that well," I said.

"Symptoms?"

"I want to throw up."

Sing looked down at the folder in his hand but made no other reference to the coincidence. The pleasures of happenstance — providence, serendipity, irony — largely elude Darun Sing. Most of us who work with him are just fine with that. From a principal investigator you want fairness, clarity and a field of interest that aligns with your own. Whimsy just ends up making everyone stay later.

"Anything else?"

"Weight on my chest. Heart palpitations. Sweating a bit more than usual."

He nodded and blinked. He would not ask me about stresses in my life, triggers I might have encountered, recurrences of intrusive thoughts. Early on I informed him of my history, in broad outlines, to establish the basis of my scientific interest and secure a place on his team. But he is not my doctor, my counsellor or my friend; there are places he cannot go.

"Take some time," he said. "Work it out with Janet." He turned to leave and then paused. "Next month we start on epigenetic mechanisms in fear consolidation. I want you on DNA methylation in hippocampal memory function."

"No problem."

MY MOTHER, UNDERSTANDABLY, found it odd that I was suddenly going to Buffalo. For years her only daughter had kept her at the perfect arm's length, the distance of a reach and a shove. Always in the same city, never leaving, but visiting her with the frequency of a distant relative from a separate continent, astonished at the local weather. Now without warning I was in her living room, announcing that I was going away. She was justified in her confusion.

"Why Buffalo?" she said. "It's such a sad little city."

"It's a research project."

"And you're going for two *weeks*?" She was sitting on the edge of the couch, knees together, rummaging through the contents of her quilted-leather purse. "What could possibly keep you in Buffalo for two weeks?"

"It's difficult to explain."

"Did you see we got this reupholstered?" She meant the couch, which was ash-blue now instead of rust. She took out a package of Du Mauriers, pulled one and gave me a conspiratorial look. "Bill thinks I've quit."

"Not if you smoke inside, he doesn't."

"Oh, yes." She reached back into her purse. "He has a diminished sense of smell, poor man. One of his hidden charms." For a second or two she further bruised her bag's inventory, then in triumph brought out a box of matches. In the midst of taking one out to strike she froze and looked at me in horror.

"Oh, darling." She smothered the matchbox in her hands. "I wasn't thinking. I heard you take that breath and I realized." With her matchbox-gripping fist she reached out and touched my knee, a gesture as comforting as it could possibly be.

"There are lighters," I said.

"I know, I know. I have one somewhere." She rose and went to her kitchen. "If you visited more often I'd be in the habit."

It wasn't kind of me, and it wasn't productive. If Lesley or my counsellor had been there they would have tried to talk me down. But they weren't. So when my mother returned with her cigarette lit, I didn't let the matter drop.

"There's something interesting in the fact that you continue to use those things, when you know."

My mother stood at the end of the couch, still and grim, and nodded. "It is strange. Can you explain it? As the expert?" She took a drag on her cigarette. "Perhaps it's subconscious. Maybe I think it's been years now and you should be over it. Maybe I'm subconsciously testing you." She waved through the smoke she'd exhaled, the colour of her new upholstery.

"I'm not a psychologist, but that doesn't sound subconscious."

"Well," she said, Du Maurier to her lips, "the brain is a mystery."

I chose that moment to rise and start toward the front door.

"Are you being dramatic now, Hope? Is that what's happening?"

My mother's sigh chased after me across the carpet she'd chosen when she and Bill had married. It had been a kind of wedding present, from him to her, which he announced at the reception with a wink and a grin. "Mildred," he said into the microphone, "you floor me."

"Sweetheart, I'm sorry," she said. "Don't be like this. You know that I'm so extremely proud of you for how you've turned your life around. And so is Bill, darling. *So is Bill.*"

At the door, I stepped into my shoes.

"Why else would he have paid for all that schooling? He said, 'Mildred, that's quite a daughter you've got.' And he was right." Though I wasn't looking at her, focused as I was on the edge of my left shoe, which kept bending under my heel, I sensed her coming toward me. "I'm just confused. That's all it is. Because you're so highly accomplished in one part of your life and I wonder how you can still be … hampered in others."

The decision I made then is one I think I'll always regret. Because it will mark me as someone unable to resist the pettiest of urges. Someone given to the ugliest, most malign impulses. Willing to behave no better than a capricious third-world dictator. The Idi Amin of daughters, *c'est moi.*

My left shoe finally accepted the foot it was intended for and I opened the front door. Halfway across the transom, I turned and lifted my face to my mother.

"By the way, I think I'm pregnant."

I was two-thirds of the way down the driveway when she recovered enough to shout after me. The usual thing. Hope. How dare you. Don't leave. Hope. Hope. Hope.

ZB Transcript 6

I HATE MY ROOM, MARCIE. Fucking hate this room. It's not your fault. Not blaming you, but this is a *shit* room.

First of all, king bed. I know most people like a king bed, but I don't. I said gimme two queens. King bed's too big for just me. Reminds me of the whole fucking ... look, one person in a king bed, that bed is *empty*, you know what I'm saying? Feels like I'm sleeping in Wyoming, for Christ's sake.

I told them. Gimme two queens. And the guy at the desk, I kid you not, fucking smirks at me.

"You want two queens?" he says. And then he looks at the girl beside him at the desk. And *she* smirks. Like I'm the goddamn joke of the week.

I said, "Hey, Derrick" — name on his badge was "Derrick" — I said, "Hey, Derrick, I hit forty-seven home runs in a season and a half with the Bisons. And I know that matters in this town because you got *nothing else* here." Not in the summer, anyway. I know they got the Sabres and the Bills, but in the summer they got shit. I mean, I didn't get into any of that with him, I just left it at "nothing else." And I said, "I would like a room with two *queen beds*, please."

I'm telling you, Marcie, if Hope hadn't been standing beside me I might have popped the guy or ... I dunno. Although now I'm thinking the whole reason they made the joke was because we were getting separate rooms. Like, no way we're a couple, right? And she's hot, so what's wrong with me?

Anyway, he said they didn't have any more queen bed rooms available. It was kings or those little doubles. Fucking Hyatt.

HEY MARCIE, LOOK, UH, sorry about that last recording. I wasn't ... you don't have to type any of that if you don't ... I guess maybe it's too late now.

I think it's just ... it's just being back in this city, that's all. I mean, it's ... I guess it's seventeen years since I was here, so it's weird. It's like being in a time warp, like I'm in a *Star Trek* movie or something, you know? I'm afraid of bumping into my old self or something. I'm just ... I'm on edge. I dunno, that's the only way I can put it.

Coming here, what can I tell you ... it was a good drive. Hope didn't say much the whole way but the traffic was okay. I like the Enclave, by the way, thanks for that. Family man car, huh? Yeah. No, it's good, it'll work.

We got over the Peace Bridge around four o'clock. That didn't take too long. Customs guy recognized me when he saw the name. He was young, so ... stats geek or something, I guess. Didn't ask for my autograph.

So anyway, we were coming in. And I was driving past La Salle Park and then, Marcie, it was like for a second it was 1998 and I was twenty-six years old. So weird. And, and I looked over at Hope and I was surprised, like I was expecting Emily to be there. Seriously, for a second it was like, Who the hell is this? Where's my wife?

Didn't say anything. Hope looked over at me and went, "What?"

And I was like, "Welcome to Buffalo."

We checked in, and the room ... whatever. And Hope doesn't want to eat dinner with me, by the way. Like I mean, never.

That's a policy. She said, "Working hours. We're going to keep working hours while we're here. No meetings before nine and nothing past five." Starting tomorrow she's gonna meet me in the lobby every morning and we'll go to work.

I think it's gonna be okay. It's good to actually be doing something, you know? It's sitting around wishing that gets to you. This is better. This is like, take charge, bam, make something happen! Right? Yeah. Yeah. It's good.

Can't wait to get started!

OKAY.

[Unintelligible]

Jesus Christ, I should probably ...

[Unintelligible]

It's uh, it's eight something. Eight thirty-three, says here. And the light's coming in all over me, and I feel like shit. Feels like my head is inside a glove or something. Like squeezed inside a glove, that's what it's ... fuck, I'm an asshole.

Stay positive though ... right, Marcie?

Yeah.

I had this coach once. I had this coach ... he used to say, "Learn from your mistakes or don't, I don't give a fuck. They just pay me to throw you the ball."

Total prick, that guy. Total prick. Never got out of A-ball though, so ... fuck him.

I dunno. All last night, Marcie, all last night all I could think about was that she's here. Emily's here in this city. And I had this ... I had this big urge — I mean, I know where she lives. Right? I could drive right over. Knock on her door.

But I can't do that 'cause I'd blow it. Blow this whole fucking thing.

So I just walked around downtown for a while. Went down,

uh, Pearl and then over to Niagara Square. I love that old city hall building there. It's like, I dunno, a piece of Chicago or something. Like a great old man you can look up to.

But walking around, I got ... I couldn't relax. The more I walked the more I ... every time I turned a corner I thought, maybe she'll be there. You know? Maybe I'll have to talk to her before I'm ready, before Hope's told me the plan.

Or worse, or worse ... maybe I'll see her with some guy. I mean, I'm always asking Pebbles if Mom's seeing anybody and she never says yes but who knows? Maybe she goes out at night. Gets a sitter and hits the town. Tries to wash her shithead ex-husband out of her mind. Maybe she lives here now 'cause she thinks she's safe from me. 'Cause it's the last place I'd ever want to be. This is her home, she's got family. All I've got here are memories of her.

Well, that and hitting the shit outta the ball. Heh ... yeah.

But, you know, what I'm saying is ... now she's here to be with her folks and put a thousand miles between us, right? Like I'm the last person she wants to see. That's why she left. And now here I show up. And all night I was walking around thinking, What the hell? What the hell am I doing here? I must be the world's biggest meatball.

And then I went to the Steakhouse downstairs and closed it.

I dunno, Marcie. Do you think this is gonna work out all right or do you think this is the stupidest thing I've ever done? I mean, I could just turn around. Send Hope home on a bus tomorrow and drive south down the 219 and take it from there. I could do that. I fucking should do that.

But fuck, Marcie. I love her. I just ... miss her. And I ...

... Shit, it's twenty-to-nine. I gotta have a shower.

Uh, listen, get on Lino, would you? I keep calling him and I only ever get his message box like I'm some loser. I wanna know what's going on with the investor dude. Feels like I should be seeing some sort of legal paper or something. Okay, that's it.

OH MAN, MARCIE. Oh man.

Fuck, I'm just out of my meeting with Hope. It's ah, it's like around noon. We're taking a break for lunch. I'm just down here in the ah ... I gotta go outside, they're looking at me. I'm just pacing around the lobby like a nut job.

Holy shit!

No, after you, sir. *After you.* Yeah, whatever [unintelligible].

OKAY, I'M IN THE parking lot. Holy shit, Marcie!

[Unintelligible. Wind noise.]

It's a bit breezy out here, I'm not ah ... [Wind noise] and Hope's got it all planned out! Oh my God, it's amazing. My head's spinning right now. She ... she booked us one of those small conference rooms, and ... and she had this whiteboard set up, right? And so she walked me through everything, the whole plan. How everything works. The brain and the chemicals and how [Wind noise] she used a lot of big fucking words and I can't remember a goddamn one of them right now, but holy shit! I think this might work!

She ah ... she says we have to take it slow. We can't rush anything. It might take a week, or it might take a month, but [Wind noise] take that long because she has to get back to work at some point so I might be on my own for part of it. Which might be okay, but we have to see. We have to see how it goes.

Okay, I'm in sort of a sheltered area now, Marcie. Sorry about that. I used to take videos of Pebbles on the beach and with the wind you can't listen to them, it's like sandpaper on the ears. So ...

But it's exciting. It's ... I mean, the way Hope explains it, we're gonna try and rebuild or, no, she said ... *resuscitate*, that's it. We're gonna resuscitate Emily's feelings for me. Right from scratch. Almost as if we're just meeting now. But that's hard because we have history. And there's a lot of bad feelings that, I mean, not on my part, but she has bad feelings, anger and that, so we have to get over that. She says it's like rebuilding a baseball swing. Which I totally get! You gotta get down to fundamentals. Basic stuff like balance. Except with Emily it's trust.

We have to — well, me. I have to re-establish trust. Get Emily to trust me. Hope says she's got some ideas. But she says first one of the things we have to do is I have to walk her through all the reasons why Emily might not trust me. Which, yeah. I guess maybe I have to, I dunno.

And Hope says I should lay off the booze, it's messing me up. She was kinda pissy about it, but I can't blame her. She's doing all this for ... well, for nothing. I dunno why.

But so, there you go — we're starting!

Okay, I'm gonna [wind noise]

Monday, April 20

MY MOTHER HAS LEFT four messages on my phone. In the longest of them, she recalled for my benefit the day she learned she was pregnant with me, and how joyful the experience of sharing the news with her own mother had been.

"It was the middle of February, Hope. The sky was a brilliant, clear blue, like a sapphire, and the sun was so bright on the snow it brought tears to your eyes. And your grandfather hadn't salted the front path, so when I ran out of the car to the front door I nearly fell for a loop. And for a second when I thought I was falling, I thought, 'Oh, no! I'm going to lose the baby before I get a chance to tell Mom!' But it didn't happen, and I got to the front door and I yelled for her, and she came thinking something terrible had happened. But then as she ran from the kitchen she saw the look on my face and she knew, and she let out a big *Whoop!* You know how Grandma can be. Just a big *Whoop!* And she had some letters or receipts in her hand, papers of some kind, that she threw up in the air. And they came down like big confetti and it was the most wonderful thing, Hope! It was the most wonderful day! And I wish you'd given us that, Hope. I wish you had. Oh, it would have been so good and so right for us to have had that, after all the difficulties. I'm so sorry we didn't have that. But Hope, we can still talk about it. And we can still celebrate. It can still be a joyful thing, Hope. So call me back, sweetheart. Please call me back. Please, sweetheart."

In the last and shortest of the messages, my mother left a simple, bleak, "Oh, Hope."

Lesley left a message too. She called while I was with Zep or I would have talked with her. I could hear the salve of care in her captured voice, the will to be helpful through distance. Apparently my mother had phoned Lesley to plead with her to convince me to return Mother's calls. "She has a point, Hope," Lesley said. "This is not really something you should be dealing with on your own." It means, of course, that Lesley learned about my pregnancy from my mother and not from me, but she didn't try to make me feel worse about that than I already did.

She did ask, however, whether the cataclysmic news had anything to do with my sudden escape to Buffalo. She doesn't know about Zep, only that I've gone to do "field research," which is a thing I have never done before in the nine years we've roomed together. The coincidence of these two events is, in Lesley's word, "intriguing."

I can't tell her what I'm doing here; she doesn't think like a scientist and so she would be appalled. But I will call her and apologize, and let her convince me to call my mother. And in this way I will give them both something.

Neither of them, in their messages, nudged the subject of the father. Undoubtedly Lesley has already made the short, logical leap. She knows about my hours with Adnan — none of their content, but the fact of them. My mother, however, has nothing, no daughterly confidences, to go on, so her bewilderment must be profound. She must now, among other things, imagine me having sex, which will require a significant realignment of what she holds to be true about her daughter. That is, unless she skips all that and assumes the employment of some university lab version of a turkey baster. That would be easier for her.

Nor did they raise the question of what decision I will be making regarding this pregnancy. There are certain things that can't be left dangling on a voice message, and it seems the fate of an embryo is one of them.

And perhaps they accept that the question is mine, not theirs. Mine not only to answer but to ask, which I haven't yet. I can't ask that question until I have answered others. And that will be a process. Scientific investigation must be built on formal, testable hypotheses with manipulated and dependent variables. If / then / because. One doesn't just decide.

The manipulated variable is Zep's ex-wife, or more precisely her brain. If Emily Good's brain can be directed or tricked into believing she is falling in love again with Zep Baker, then I have nothing to worry about, because it will prove love is merely chemical, a simple, amino acidic call-and-response. Therefore meaningless. And I can base other hypotheses, other questions, on that knowledge.

I won't have to consider factors like fate, or hope, or desire. I won't have to imagine the possibility that certain kinds of lives can change for the better after all, or that happiness might hinge on the infinitesimal chance of two particular people finding and believing in each other. I won't have to consider the potential for happiness at all. If love can be made, if it can be imposed on someone, then love doesn't matter.

If yes, then no.

Zep has no questions, except "When do we begin?" He has put himself in my hands. I'm his coach and he has faith in my game plan. I've neglected to mention that in this particular field of play, I've never been anything but a spectator.

With Zep, I have the challenge of managing his expectations and ensuring that he doesn't try to move too quickly. Testing the hypothesis properly depends on methodical progress. We will create Emily's love bit by bit, through careful, incremental provocations of neurochemicals in specific regions — nucleus accumbens, caudate nucleus, ventral tegmental area and others.

I'm certainly not the first to explore the subliminal induction of emotion. But I think it is safe to assume that I'm the first to attempt it outside a lab, without the awareness of the subject, assisted only by an excitable former third baseman who has everything to lose, or gain. I will have to give Zep explicit instructions at each stage, and I will need to observe him. He can't just be Zep in all his Zepness.

ZB Transcript 7

FUCK, MARCIE. You know what I'm doing right now? I'm sitting here watching a total asshole screw up his life.

He's sitting right across from me with his wife. I guess it's his wife. I'm in the Steakhouse here, having dinner. I can't talk too loud or they might hear me.

[Woman's voice. Unintelligible.]

No, just water's good. Thanks, sweetheart.

So ... anyway, uh, Hope and I worked on planning all day. It's all set up. Like as much as it can be. I know Emily's working at this tent rental company, The Tent Event or something. They do company spreads and weddings and shit. I found her bio thing online — you know, "Meet Our Team" or whatever. She's an event consultant, which is good I guess, for her. I mean, like I always said, she's got a killer smile. She knows how to talk to people. And Pebbles says she's still working out, so she's got that tight bod. Put one of those sharp suits for women on her? Sure, I can see that. Just fucking rips me up she's working for some two-bit company in Buffalo when she could be on the beach in Florida with me. Like that's the life she wants? Tromping around parking lots with a fucking clipboard? But, whatever. That'll change.

No, I'm fine sweetheart. Thanks.

[Woman's voice. Unintelligible.]

I'm just dictating here … Dictating, see? [Unintelligible] Right, sorry. Yeah. I'll keep it down.

Sorry, Marcie. They don't like me swearing in here.

So, point is, I know where she lives and where she works, and I pretty much know her hours, when she comes and goes. Don't know about lunch, but we'll figure that out.

Hope's all over me about taking it slow and I keep telling her, Don't worry. You're the boss. You tell me what to do, I'll do it. I mean, it's not like I don't know I fucked it … effed it up the first time on my own.

So, that's all good. And now I'm here eating a rib-eye. I think this is gonna be my place while I'm here. I mean, it's close. From the hotel it's easy. And it's a classy place, waitresses are nice enough, most of them. And they do the steaks right. Got a nice char going on the outside. Spice rub. It's good. Kinda like how Ramone does it. Except his has that Cuban vibe to it.

Yeah, and it made me think, you know, about that time when you guys had me over. It was like … I guess it was three days after Em said she needed me out and … I mean, that was a shitty time. But you guys were great. Just … made me feel welcome somewhere, you know? And, and you made those potato balls? Deep-fried and all that stuff in there? Shit, those were good! And what'd we drink? Cuba … Cubanitos? With the lime and the hot sauce? Yeah. Oh man, I could use a couple of those right now. But I promised Hope so, that's out I guess. I wanna do this right.

Yeah.

Jesus Christ.

This couple, Marcie. I'm telling you. I keep looking at them. They're right across from me in one of the booths. They're, I dunno, late-thirties or something, a little younger than me. It's a night out for them, you can tell. Wife's all dressed up. She's got this black dress on, kinda low-cut, gold necklace of some kind. Shiny shoes, lipstick. She looks great.

The guy, though. This guy, I'm telling you, Marcie ... he's a schlub. *Schlub*! That's the only word for him! No jacket, first of all. Maybe it's on the seat beside him but I can't see it. Anyway no tie. Shirt's open down to his chest hairs. Pants aren't jeans but they aren't much. Shoes, they're okay. Hair's like, "I'll just put my fingers through and that'll be good." You know?

So, right off it's obvious: she's trying, and he doesn't give a ... an eff, okay? And it's not like he shouldn't be working at it. Like, she's *way* better looking than him. She's not Emily, but she's pretty damn good. And he's just some guy. Right? But, Marcie, that's not the worst of it.

The worst of it ... oh man. I mean ... sorry, drink of water here ...

The worst of it ... is that she's talking to him. Right now I'm watching her. She's got this smile on her face, right? And she's talking to him. She's talking like she's really happy to be here with him. And she wants to tell him stuff. Like about her day. Or maybe they have kids and she's telling him what little Joey did today or whatever. Drew some picture or something. Something that isn't important, but it is important, you know? And she wants to share it with him.

I mean, I can see her, right now. She's talking. She's talking, Marcie, and ... he's not listening. He's not. Fucking. Listening.

He's looking down at his food. He's looking off at the other people. He's looking at the waitress going by, right? The girl behind the bar, the pictures on the wall. He's nodding like that's all he needs to do, just make his head move so it looks like he gives a shit, but he doesn't. He *doesn't*.

You know what I wanna do? I wanna go over there. I feel like right now, this minute, I should just go and push in beside him and tell him, Hey, you're a fucking asshole, you know that?

Don't you see what's happening here? Your lady is talking to you, asshole. Why don't you lift your head up and fucking look at her. Why don't you ask her a question or something, show her that you give a shit.

I wanna say, like, maybe you don't understand, maybe you're stupid. Maybe you don't get that all this stuff she's saying is important. That it's like, you know, pieces of her life that she's giving you. Right? And so maybe you should treat them with some respect. Because guess what's gonna happen if you don't, asshole? One day she's going to stop. Okay? One day she's going to stop talking to you, because she can't be bothered trying anymore. Because why the fuck should she? It's hopeless. Because you're fucking hopeless. And then after that she's going to leave. She's going to walk away and then what? Then your life is fucking over. Because no one is ever going to work as hard to be with you as she is right now.

I should do it. I should say to this guy, Look at me, right? Look at me, I'm eating alone here. I should go over and say that to him. You see me at that table by myself? That's you in five years, asshole. Because your wife has maybe two, three more years in her of trying as hard as she can. And then she's gonna give up. She's gonna say who the fuck cares anymore? And then she's gonna coast for a couple of years. And you're gonna think hey, this is okay. Everything's fine. But it won't be. It won't be fine. Because she's only coasting to get her strength back. And when she's done that, she's going to walk the fuck out. And you're going to be shit out of luck, asshole. Because most people don't get a second chance.

[Unintelligible]

Sorry. Yeah, sorry … No I understand. It's my fault.

They're kicking me out, Marcie.

Probably a good thing. Probably saved that guy's ass.

Tuesday, April 21

SCIENTIFIC STUDY IS DETECTIVE WORK. Studies are called *investigations*, and the head of a study is the *principal investigator*, often shortened to *P.I.* So I am Hope Riopelle, P.I., hot on the trail of a slippery operator called Love, a.k.a Adoration, a.k.a. Eros, a.k.a. The Heart's Immortal Thirst, a.k.a. The Blood of Life, et al.

Since I'm playing detective, it seems only appropriate that I'm on a stakeout. Sitting in a dark grey car with tinted windows, parked at the curb of a city street at eight-fifteen in the morning, waiting on a dame. All I need are a snub-nose .38 in the glove compartment and a mickey of Scotch under the seat. And a penis, I suppose.

There have been, in fact, one or two occasions in my life when all those things would have come in handy.

Zep sits beside me in the driver's seat, his legs bouncing like crows. We have been here for only half an hour and already his stress hormones have pushed the powers of his deodorant to their limit. Citrus and sandalwood are holding on by their molecular fingernails. When his eyes aren't trained on the entrance to the parking lot of City Honors School, they jump to his Cadillac's mirrors — side, back and side — and then to me. To my lap, specifically.

"What are you doing, taking notes?"

I tell him I wouldn't be much of a scientist if I didn't.

"Nothing's happened yet." He grips and regrips the car's steering wheel. "It's weird, huh? Being here, in this car? For you, I mean.

Me, I've sat in cars waiting on women before. But you're probably more used to being in a lab, working with rats or something."

This is atypical, I agree.

I had wondered (not worried, particularly) about the extended time we would be spending in the car, in close proximity. It's only been a couple of hours so far, including the drive from Toronto, so results aren't definitive, but to this point it hasn't been a problem. The pressure is mostly on Zep, not on me.

"I could use a drink," he says. "Which, you know, I wouldn't even do 'cause it's the morning. But, I'm saying, if it was the afternoon, and I hadn't already said that I was gonna try not to drink, then, you know, I would drink something. Calm the nerves a bit." He shakes his head slowly, ruefully. "Never needed it when I was playing."

I have told him that smell is a powerful trigger of memories, both good and bad. We will be using that, at some point. For now, and realizing it makes me sound like an emissary from the nineteenth century, I simply ask if he would want Emily to smell liquor on his breath. He thinks about that, staring through the window, his thumb worrying an edge of the steering wheel.

"My drinking wasn't really the problem."

Zep has told me some, but not all, of the factors that led to the disintegration of his marriage. I know it's not all because he holds himself tightly when he talks about it. He has not fully acknowledged every flaw in the fuselage, at least not to me. But there was no violence. He was adamant about that, and although I have nothing more than instinct to go on, I have faith in that, and I believe I can take him at his word. He also insists he was never unfaithful, and while intellectually I find this harder to believe, given our initial interaction years ago, a story he told me makes it plausible.

Two years before the end of the marriage, he found himself drawn to a young woman who worked in the sales department of a local TV station in Tampa. Apparently Zep does his own TV commercials for the chain of car washes he owns. The woman, whose name was Sonja, had recently joined the department and she told Zep she wanted to produce a great new spot for him, something that would "win awards." And she took on the project with such zeal — arranging for special scripting, costuming — that he was caught up, he was flattered. It's clear he confused the attention this woman paid to his commercials, and his business, with attention to him. It had been a few years, he said, since he'd felt special in the eyes of a woman. That's not quite how he put it. A few years "since I'd been more than meat" was Zep's phrasing.

Did this include his wife? I wondered. He nodded.

"She hadn't been into me much for a while."

What makes me think this story is true, and makes it possible to think that Zep was never actually unfaithful to Emily, is his admission that, in the case of this Sonja, he wanted to be. "I thought about her a lot, what it would be like to be with her." But she was married, he said, and she rejected him. It was around that time that Zep was arrested for impaired driving.

"Couple of months there," he said, "I was pretty fucked up."

He insists Emily never knew the real reason behind his behaviour, but it added strain to whatever they were already going through. For a while, Zep admitted, during his Sonja period and after, he "checked out" of the marriage. Put what energy and focus he had toward the car wash business, and his daughter Pebbles. "That part, being a dad, that never changed."

Apparently the trigger for Emily's decision finally to end the marriage was a small, fateful decision Zep made. He bought himself a suit.

By this point they had begun to have repeated, vexing arguments about money, a theme of which was what Emily saw as their conflicting priorities. This is Zep's account, of course, but he seemed to make a good-faith attempt to tell it fairly. Apparently Emily wanted their disposable income to be spent on quality-of-life things — travel, family — and to her, Zep seemed more interested in appearances. A week before, for some reason that seemed defensible to Zep at the time, he had refused to pay for Emily's parents to fly first-class down to Tampa for a visit.

A few days later, he spent $4,700 on a suit.

"Lay it all out like that," he said, "it looks pretty stupid on my part. Selfish. And I'm not saying it wasn't. But where we were at the time ... I knew her folks were just coming to gang up on me." During our session in the airless conference room, Zep had taken off his jacket, loosened his tie and opened his pale blue shirt at the neck. Since his playing days he had obviously gained some weight, and so his extra bulk strained against the fabric of his shirt. He had a habit, while talking about the past, of leaning on his elbows on the conference table and rubbing his hands over his head, and by then he had done it so much his hair was pushed into haphazard tufts, like trampled grass. He appeared utterly unselfconscious, an earnest, big-shouldered boy.

I repeated to him that he didn't need to explain himself to me. It wasn't important for him to describe in detail what happened. He just had to give me the information necessary to understand what Emily's attitude would likely be toward him now. And where her negative associations would lie.

"I'm a selfish jerk," Zep said. "That'd be her attitude."

The objectives of this investigation are as follows:

1. To provoke in the subject, Emily Good, emotional responses that "feel like" love to her.
2. To accomplish this to the degree that Emily Good believes herself (however briefly) to be "in love" with her ex-husband, Zep Baker, and communicates this to him.

3. In achieving objectives 1 and 2, to substantiate the hypothesis that "love" is a predictable biological process, neurochemical in nature, and possible to simulate.
4. In achieving objective 3, to prove that the emotions described or summarized as "love" or "being in love" are open to misinterpretation by the healthy conscious mind and therefore unreliable.

Notes:

a) We know that human emotions are the conscious product of underlying chemical actions in specific regions of the brain. But it is possible that "attraction" may be influenced by transient factors. What makes a specific woman attracted to a specific man may depend on genetics, family history, the imprint of individual experience, either recent or buried in the past. The totality of this component may be described as a "love fingerprint" and it is possible that whether one man or woman can be a candidate for love with another depends upon the presence of this love fingerprint. That factor is beyond the scope of this investigation and not relevant to its findings.
b) We can assume, given the history of Zep Baker and Emily Good — they were once in love and married — that whatever a man requires to be "attractive" to Emily Good, Zep Baker is proven to possess, i.e. they have the necessary love fingerprint. What are currently missing in the brain of Emily Good, because of recent negative experience, are the necessary chemicals, the feelings they produce, and the conscious associations — the stories, images and assumptions — to go with them. Emily Good lacks the "feeling" of being in love

with Zep Baker and, in all probability, understands this condition to be permanent. She may in fact consciously wish this to be so. All these factors considered, she is the ideal subject for an investigation that will undertake to prove that the conscious mind can be fooled into believing it is "in love" by counterfeit stimulations.

c) It is important to note that the circumstances of this investigation — specifically, the involuntary, unknowing participation of Emily Good — prevent the direct application of controlled doses of neurochemicals, via injections or pills, in a lab environment. We are limited, therefore, to a more indirect and inexact method: provoking the brain's responses via orchestrated experience. Put simply: We must cause Emily's brain to dose itself.

"I REMEMBER THIS OTHER TIME in the car," says Zep. He's staring out the window, his thumbs working the wheel edge. "Can't remember what I was driving. Maybe the Range Rover. Pebbles was with me. She was little, about four. It was summer. We were waiting on Em to come out of a store somewhere." He drops his head in thought. "It was Tampa. I remember 'cause I was suspended for fifteen games so they said, 'Go home,' so we went."

Zep lifts his head. "Anyway, we're waiting for her. It's taking her so long Pebbles falls asleep in the car seat. And, you know, I'm checking my watch. Where the hell is she? I'm thinking, should I go in and check? I got the kid, so that means I gotta wake her up and get her out of the seat. It becomes a big production. So I stay put. And then I start having these weird thoughts, like, what if she's never coming out? What if she died in there and they're calling an ambulance right now? So I start listening for that, you know, the siren. Sitting there in the car. Then I think … what if she just skipped out? Like maybe she went in the front door and straight out the back and now she's in some guy's car and they're headed to New York or some place.

"I figure that's it. Still got my ear cocked for an ambulance though, just in case. But, pretty sure she's gone. Heart's going like mad. I'm looking in the mirror back at Pebbles, like, 'It's just me and you now.' And I'm thinking, 'Holy fuck, I gotta tell my mom.' And I'm thinking about how to tell her. And I start going crazy about that, like, do I call her or wait till I see her? How do I tell her? And I feel this, like, shame. Just … hot mud sliding over me, all this shame."

Zep pulls a deep breath into his chest. Shakes his head.

"Then she comes out with two big bags. Gets in the car. Says, 'Look what I got us.' And I'm wiping tears out of my eyes."

I ask him what it was she'd bought.

"Don't remember." Zep pushes himself straight in his seat. "Some fucking thing."

PHASE 1 — Interest

This morning, Zep's assignment is simple, but he must execute it flawlessly in order to set up all that is to come. It has two main components: 1. Ambush, and 2. Injury.

We are waiting for Emily to drop their daughter off at school. She will be driving, Zep is sure, a champagne-coloured Honda CR-V. When she turns into the parking lot he is to wait a moment, then follow. He is to park or stop the car in a way that prevents Emily from seeing me through the windshield. (Only the Cadillac's side and rear windows are tinted.)

It's unlikely that Emily will exit the CR-V when she stops. When Pebbles emerges from the passenger side, Zep will get his daughter's attention and run toward her, smiling. This will be a surprise for Emily and Pebbles both, and surprise is critical. If Emily were to anticipate seeing Zep, her negative associations with him would, for hours prior to the meeting, stimulate the release of cortisol by the HPA axis. She would arrive on the scene angry, irritable, ready for battle, and this would eliminate any chance of a positive reaction during the following two stages of the encounter.

First, Emily will see Zep and Pebbles embrace. It has been nearly a year since Emily has witnessed Zep and Pebbles interacting. (Since she and her mother began living with Emily's parents after the separation, Pebbles has generally been flown to Tampa for visits with her father.) So the quality of the embrace is important. This is why it's necessary for Zep to smile as he runs toward Pebbles. She doesn't have negative associations with her father, so the surprise of seeing him should be a happy one, as long as he gives her no signal to be concerned.

In addition, Zep's running should trigger Pebbles to start running toward him. Rather than being hesitant and uncertain, their embrace will be enthusiastic and joyful. So immediately after Emily registers the unexpected presence of her ex-husband, she will see Zep receiving love.

This will give Emily a striking mental image to replay later, as she thinks about the encounter. It should also prompt her brain and pituitary gland to release oxytocin. Normally a neurochemical associated with bonding, affiliation and trust, oxytocin release can also be stimulated when the subject experiences empathy. Watching the emotional reunion of Zep and Pebbles will be Emily's first empathy trigger.

It is likely at this point that Emily will get out of the CR-V to ask Zep why he's in Buffalo. He will tell her that he is here to do some charity work for the Buffalo Bisons, one of his former teams. He will mention visiting sick children in hospitals. This will give Emily another positive association for Zep and another prompt for empathy. It should also give Emily's neocortex enough information to process so as to ward off for a moment the intrusion of negative thoughts or anger at his surprise appearance. This should give Zep enough time to say goodbye to Pebbles and to proceed to the second main event of this encounter: Injury.

After waving goodbye to Pebbles, and after her back is turned, Zep will move away from Emily's car. He has been given clear instructions not to move toward Emily or to initiate any kind of physical interaction at this stage. When it is safe to do so — with Pebbles out of sight, with Emily's eyes still on him, and with no other cars or parents too close — Zep will stumble and fall heavily. This will be Emily's second empathy trigger.

During his fall, Zep will attempt to tear part of his clothing and, if possible, draw blood. It may be a knee or an elbow, but knee is best because it is more potentially debilitating. It took some explanation to get Zep to agree to this part of the encounter. It wasn't pain he feared, apparently, but embarrassment. He didn't like the idea of appearing weak in front of the woman he's trying to impress.

Eventually he was made to understand that allowing Emily to see him weak and injured will help him in three ways: 1. It will trigger a second and more significant release of nurturing oxytocin in Emily's brain. 2. It will provide the seed of an image/idea to counter Emily's negative view of Zep as "concerned with appearances." 3. A visible injury to Zep's knee should prompt Emily to approach him and help him to his feet. Thus, Emily herself will initiate the first physical contact between the two, ensuring there can be no negative associations — no fear or reservations — with this initial touch.

BY 8:25 A.M. PARENTAL DROP-OFFS have become steady occurrences in the City Honors School parking lot, about five per minute. Finally, at 8:33 a.m., Zep announces Emily's arrival with a sharp intake of breath.

"There she is. Fuck."

Several blocks away, Emily's CR-V can be seen turning onto East North Street from Jefferson Avenue. For a moment Zep hesitates, then he reaches up and starts the SUV's ignition. I counsel him to wait.

"Yup."

I remind him to run toward Pebbles around the front of their car, not the rear, so that Emily can see him.

"Right." He turns to me. "Do I look okay?"

ZB Transcript 8

HEY MARCIE. SO ... GUESS, uh, guess where I'm talking to you from. I'm gonna give you a few clues. It's sorta green, and there's a lot of tile, and I got a curtain around me, and it's not my hotel bathroom.

Yeah, I'm in the emergency ward at Buffalo General. Ha! I'm betting you weren't expecting that. I'm in an exam room now or whatever they call these. I was in the waiting room for about three hours and they just transferred me. But I'm still waiting.

Don't worry or anything. I really fucked up my knee though. It's all part of the plan or something, except, I don't think it was supposed be this bad. But the good news is the hospital was only like three blocks from the school, so — okay Marcie the doc's here I'll pick this up later!

OKAY, SORRY MARCIE, I'm back and so what happened is — okay, I should start from the beginning. Uh ... *fuck*. You wanna know something? Jesus Christ. Don't ever try and drive with a knee brace on. It's fucking awkward as shit. It's a good thing I'm not in the Ghibli right now, I'm telling you. They put me on some heavy painkillers too, which, technically I guess I shouldn't be driving but ... whatever.

Hope's back at the hotel right now. I guess she's cooking up everything we're gonna be doing tomorrow.

So I guess I should give you the story here.

I won't get into all the, like, science stuff 'cause I gotta admit whenever Hope's talking to me it's like a bunch of F-35s screaming over my head. But we set up this whole situation with Emily and Pebbles and it pretty much went how it was supposed to I think. Except for a couple of hiccups.

Fuck, I'm telling you, Marcie, I was so fucking nervous it was like Cleveland in '97, my first big league at bat. It was just like that! When Emily pulled into the parking lot I seriously thought I was gonna pass out for a minute.

So the whole thing was —

Yeah, yeah! Gimme a minute to get my *goddamn* leg on the *goddamn* pedal. Jesus Christ. Everybody's in such a fucking hurry.

So, we had to spring this surprise on Emily and get her to start seeing me in a good light or at least give her something good to think about. Right? 'Cause otherwise she doesn't want to have anything to do with me. And Hope had this whole scenario and it was ... awesome. Seriously, Marcie, she should be planning military raids or something.

So, okay, we're parked on the street opposite the parking lot for the school, Pebbles' school, and Emily comes with the CR-V and she pulls into the lot and I gotta wait for a minute to see where she's gonna go. Like is she gonna just pull up to the door or is she gonna park the car, we couldn't be sure right? And it's all gotta go smooth. So I gotta wait to see and then I'm gonna pull in and some asshole, I mean, probably a nice guy, you know, he's a parent, he pulls into the lot in front of me with his kid! So I can't really see where Em's going. So already this isn't going well, right?

And I'm thinking, fuck fuck fuck. But then I see the cars all have to go in one direction, like in a circle. That means Em's gotta come out the other way. So that's where I go. Split-second decision, I go the wrong direction, deliberately. And I put the car where she's gotta work to get around it when she leaves. Just in case, right?

Great, so then I get out of the car. And I'm about, I dunno, a hundred feet away from where Em's stopped her car, and I see Pebbles getting out of the passenger side. And that's my cue. I gotta call her name, like "Hey Pebbles!" And then I gotta start running to her! But I'm kinda far away so fuck, I shout it. "Pebbles! Pebbles!" And then I start booking it! Fast as I can!

And she turns around and she's, like, startled, right? The look on her face is supposed to be "Hey cool, it's Dad." But really her face is like, "What the hairy fuck?" So then I'm thinking, holy shit, it probably looks like some big emergency! Like I heard there's a bomb and I'm running to save her from terrorists, like SLOW DOWN asshole! Right?

So, okay. Just a minute, I gotta ... feels like this brace is cutting off all the circulation in my leg.

SO ANYWAY, I SLOW DOWN into a nice trot. I'm thinking home run speed not infield-single speed. And I wave and I smack a big all-star smile on my face like Hope told me. And just like Hope said, Pebbles starts grinning and running to me and man that was cool, Marcie. That was so cool. When your kid runs to you with a smile on her face? Jesus. That's something you could sell as a drug, I'm telling you. I haven't seen that from Pebs since she was eight years old. And we have this great hug. She totally forgets her friends are watching her. She's got her face squished in my chest and she's saying, "Dad, why are you here?"

And then Emily gets out of the car. And my first reaction, Marcie, seriously, it's ... Is this my wife? 'Cause I haven't seen her in about eight months at least, and she's totally different. She's just ... I mean ... it's hard to describe. I want to say "more beautiful" than I've ever seen her but it's more like "the most beautiful," you know what I mean? Like the best Emily has ever looked, all the times and all the years I've known her, all put together. Bam! That's how she looked. And I'm not lying, it hit me. It hit me so hard it shoved me backward. And it was all I could do not to blow it. You know? I just wanted to go up to her and grab her and just ... Honestly? I just wanted to look at her. Just look, that's all. Because, *man* ... And I wanted her to look at me like she used to. When she loved me, you know, she looked at me a certain way. I don't know how to put it in words but it was like ... sunshine or something. That sounds stupid. But how sunshine makes you feel.

Jesus Christ. *Take another asshole pill, asshole*! You hear that horn going, Marcie? Fuck me ... I guess, I dunno, maybe I am going kinda slow here. I'm just driving around like an idiot. I should just pull over.

Here's a Wendy's, this'll do ... Give me a second here.

Okay. Off. We're good. Just take a breath.

So Em comes out of the car. Looking amazing ...

And I'm trying to remember, what's my job now, right? What'd Hope tell me to do? Like everything's just wiped outta my brain. And Em's coming closer, got this confused look on her face. Not mad but maybe a little.

"Zep," she says. "What are you doing here?"

"Yeah, Dad," says Pebbles.

And I'm thinking shit shit shit, what's my story? And I totally blank. Totally gone. Like I missed the sign completely. I even look over to the car for Hope but I can't see her. And you know what I say, Marcie? You know what I say?

"Nothing."

Like I'm some kid caught looking at porn and his mom says "what are you doing!"

"Nothing."

Fuck.

So Em says, "*Nothing*? Zep, Pebbles isn't visiting you till the summer. What are you doing in Buffalo? Why are you *here*?"

And Pebbles backs up a bit, like to get a better look at me. And Em's giving me this hard suspicious stare and I know that's, like, not what's supposed to be happening at all. And I look at the car again and Em looks where I'm looking and I'm thinking, shit, what if she sees Hope? It's all over! And the only thing I can remember is I gotta screw up my knee. That's my job. Take one for the team. That's the only thing in my brain!

So I turn. For who knows why? To look natural or something. I just turn, and then ... I go down. I mean I go *down*! Like my knee's a Howitzer heading straight for the pavement.

And I think I might've blacked out for a second, from the pain. 'Cause the next thing is I'm looking up at two faces, Em and Pebbles. And Pebbles is crying. And Em's looking worried, and there's other people around too. Like other parents, and kids. They're all crowded around! And then it hits me.

Bisons. Hospitals. My story is Bisons and hospitals! So that's what I say, while I'm on my back in the parking lot.

"I'm going to the hospitals."

And Em says, "It's okay, Zep. The hospital's close. I'll take you."

So it worked out, Marcie. It all worked out. And the doctor said I got a fractured patella.

These, uh ... these painkillers are really kicking in, Marcie, so I'm just gonna ... I'll talk to you later.

Tuesday, April 21 /cont

WE KNOW HOW MEMORIES happen. We know what makes them stay. We know where memories live.

Something happens when you're ten — your mother slaps you — and when the cerebral cortex registers this, the brain says oh, interesting. The brain says let the hippocampus team have a look at that. Put a light on Your Mother Slaps You. Let's retrace that event. The rest of life goes on, all the things you see and hear and feel, while the hippocampus team examines Your Mother Slaps You, measures it, reflects it in mirrors, redraws it in pencil and ink, carves it into plaster, cuts it into stone. This is you thinking about how your mother slapped you, what it felt like, what it sounded like, how her eyes looked, how her perfume smelled. This is you dreaming about it. This is you wishing it had never happened. This is you hating your mother for slapping you.

Memories that provoke our emotions get carved the deepest.

And when the hippocampus has examined every angle, carved along every line, Your Mother Slaps You takes its permanent place in the cortex, in the same spot it first happened. Because for you, that's where it did happen. Your mother's hand struck your cheek in the three-dimensional world, but as far as your brain is concerned, it happened in a matrix of cortical receptors. And if it's carved deep enough, that's where the experience remains. So when you remember Your Mother Slaps You, you are, in fact, reliving it.

This happens with every important memory we hold, from the

best to the worst. Each wondrous event, each terrifying experience, gets retraced over and over, carved deeper by our thoughts and our dreams, until it can never be washed or worn away.

Where my thumb stuck to Adnan's hand, it left a print. And for some hours he tried to keep it safe, using his hand awkwardly to avoid ruining it. My joking about it only made his face darken. He said, in a voice so low I could barely hear it, "Maybe this is all I will have of you."

I wanted to tell him, but he would have misunderstood: More likely, you will never be rid of me.

Initial assessment of the events of April 21:

It's hard to know whether the validity of the investigation has already been compromised by what happened in the parking lot of City Honors School. Very little went according to the plan I established with Zep, and now his injury may impede further progress. Admittedly, it might have been worse. There was a moment, after Emily Good emerged from her vehicle, when Zep appeared to freeze. I thought then, as I watched at a distance from inside Zep's car, that he might reveal the entire project, and his hopes for reconciliation. In the midst of what apparently was a moment of panic-induced amnesia, he did turn and look directly toward me. And the gaze of his ex-wife, Emily, followed. Uncertain how well my presence was obscured by the car's tinted windows, I remained as still as possible. I was able, consequently, to see Zep fall to his knees, so I knew that he was attempting to follow the plan we'd established, although his actions throughout in almost no way reflected the instructions I had given him. (The chief deviations being: 1. He ran toward his daughter, Pebbles, far too aggressively, which could well have provoked anxiety in her rather than

> joy. 2. It's not clear that he ever gave his ex-wife the story designed to explain his presence in Buffalo. 3. He attempted to injure himself in the presence of his daughter, who reacted with predictable anguish, thereby rendering Emily's emotional response as much a reaction to her concern as to Zep's injury. 4. He injured himself excessively, forcing Emily to transport him to the hospital, thereby extending the time they spent in each other's presence and increasing the chances that Zep would speak or act in such a way as to compromise Emily's neurochemical activity.
>
> It will be, likely, some days before it's clear whether, and to what extent, these deviations from the plan have compromised the investigation.

I WAITED A WHILE to contact Zep after he was helped into Emily's car and driven out of the parking lot. My assumption was that he was being taken for treatment — from his hobbled movements his injury seemed to be significant — but there was no way for me to follow. Zep had taken his keys.

After twenty minutes, he called me. He explained that he was waiting in the emergency room of a hospital only a few blocks away, and that after dropping him off at the entrance, Emily had continued on to work. I agreed to meet him there.

When I found him sitting in the waiting area at Buffalo General, he was smiling to himself. This was in spite of the fact his knee appeared to be painfully swollen. He looked up when I sat down beside him.

"Did you see her?" he asked.

I said yes, I had, although not in any detail because of the distance. (It occurs to me that if we continue I should get a pair of binoculars.)

"She was beautiful, huh?" His eyes seemed to search for confirmation, and when I nodded his smile grew wider.

"Look," he said, "I know I kinda fucked up this whole thing. But I think it worked okay." He began counting on his fingers. "Pebs hugged me, Em saw me hurt, and she helped me up. It's the result that matters, right? I mean, I missed the bunt, but I still got the runner over."

It seemed best, at that moment, not to review all of the ways the results might have been tainted. I asked what they'd talked about in the car.

"Nothing much. It was just a few blocks. I tried to tell her the whole charity, hospitals thing. But mostly she was on the phone to her office about how she'd be late for some meeting." He began to rub his knee then, the first time I'd seen him acknowledge any discomfort, and stared toward the floor, looking somewhat lost.

"Zep?"

"Yeah? Oh. I was just thinking, it was kinda like I wasn't there, in the car. Hey" — he clapped his hands — "what's the next step? What're we doing?"

I told him I would take a cab back to the hotel and review where we stood.

Wednesday, April 22

APPARENTLY, OPENING THE CURTAINS of a hotel room in the early morning can be an act of desperation. Flickering lampposts, empty streets, pink sunlight slipping over flat, granular roofs … the sight of these things can be comforts when you spend your nights in an anonymous, carpeted space and the only familiar things at hand are your own thoughts.

Last evening, for a change, rather than order room service, I ate dinner downstairs at the restaurant Zep told me about. He said he'd been banned for using profanity — "For swearing like a motherfucker, as usual," he said, seeming somewhat chagrinned — so it was safe for me to be there. It's not that I'm afraid of Zep, but I'm wary of lines blurring between the professional and personal. He does not strike me as someone who is skilled at the observation of boundaries.

What I discovered, which I had not known before, is that at certain restaurants — one such as this, all linen and dark wood, held back in time — a woman eating alone is like the weakest hatchling in the nest. Something to be worried over, pecked at and prodded until it comes to welcome death as an alternative to continued attention. The young waiter assigned to me made a sad, quizzical face as he approached the table. "Are you waiting for …?" he said, his hand wavering spell-like over the opposite place setting. I wanted to finish his sentence: "… a crystal ball? … some entrails?" When I told him I was alone as intended, he smiled as if I were lying. Soon he was treating me like an old familiar, lingering with his tray on his hip to see if there might be anything about my Alaskan Halibut I wanted to discuss, and revealing secrets from nearby tables. ("That couple in the corner? She's on her third Bloody Mary, and she's through taking his sister's crap.") Eventually my waiter, who confided that his name was Craig, thought it worthwhile to inform me when he was getting off shift.

At such Craig moments, I wonder what encouraging signal I could possibly be giving off. Is politeness enough? I don't want to be rude. Rudeness demands a courage I don't possess. Saying "Go away" seems to me as likely to attract unwanted attention as a smile. When the Craigs come at me, I do my best to give them nothing to react to. I listen without comment, keep my face as still as possible. Sometimes, after a Craig experience, I check my expression in a reflective surface — my phone, an elevator's mirrored wall. Was I smiling without being aware of it? Did my face betray me?

During those precious moments in the Steakhouse when Craig left me alone, I was observed by a table of two men seated by a bank of red-silk rhododendrons. They looked at me alternately, never together, so that I felt passed between them. A man dining with his wife sat across from me on the other side of the room. His back to the wall, he was able to stare at me over his wife's shoulder as she looked down to slice her teriyaki-glazed salmon. And three middle-aged women in running shoes twice asked me to join them because, they said, I looked "lonely."

Stupidly I'd left my phone in my room, and when I returned I saw that Lesley had left a message. "You're not answering and it's dinnertime so … I guess that's a good sign?"

She wanted to let me know that Adnan had called again. "I have this funny idea that he may be the father of your unborn child, so I'm a little torn about leaving him completely in the dark." She assured me all she'd told him was that I was out of town. But after she did, Adnan asked if he could send me an email. He understood that I didn't want to be reached directly. He was asking only that she forward his email to me. It was more a plea, said Lesley, than a request.

"So, Hope, this is me checking. Are you okay with me forwarding an email? There is a man here dangling at the end of a string and I am rather loath to leave him like this. Call me back or email me. But it would be nice to talk to you."

I emailed and told her to go ahead. Adnan's email arrived just over an hour later.

Dear Hope,

Thank you for let me speak to you in this letter. I have been think about what I wish to say to you for now three weeks.

The phone call we had some days ago was not enough. We did not talk about any important things. So that is why I am need to send you this letter.

As I have said to you please forgive my language and also in this letter. English is not my first language because I came here with my parents when I was sixteen years old from Syria but I have always tried very hard and I have done my best. I use the spell check and I think clearly and most times it is enough but not when I speak to someone who deserves better words, stronger words, and that is what I believe about you.

I do not want say silly things in this letter. You are not a woman who wants silly things. I know that. But I want to say all from what is in the heart. When you touched my hand where it stuck to the syrup that day was special to me. It was only one small thing but if that was only what happened, then that day would be special. Because I already know at that time that you are a good woman. I don't know why. I don't know what tells me. But I know. And that is why I gave you the things that night when I cooked at the party. You were alone. You had friends but no special friend beside you. And I saw you then and wanted to be that special friend. But how? So I made you things that night and that was good because it was why you talk to me at the market.

And so we were together. One time together for a small few hours. Not enough. But it was all the best times of my life for me. That is what I feel. And maybe that is a silly thing. But for me it is what is true. And what we did, all the things in the kitchen, and cooking, and what I made for you and we ate and all of that time was very good. It was very good,

Hope. And all of that would be enough.

But then you put your hand to my mouth and we kiss, my Hope, we kiss. And then we make love on my mattress. On my bad bed which was mess and nothing you should see but you said it was okay.

And you gave me a gift of trust Hope. A special gift. You said for me to look. And so I look and what I see can never make me feel good about the people of this world. I am sorry for crying. I am sorry to not be brave like you. And I said then forgive me and I hope you have forgived me but I think you have not Hope. I think because I cried is why you will not talk to me or see me now. Or maybe something else I did wrong. So I am very sorry Hope. I want to make it better. I will not cry. Never more will I cry Hope I promise!

I promise to you Hope. I promise to be good for you. And I am a man who keep all his promise every one.

Please let me come where you are.

Adnan

THIS IS MOSTLY, I THINK, the effect of a changing ratio between dopamine and serotonin. High levels of dopamine are released from cells in the VTA — the ventral tegmental area — which project into the reward systems of the striatum, driving motivated thinking. "I want what I want." And high dopamine levels may work to suppress serotonin, leading to depression and anxiety. "I feel bad without the thing that I want." And low levels of serotonin trigger excessive activity in the anterior cingulate gyrus which has been associated with obsessive thoughts and behaviours. "Only what I want can make me feel better." This is how the brain creates infatuation, the fixation on the object of affection. It's a model for the effect we will try to induce in Emily.

I can think about it only like that, if I try. I can think about this man's pain as a natural product of biology, as evolutionary wish-fulfillment, nothing really to do with me. If I think about it like that, then it could have been any other woman. A Sally in that chair at the dinner table. An Anne. Alone, conventionally attractive, overdressed, trying too hard to relax among people she barely knew. An object for this man's VTA to latch on to.

Biology can explain why he noticed me, and wanted me, and why he thinks he needs me still. What it doesn't explain is why I spoke to him in the market. Why I touched his sticky hand. What it doesn't explain is why I went with him in his van, let him do the things he wanted to do. Let myself let him. Why I allowed him to see what even I won't look at: the empirical evidence that I am not any woman, as much as I might wish to be.

And it doesn't explain why, on the bottom shelf of the bar fridge in my hotel room, sits a tinfoil package of crumbling tarts. Or why I open this package each night, and take these things he formed with his hands, and in the dark, lay them on my breasts.

ZB Transcript 9

MARCIE WHAT THE FUCK is going on with Lino?

Jesus Christ, it's been like a week since I heard from him. He won't answer his phone. He won't return my messages. Last I heard the investor dude was ready to go and now it's like total radio silence. I want to see papers! Like, contracts and shit. I want this guy's money in the bank. I want my formula guy working on tastes. Has he given you anything? Lino I'm talking about. Or shit, formulas even. Tastes. Cranberry Quench, for fuck's sake. A list of ingredients. Anything you can fax me, send it through the hotel. I wanna know something's happening.

Right now I'm just sitting here. I'm in the conference room waiting for Hope, watching a goddamn tube light spazzing out over my head. Yeah, that's first class, Hyatt.

Hope called me about eight this morning and said she needed a few hours because she hadn't slept. Like I did any sleeping the way this goddamn knee is killing me.

Anyway, she gave me an assignment. The next deal is we have to make Emily laugh, so I have to come up with some things that'll get laughs from her. And they can't be like chuckles, either. They have to be big laughs. She had some French word for it.

So that's what I've been trying to do all goddamn morning. I went outside and I walked around like the doctor told me, because he said the knee might seize up on me if I don't. Gotta keep moving. So I'm out there walking around like an idiot trying to remember what gets Emily laughing. And she has a great laugh, you know? I mean, get her going and she'll be holding her stomach and gasping and tears'll be running down her face. So, it should be easy, right? Yeah. But I can't come up with a damn thing.

Pebbles is the only thing I can think of. She'll do something goofy and for sure that'll crack Emily up. I mean, thinking back ... that was probably the only thing that got us through the last year. It's like Pebs knew it was close, you know? She knew something was up. And she just worked like hell to keep Emily laughing. She'd haul out an old Hallowe'en costume or come up with some stupid stunt. I remember ... I remember one time they were learning levers or something in school and she rigged up this lever to fire those squishy candies into her mouth. You know those gummi things? She got Em to sit down for this and started pelting her face with these gummies and pretty soon Emily's howling. Just fucking howling, she can't catch her breath. Pebs was ten or eleven then but ... she had some goddamn degree in keeping her mom happy.

But I don't wanna rope Pebbles into this, you know? It's on me. It's all on me.

Pisses me off I can't think of anything.

Probably if a piano fell on my head Em would find that pretty funny. Or got arrested for tax fraud or something. That'd be a gut-buster.

OKAY, I GOT one thing.

I figure it can't be like taking her to a funny movie, right? Because that'd be a date and no way she's going for that yet. I mean, that's where we're trying to get to. Trying to get past that, even. But one base at a time. You can't score direct from first.

So I'm thinking it's gotta be a surprise, something unexpected.

Like we're doing one thing and something else happens. Walking down the street and a bird shits on me or something. I mean, she'd laugh at that. Guaranteed she'd laugh. And if I was wearing a new suit? Oh man, she'd kill herself. But it's not like I can get a trained bird to shit on cue in the next twenty-four hours.

Something along those lines though, I think that might work. It's not much, but maybe I can talk it through with Hope. Whenever she gets down here.

Wednesday, April 22 /cont.

I CALLED MY MOTHER FIRST. It seemed easier that way, starting with what I thought would be the smaller bite of penance. And it was important to me that I be able to tell Lesley I had made that call. That I hadn't ignored her advice. My mother may no longer be (if she ever was) a mast to which I can rope myself. But I fear the loss of Lesley. Without her observance, and her sturdy presence, I would feel windblown.

Lesley and I have been friends since my second hospital stay, which makes it ten years. She was assigned to me as a peer counsellor and we hit it off. I forgave her her woolly eccentricities, her vaguely vegan diet (mouldy cheeses her weakness), her tendency to drop her voice to a comforting murmur whenever I showed any anxiety (so that sometimes I was only made aware of my anxiety by the low hum in her words), and her ridiculous love of fringes in all things — clothes, throw pillows, theatre. She, for her part, forgave me my eight fewer years, my ninety fewer pounds, and my tendency to bolt from certain kinds of pressure like a cat unable to forget being stepped on.

When I left home, seven months after the hospital, it was because Lesley had offered me a room in her third-floor apartment. Together we endured a rotation of downstairs neighbours, including a singer of Chinese opera, a pot-smoking professor of environmental studies, and a single mother of one inconsolable toddler. At any hour this desperate mother would scream at her wailing child to stop crying, which had the effect anyone but apparently her might have expected. And Lesley and I would sit in the dark listening for a change in the tenor of the mother's voice that would signal a need to intervene. We didn't know precisely what we were listening for, but felt we would recognize it when it came. And for me it was oddly comforting, those minutes or hours with Lesley, listening to the anguish of a mother and her child. It was an anguish bound within limits. You could perceive the borders of it, and know that this pain, while real, could never touch you. I sometimes imagine that men find a similar consolation in watching football.

We left that apartment before we heard the telltale change, but not because of the noise. A larger apartment opened up in a house Lesley had long admired and so we moved, and we have lived and moved together ever since. Over the years Lesley has taught me to love Houjicha tea. She has introduced me to writers, both living and dead. She has brought me ginger ale when my stomach is upset, and she has taken small, sharp implements from my hands.

So I needed to speak to my mother first. And when the morning had aged past its pink and I knew she'd be up and sitting with a coffee and a Sudoku, I called.

There was a pause when I said hello, and I understood that she was standing in the kitchen, calibrating her reaction. Her first word or two were important. She was undoubtedly angry and hurt, still, but knew better than to unleash it first thing, all at once. And I'm sure some part of her was relieved too, and grateful, simply to be allowed to hear my voice. This is the terrible power of the damaged daughter. The confusion, pain and yearning that we invoke simply by being. We're like gods.

"Darling," she said. And I was proud of her for that choice, a kind of masterpiece of caring and distance. "How are you?"

"I'm fine, Mom."

"Are you still in … was it Buffalo?"

"It was and is."

"Working."

"In a way."

She chirped a little laugh, more, I supposed, from tension than anything. I wondered if she was eyeing her cigarettes.

"And the weather's good there?"

"Mom, it's not even two hours away. It's the same."

"I think that's not true, actually. But it's … not important."

For a moment there was no sound. Only the loud, empty silence of the wounded parent.

"So, Hope —"

"Mom, I want to say I'm sorry for walking out on you —"

"For walking away, yes. With such …"

"It wasn't fair."

"No."

"So that's why I'm calling, okay? I'm sorry."

"All right, well." She took a deep breath. In the background I briefly heard the sound of running water. She cleared her throat. "And so … you're pregnant. You're sure?"

"Pretty sure. I had some morning sickness, and I did a test that came up positive. But I haven't been to a doctor yet."

"Well, you definitely need to do that."

"I know."

"So, sweetheart … I've been wanting to ask you and I didn't get a chance to before —"

"Mom —"

"Are you happy, darling? Is this a good thing?"

We breathed on that for a while, my mother and I.

"Perhaps you don't know yet," she said finally. "It can be a shock for anyone. Have you talked —"

"You're ...," I started. "Mom, you're the only one I've said anything to about this."

"Oh. Not even Lesley?"

"Not yet."

"Oh, so ..." I could tell she had started to cry. "Well, thank you, Hope. Oh, that's ... thank you. What about ... what about the father?"

"No."

"Well, when are you coming back, darling? Because I don't —"

"I don't know exactly."

"Hope, you must come home," she said. She was crying openly now. "Because right now you're alone and I ... I don't want you to be alone!"

I waited for a moment. Experience had taught that it was better to let the space between us expand with quiet than to try and shove words around my mother's weeping.

"I just ...," she said eventually, "I would like to see you, sweetheart. And know you're all right. That's all. I want you to be safe. And ... there are things that I can do."

"Okay, Mom."

She tried to chuckle. "A grandmother can come in handy, you know. I mean, if that's what you decide."

We were like snap-off pieces, my mother and I, displaced from the home and the life we had known, she in the granite-countered kitchen of a house that held no history for her, with a man who could never be blamed, me in a hotel room cleansed of memory at the same time every day. We were loose parts detached from what had formed us, waiting to be assembled into something new.

"Well, I'm going to make Bill his coffee now, darling," she said. "Please call if you need anything at all."

BEFORE I PICKED UP THE phone again I stood in the shower for fifteen minutes, against the impersonality of its streak-free porcelain, the brittle smile of its buffed chrome. The bathroom light was off, in contempt of the wraparound mirrors. In my life, I have made friends with bathrooms. We achieve intimacy incrementally. If we have time enough, we become familiar, we share secrets. This hotel bathroom will never know me; it will never earn my trust.

When I called Lesley, she was in her least forgiving mood.

"You are better than this, Hope," she said. "It's indefensible what you're doing."

I told her I wasn't trying to defend myself.

"This poor man."

"Did you read the letter?"

"Yes, I read it. I didn't feel bad about it either, and I still don't. This is a situation you created."

She sounded as if she were putting away groceries; her breathing had the huffiness of exertion, of cans shoved into place, cupboards slammed shut. But what she was closing off were my paths of avoidance. There have been times in the past when Lesley has gripped my face in her hands and forced me to look her in the eye. I could tell it frustrated her now that she could not grab hold of my cheeks.

"What are you telling yourself?" she said. "What tape are you playing?"

"I'm not."

"Do you think he's dangerous?"

"No."

"What do you fear?"

"Nothing."

"Bullshit, bullshit. God, I'm not even going to talk to you."

I waited for her to hang up but I knew she wouldn't. Lesley would never abandon me. But I also knew that I couldn't tell her what I feared more than anything in that moment — that whatever I said would be used to build an argument against delay, against hoping for my problems to vanish. Pregnancies didn't always take, wasn't that true? Did things not sometimes slip away? Might I not soon stand up in the bathroom, look down and see my immediate future resolved? Lesley has never believed in handing one's keys to circumstance.

"Let me ask you this," she said. "When I say his name, when I say 'Adnan,' what do you feel?"

For a moment I said nothing. I knew she wanted honesty, and by now, after ten years of the drama of me, she had a right to expect it. And then I said the cheapest, most counterfeit thing of all.

"I don't know."

"Adnan, Hope. *Adnan*. What's going on right now?"

"I have to go."

"Hope, stop."

"I have to go! I'm late!"

She waited. She waited. I might cry. I might blurt out something useful. A scale or two might flake off and reveal something damp and fleshy underneath.

"Fine then," she said finally. "Go."

I hung up.

ZB Transcript 10

HEY, MARCIE, I'M IN THE CAR on my way to dinner. There's this Italian place up on Bryant that looks good. Not too far but I figured I'd drive, 'cause why the hell not? I'm not drinking, right? Maybe I'll head over to the waterfront later. What the hell else am I gonna do with myself around here? I gotta find a poker game or something.

Anyway. Hope and I talked this afternoon. Man, was she in a shitty mood. Jesus. I was thinking maybe "time of the month" or whatever 'cause it used to be a deal for Emily, but who knows? I sure as hell wasn't gonna ask her. "Spitting glass and porcupine quills," that's what my mom used to say. Hey, Marcie, you ever meet my mom? She's still kickin' over in Clearwater. I talk to her every once in a while. Great old lady, I gotta say. Flora Baker. Kept the house running whenever my dad went off on his fuckin' ... whatever. Got a job taking calls at a real estate office. Put up with no end of shit, the way she tells it. Fuckin' scuzzbags at that place.

So, what is this, I gotta turn left here? Shit.

Yeah, my mom. She was pretty mad when Em called it quits. I had to talk her out of writing a letter. She kept saying, "You deserve better! You deserve better!" Which, you know, I didn't want to get into the whole story with her. It's nice to have your mom on your side sometimes.

So, that's way off topic. Back to Hope.

Good news is — no I'm waiting for you, buddy. Waiting for you! Rules of the road, for fuck's sake ... Yeah, so, for this whole laughing thing, Hope says I don't have to get something dropped on my head. She said I might want to avoid, like, risking injury for a while. I said fine by me! It could be a story, she said. I could bump into Emily and start talking about something funny that happened, maybe something from way back. Whole point is to get her laughing, doesn't matter what. So I was thinking about that time at the drive-in, back in '97 I think. I ever tell you that story, Marcie?

It was here in Buffalo. Em and me had just started going out. I was like twenty-five and she's three years younger, so twenty-two, right? And there was this whole thing with the Bisons where, I guess some guys had come in late a few times, there was a lot of partying, so they were cracking down. They put a curfew on the whole team for, I dunno, two weeks or something. Everybody had to be home by midnight. But these two guys, two relief pitchers — it was Mercin, Bobby Mercin, good fastball guy, and, uh, Hernando Gabrey, we called him Gabbers — they were the real partiers. So they had to be in by ten. And it was pretty serious 'cause they were gonna get cut if they broke this curfew. And Gabbers had these kids back on the island he's from. Two or three kids I dunno, but, you know ...

Yeah! So it was a Saturday, and we had a day game. And then that night a few of us wanted to go to the movies with our girls, right? Somebody said, I guess it was Rick Kelsoe, said let's go to the drive-in. There were still a few of them around then, and I think one of them was playing *Happy Gilmore* so we said let's go. And Bobby and Gabbers said they wanted to come along. But, so, we tried to talk them out of it. The movie only started at like ten. But these two guys, they were fuckin' determined. I dunno, they loved the danger or something. So we said okay, we'll smuggle the guys into the theatre in the trunk. 'Cause we couldn't let anybody see them, right? This is Buffalo, so everybody knows their faces and everybody knows these guys are in the doghouse — I mean, all that stuff gets reported here, so anybody sees them after ten it's gonna get back to the team.

I think ... Is this the place? ... Yeah.

Just a minute, Marcie, I'm parking ... Popular place by the looks of it.

Okay.

So anyway, I'll finish this before I go in. Don't want to get turfed from another restaurant.

These guys were living in some shitty apartment in Tonawanda, so we picked them up there. And fuck, they were already drunk! And we already had five or six people in the car — it was me and Em, and Kelsoe and whatever chick he was seeing then, and somebody else ... Ham Tacada! Called Ham for obvious reasons. So it was five but it seemed like six, if you know what I mean.

And so we pick these two up and they're pissed, so we said, "Get in the trunk, assholes." Rick was driving this big Chrysler so he had a trunk like a motel room. And they were gonna have to get in anyway eventually, before we drove into the theatre. So we just said, "Get in now." And we're already killing ourselves, right? These guys are climbing in and hitting their heads and stepping on each other trying to sort themselves and the two girls, they don't know what they've got themselves into. But Em seemed to be having a good time. She was laughing, kinda nervous.

Anyway, so we shut the lid on them and drive to the place. It's like twenty minutes or something. And we can hear them complaining back there pretty much the whole way. Just stupid stuff. And then Gabbers starts shouting, "Agh! Agh! You fucking asshole! You fucking asshole!"

And we're like, "What! What is it?"

And Gabbers shouts, "He farted! He farted! Fucking asshole farted back here! I can't breathe!"

And Bobby — and it's all muffled, right? — Bobby shouts, "I can't help it! I ate your burritos!"

So we're just dying by this point. And then we get to the theatre and we tell them like, "Shut up! Shut up! We're here!" So they go quiet. And then we drive around looking for a place. Rick's in the front with his girl and Ham's in the back seat with Em and me. I don't know where we thought these two guys were gonna sit once they got out of the trunk. But anyway, we find this spot, and drive onto the hump, you know, so the front's higher than the back. And Rick turns off the car and it's all quiet for a second, totally silent, and then we hear in the back: *Ffffrrrrrrrt*!

And then: "Agh! Agh! He did it again! He did it again! Motherfuckers let me out! Let me out!" Gabbers is banging on the trunk lid, pounding on it, shaking the car.

But the thing is, we wanted to teach these guys a lesson. Like they were fucking around with their careers, right? But also we were playing good that year and we didn't want to mess with that either. So we wanted these guys to just stop being such fucking idiots. So we said screw it, we're not letting them out. We called back and said, "Gabbers! Shut up! There's a coach here!"

He said, "What?"

We said, "There's a coach here!" I forget which one we said, maybe Altworth, Doug Altworth, the hitting coach. We said, "He's sitting two cars over, with his wife, we can't let you out!"

So Gabbers starts moaning like he's in pain or crying. "Awwwww, fuck! Awwwww. I can't believe you guys, man. I'm gonna die in here, man!"

And then it goes quiet. Pretty soon the movie starts. We're trying to get comfortable. I'm checking to make sure Ham's way in the corner and his hand isn't anywhere near Em's ass. Shit like that. And it's so quiet in the trunk I'm thinking maybe the two of them are asleep. And then, outta nowhere, Bobby Mercin starts going crazy!

"What the fuck! What the fuck!" And the car's bouncing and we're like, What's going on? And then he starts shouting, "He's pissing on me! He's pissing on me! Fuck! Fuck! He's pissing on me!"

"That's what you get, man!" Gabbers is saying. "That feel good? That's what you get!"

Oh, God. Oh fuck. So goddamn funny. And they're wrestling around in there. It's like we got two alligators in the trunk. Gabbers starts shouting, "You kicked my dick! Fuckhead, you kicked my dick!" And I say to Rick we should get out of there.

Like, just take off. Forget the movie. We gotta let these guys out — they're gonna kill each other. So that's what we did. Rick got them back to their apartment and that was it. They never went out drinking together again.

What d'you think, Marcie? Think it'll get Em laughing? I think it's fucking perfect.

Okay, I gotta get something to eat, I'm starving.

Thursday, April 23

LOVE CANNOT ENTER through a guarded perimeter. That's what my research tells me. It isn't a battering ram. It hasn't the monkey strength to climb over walls. It doesn't seep in through cracks like the smoke of siege fires. It comes in only through open doors, and only when invited.

Yesterday I asked Zep to show me a piece of Emily's writing, a letter or an email that would reveal her current state of mind, her attitude toward him. We were sitting in the conference room. The far light panel had been flickering the way it often does, but it went steady just about then, as if the room itself were sitting up to take notice. Zep struggled with his phone for a while, searching his email, until he found something.

"I guess it's like this," he said and, without looking, handed the phone to me.

It was an email Emily had sent him in November, when it seemed he'd been trying to negotiate with her to let Pebbles stay with him an extra week over American Thanksgiving.

Zep,

You say you want more time with Pebbles around Thanksgiving as if it's your right. It's galling! What rights do you think you've earned? And what planet are you on that you think I'd be inclined to give you anything where she's concerned? I don't care what the court said, what you did was despicable and you should feel blessed and grateful that I haven't told her. The only reason I'm letting her fly to see you at all is because if I didn't I'd have to explain why and then everything would be known and the only person that hurts now is her.

Stop asking.

E.

I HANDED THE PHONE BACK to him and waited. Over the years Lesley has used this so many times with me, therapists too — the vacuum effect of silence. But I can't remember ever having used it on someone myself. It felt oddly coercive.

Zep held the phone for a moment, twirling it like a poker chip in his large hand. Then he laid it on the conference table and began spinning it with a flick of his fingers, over and over, all the while staring ahead to some place beyond the room, his face utterly blank. After a minute he glanced over at me and gave me a sheepish grin, as if he'd just remembered I was there.

"My dad," he said. "His name was Harrington. Harrington Baker. Kinda name you think you might see on a business card or something, like a company president. But my dad, you know, he was a piece of shit. He couldn't keep a job. He worked with big machines, like in factories. Hydraulic presses and that. Maintenance technician I guess, that's the name for it. He had a talent for it and he liked it but he was always getting fired. Or he'd just fuck off because whoever it was, whatever company, was making him work too hard. Making him come in on weekends or just generally keeping him busier than he thought he should be. And he drank, you know. That figured in sometimes.

"So there'd be a morning when he'd just stay in bed and that'd be the signal for my mom that she had to get a job for a while so we could keep the groceries coming and didn't get booted out of our house. And then that'd piss him off, like she was showing him up or something. So when he was drunk he'd hit her. Real win-win situation for her.

"He drove a Chevy Impala. Every three years he'd get a new one. Never bought anything but a Chevy Impala. Usually dark blue but sometimes he'd change it up and get a white one. After he hit my mother a couple of times he'd get in his Chevy and drive off for two or three days. No idea where he went but I used to think he was going to some woman who'd make him feel better about himself.

"And then, you know, he'd come back. You'd get home and that Chevy would be in the driveway and nobody would say anything and life would go on. He'd hang around the house for a few weeks, or months sometimes, doing odd jobs. He called them 'property improvements.' One year he put up a metal fence around the backyard. Another year he tore it down and put up a wood one. Dug out part of the backyard for a garden. Put up panelling in the basement. Installed a new railing or new taps. Fixed the grouting in the upstairs bathroom. These were all apology jobs, and there were a bunch of them. Every one of them meant he'd hit my mom. You'd look at the fence or the garden or the cupboards or whatever and you'd think about him hitting her, how he hit her. Pretty soon we were kinda surrounded in that house with all these fucking improvements."

Zep said all this while staring down at the phone he was spinning on the table. Eventually he stopped talking but kept spinning, as if he were caught in the grip of an endless fascination.

I asked him why he was telling me about his father. What did his story have to do with the email from Emily? He took in a deep breath, and the phone went still in his hand.

"My mom stayed with my father until the end, until he drove off drunk one time and took himself out with a hydro pole, but I knew she was never happy. 'Cause he was a wife-beating, cheating piece of shit. And so it was pretty clear to me what a bad husband looked like. Whatever my father did, that's what no woman would want. Right? So when I was married, I always thought, if I could just be better than my father, as a husband, that'd be good. Just don't do what he did. And I made sure, whenever I got angry or shit happened, I had this picture in my mind of my dad, and no matter how I felt or what I wanted to do, I never matched that picture. I was never my father. You know? And I always congratulated myself for that.

"But I guess ...." He turned his phone over once ... twice. "I guess I didn't set the bar high enough."

I asked what Emily was talking about in the email, what had he done that was despicable? I told him it was important for me to know what kind of challenge we were up against. That if he wanted me to help him he couldn't keep important things like this a secret.

"And if I don't tell you?" he said.

"Then this is over and I go home." I began to gather my notes into an orderly stack.

He stayed silent for a moment. And then, strangely, he grinned, and his sun-worn cheeks creased into parentheses around his mouth.

"Man, you're tough," he said. "This is like having to steal a base with two out. You know what I'm talking about? A lot of ways this can go wrong for me."

"Zep, I just want you to be honest."

He was nodding. "Yeah, I know." For a moment he sat still, his eyes gazing at the sheets of paper in front of me. He seemed to be weighing risk and possibility. "Okay, look." He shifted abruptly in his seat. "It's about money. All right? It's a money thing."

I stayed silent.

"She's pissed off about something I did with some money that we had. That's all." He watched me for a moment. "That's all it was."

"Despicable is a strong word."

"For sure. But, you know, couples argue about money. That's what we do. You've probably done it too."

I looked down at my papers and shuffled through them.

"Is this like the suit you bought?"

He shrugged. "Kind of. Probably. Little bigger scale … but, yeah."

"It's something Pebbles doesn't know about, but if she did, she'd be hurt."

"Right, well, maybe. Who knows with kids?" Zep leaned forward, his hands sliding over the surface of the table toward me. "Point is, it's just a money argument. Em and I disagreed about how to spend some money, and that's it."

"Do you think she can forgive you?"

He grinned. "I guess we'll find out."

We must get Emily to relax. She can only feel love toward Zep once she allows herself to trust him, and she can only trust if her guard is down. If you expect the worst, if you fear where the path will lead, you will never set foot on the path. You will cut off your foot if you have to.

PHASE 2 (preliminary)

The key to drawing Emily toward positive feelings for Zep lies in her hypothalamus and her pituitary gland. We need them to produce endogenous opioid peptides, or endorphins, when she is in Zep's company. An orgasm would work for this, but that's leaping ahead. A hot curry lunch would work as well, or an eight-kilometre run, or pain. Any kind of stress on the body can prompt the release of the body's own compensatory "morphine," from the pituitary into the bloodstream, and from the hypothalamic neurons within the brain. But for the greatest benefit to our purpose we need Emily to associate the sweet, analgesic feeling with Zep. So we will use laughter.

Zep's assignment, once we get him into position, is to tell Emily a story that will prompt her to laugh heartily. A chuckle or shy titter won't achieve the desired effect. It is important for her to laugh loudly, without inhibition — the so-called "Duchenne" type of laughter — because it engages the diaphragm. This particular body stress quickly triggers the release of endorphins and produces, as a by-product, a feeling of well-being and generosity, emotions that Emily will subconsciously apply to Zep.

All of this has been explained to Zep, and he insists he has a story to tell her that will elicit the necessary laughter.

In order to allow this, however, we must first create another opportunity for Zep to encounter Emily. This can be an "accidental" encounter, such as Zep bumping into Emily in the street. It would be preferable, however, if the circumstance itself were to suggest future opportunities for the two to meet. If we rely on apparent chance, then as the project progresses and our need for encounters increases, it will become more difficult to explain the coincidence of their meetings, and more likely that Emily will begin to view them with suspicion.

I asked Zep if he could think of a reason that he and Emily might meet, or encounter each other, regularly. I advised that whatever brings them together should be something unlikely to generate conflict. They should not, for example, be meeting to "negotiate" anything. Ideal would be meetings that allowed them to concentrate on something other than themselves, so that their proximity to each other would be the circumstantial result, not the purpose, of their being together. This would allow the effect of our initiatives to seem more incidental.

ZB Transcript 11

HEY MARCIE, SO HERE'S THE PLAN. I'm gonna be Pebbles' chauffeur. Yeah, I'm gonna take her to school in the morning. While I'm here, I mean, not like forever. It's just a morning thing 'cause after school she comes home with one of her friends I think. And Emily's at work anyway when school gets out so there's no point.

Hope said I have to be able to see Emily on a regular basis if we're gonna be able to do anything, like with her mind, right? And so I can't just bump into her all the time, I have to have a good reason to keep meeting up with her. Makes sense. So I was thinking what it could be. Like, something with her job? Something with where she lives? Like, do I rent a place near her? And then it's like, of course, *your fucking daughter*, asshole! Right?

Staring me in the goddamn face. Sometimes I think too hard for my own good.

Only thing is, I haven't told Emily yet. We haven't talked since she dropped me off at the hospital. I don't know if she even knows I'm still in town. So I have to call her and set it up.

Hey ... maybe I could do that now ... Yeah, what if I did it now so you could type the whole thing! I could try holding the phone and the recording thing up together and maybe you could hear her too. It's worth a shot.

Wait, I'm just getting the phone out. Okay.

[Unintelligible sounds]

I dunno, Marcie. It's pretty awkward. 'Cause I have to hold them both in ...

[Sounds like scratching against the recorder.]

Naw, that's ...

[Unintelligible sounds]

I could try putting the recording thing on the table here and then, like, leaning down so the phone's right next to it.

[Loud bumping sound]

How's that? I know you can hear me, I just … it's hard to get the speaker part on the phone to be close to … I have to put it like half on my ear and lean …

Okay, fuck that. That's bullshit. I can't even breathe if I bend down like that.

I'm just gonna leave the recording thing on the table and you can hear me and that's it. Okay? All right. So, give me a minute here. I gotta walk through the whole thing in my head first. I dunno this is probably stupid.

Jesus Christ. *Stay positive*! I'm such an asshole.

Okay. Here we go … Breathe.

It's ringing … I'm a bit nervous here. Like I'm calling her for a date or something … Ringing again. She's probably stuck her phone in her p—

Hey, Em, it's Zep!

Yeah. Is this a good time? You busy? This'll just —

I'm still in town. Yeah … Oh, thanks, it's better. Yeah it's a bit stiff but … I cracked my uh, the kneecap. Yeah. Stupid. I dunno what happened. I have this, like, brace on it now. It's better. Doctor says I'm only going to be, you know, partially crippled. [Laughing] Right. For the rest of my life! [Laughing] Right.

So listen, Em, I'm calling to —

Yeah, I said I'm still in town. 'Cause of the hospitals thing … No I told you. In the car. You were kinda busy you weren't … Well, the whole reason I'm here is to do some charity stuff with the Bisons. Yeah. Visiting hospitals and stuff. Doing good deeds. Yeah … Just for the hell of it! I thought, why not? They asked, so …

Oh, thanks. It's all right.

But listen, speaking of good deeds, I was thinking. While I'm here … see … okay, just, I thought it'd be cool to help out a bit.

With Pebbles, I mean … Well, I was thinking I could take her to school in the mornings. You know, while I'm here. It could be a week or two. Or maybe more, I'm not sure.

No, I want to.

Honest, Em, it wouldn't be. It's no trouble. I'd get to see Pebbles a bit and you — you know, it'd be good. It would. Just for a couple of weeks, while I'm here. It's like, one less thing you have to worry about.

Come on, just let me …

Well, after school I dunno. It might not be … I thought some other parent drove her … Well, yeah, I guess, if it's your turn to do it … yeah, sure.

Great! Great! Okay, so I'll be there tomorrow. What time? … Really? Fuck, okay. That means I'm getting up at — your folks are still in Kenmore, right? That place on Woodcrest?

Great, so … guess I'll see you at eight tomorrow. Right … Bye.

OKAY, MARCIE. I'm in.

Friday, April 24

I HAVE WRITTEN A LETTER to Adnan. I have not sent the letter, but it exists. Last night I spent the hours after meeting with Zep sitting in my blank room, deciding on the words. And now, at any moment, with some unprecedented gust of certainty, I could hit *send*. And he would never call or write to me again.

And that would be better for him.

He clings to some idea of me. This thing called "Hope" that he has seen and touched. He knows what I am on the outside. He lifted me, weighed me in his arms like apples, peeled me and pried me with his chef's fingers, and did not always like what he found. He discovered reasons, at least one, to reject me. But somehow he has not. Perhaps he thinks his talent, or his passion, will overcome my flaws. Perhaps he imagines that, having examined the whole surface of me, he knows what lies within and has already decided what he will make of me. Perhaps he thinks I will be good.

If I press send, if I only do that, he will never be disappointed. Whatever alchemy of sense and memory and desire is working on his mind, whatever he imagines I might be, will remain. I should send the letter for that reason alone, as an act of pure selfishness. My chance to be that good.

But I hesitate, and there's no reason for it except selfishness again. Evidence of my weakness, my failure as an ascetic, my inability to fully purge the stupid, futile dreams of a child who thought finding happiness was merely the natural, inevitable consequence of wanting it. And I hate myself for it. I don't even know if what I want is real. Empirically real. I suppose that's what I'm here to find out. But even then I still won't know whether it can ever be real for me.

While I wrote the letter to Adnan, a wall of bricks like *don't* and *can't* and *stop*, I heard voices outside my room. A man shouting, at first that's all I heard. I couldn't tell for certain if he was shouting in anger, but I assumed so. And I was reminded again that I am not at home, that there is no one here for me, and I was torn between stupid fears. The possibility that whatever anger was out there might somehow smash through the double-locked door and finally consume what's left of me on this oatmeal-coloured bedspread. Or the possibility that it would remain where it was, inchoate but eternal, so that I would be forever trapped in this awful room.

Perhaps this is why I don't travel.

I went to the door, put my hands against the cool slab and peered through the eyehole, felt my eyelashes flick against the hole's metal ridge. The shouting man was there, captured alone for a moment in my fisheye lens. He seemed to be shouting for no reason at all, an aimless, scattered fury, and this is the most worrisome kind — anger like a burr hoping for anything to catch on to. Then he was joined by a woman. They were drunk and staggering and the man momentarily leaned against the wall opposite me for support and it became clear (if *clear* could fit, given the indecipherability of his words and the warping distortions of the lens) that his anger was directed at her. She had done or said something to offend him. And in that moment, God forgive me, I was relieved. I was relieved. The burr had already caught. It was no threat to me.

Phase 2 — Attraction

Zep has arranged to see Emily regularly by becoming, temporarily, his daughter's transport to and from school. This, he expects, will afford him at least one opportunity a day to encounter Emily. There are obvious limitations to this arrangement, including the fact that it prevents my travelling in the car with him, making close observation difficult or impossible. In order to observe his interaction with Emily it is necessary that I place myself nearby, perhaps on occasion by posing as a pedestrian, or by situating myself in a car parked at the curb. If this becomes impossible, I may have to rely solely on Zep's own accounts of their interaction, although clearly this option is not preferred.

There are, however, benefits to the arrangement. Behavioural factors suggest that by performing a regular service involving their daughter, Zep will appear to Emily inherently more trustworthy. As he acts the role of protector (to their daughter) and helper (to Emily), the qualities of reliability and strength will accrue to Zep in her re-estimation of him. This positive conditioning, and the habituation of her contact with him, may work to speed up the process of reintegrating Zep into Emily's existential framework — what she understands to be true of her life — so long as Zep never falters or fails in his task.

The primary goal of Phase 2, however, does not change under this new circumstance. Zep understands that his responsibility, during this morning's encounter with Emily, is to provoke in her a spasm of Duchenne laughter lasting at least eight continuous seconds, preferably more. (Eight seconds being the minimum length of Duchenne laughter required to initiate a release of endogenous morphine sufficient to induce positive associations and a sensation of well-being. See Grossmore, et al, 2011.)

Phase 2, Log A

(Notes: 1. Site of this phase was the driveway in front of the residence of Joyce and Raymond Good, 126 Woodcrest Blvd.,

Buffalo, NY. 2. The importance of timing the duration of Emily's laughter required that I observe the encounter. I rented a car for this purpose, parked on Woodcrest Blvd. opposite number 126 with a clear sightline to the front door of the house. 3. Observations (enhanced by the use of 12x42 power binoculars) were logged as they occurred with the time indicated.)

7:55 a.m.: Emily's Honda CR-V is parked in the driveway. Zep Baker has not yet arrived.

8:01 a.m.: No sign of Zep.

8:09 a.m.: Zep arrives in his Cadillac, acknowledges my presence with a wave through the window (which he should not do), and pulls into the available space at the end of the driveway.

8:09 a.m.: Zep's daughter Pebbles immediately emerges from the front door of the house and runs toward Zep's car as he is getting out of the vehicle. She carries a pink and green backpack and appears ready to leave. Zep stands beside the vehicle, speaking to Pebbles, who stands on the other side of the car, apparently ready to get in. Zep gestures toward the house. (He must have time with Emily in order execute this phase.)

8:10 a.m.: Emily emerges at the front door of the house and waves. Zep begins to walk toward the house then stops in response to something Pebbles says. Zep throws up his arms and returns to his car, glancing toward my location as he does. Both he and Pebbles get in the car.

8:11 a.m.: Zep sends a text to me: "Fck Peb says shes late."

8:12 a.m.: I send this response: "Find out where E has lunch. Does P know?"

8:12 a.m.: Zep's car backs out of the driveway. He glances at me as he drives away.

8:19 a.m.: Zep sends this text: "Peb no clue."

8:19 a.m.: I send this response: "Meet hotel as planned."

ZB Transcript 12

SON OF A BITCH, Marcie.

I don't think this is gonna work. Probably shouldn't even be doing this right now, I'm so pissed. Like what the hell? I'm ten minutes late picking up Pebbles 'cause you can't get a second wakeup call at this goddamn hotel. You get one shot and if you don't wake up *right then* you're fucked. So I'm ten minutes late and everything goes to shit. The whole plan goes out the fucking window 'cause Pebs has to get to school for some music practice thing. So there's Emily at the door and I got my story and I can't even talk to her because Peb's like "*Dad*, we have to *go*!" And I can't say to her what's really going on because the whole thing is I'm supposed to be spending time with her, not Em, which, like, fine. I want to spend time with her but fuck! Fuck fuck fuck!

[Unintelligible sounds]

Sorry, Marcie, I dropped the thing.

And by the way, if you can get Lino on the phone, tell him if he doesn't call me back today he's fucking fired.

Friday, April 24 (later)

AT ABOUT 9:30 A.M., Zep and I met in our small Hyatt conference room. Though he had had some time to consider events, he remained extremely frustrated. Slumped in his seat, with his suit jacket bunched around his shoulders, he twisted his car keys in his hand.

"What a fucking disaster. There was nothing I could do!"

I said then what I should have said earlier, which was that involving a child in any plan was inevitably going to add an element of unpredictability and potential disruption. But I explained that scientific investigations frequently encounter roadblocks and setbacks, and that this was something that could be overcome.

"You're saying 'stay positive.'"

"Negativity isn't going to help us think our way through this."

He nodded, but he appeared unconvinced. He stared intently at the keys that rattled as he turned them over and over in his hands. After a moment of this he glanced up at the binoculars I'd set on the table.

"Those working for you?"

"They're fine, thanks."

"Three hundred bucks, they'd better be." His gaze returned to the keys in his hand and he shook his head morosely. "Jesus, all I'm doing in this thing is spending money, and so far what's happened? What have we accomplished?"

"I can go through the list if you'd like."

Zep shrugged.

"You have re-established contact with Emily. You've communicated a plausible reason for being here, a reason that could potentially raise you in her estimation and certainly won't hurt. You have elicited empathy from her and, in fact, caused her to act on your behalf. You have set up opportunities for future contact —"

"Not if Pebbles won't let me talk to her."

"That happened because you were late, did it not?"

"Yeah."

"So next time, be early."

A small grin showed itself at the corners of Zep's mouth.

"You sound like one of my old hitting coaches."

I reminded Zep then that, while we had some time, it wasn't an endless amount. We still had a number of phases to go, and the lab in Toronto would likely need me back at work within two weeks. There were also some other matters in my life I had to resolve. At that, he looked up at me, and I felt instantly that I had revealed too much.

"Personal stuff?"

I began to gather my notes.

"It's weird," he said. "We're working on this thing together, spending all this time, and it's all about my personal life. I mean, it's the most intimate shit, right? Love? And yet I don't know anything about you."

I put the binoculars in my satchel. "That's the way it should be."

"Why?"

"Do you know anything about your doctor or your lawyer?"

He raised his hands in surrender. "Don't be so touchy."

It is possible I sounded more agitated than I'd intended. The buckle on my satchel snapped closed under my thumb. "Just stop thinking of me as a person," I said. "Think about me only as the function I perform."

Zep stared at me. Or perhaps I remember that inaccurately. Certainly his eyes were on me. "You don't want to be a person."

"I'd rather not. In this situation."

"That's stupid." He waited a second for me to respond, but I didn't. "And anyway, it's not how I work. I'm a people person! I'm naturally curious. Like I have all these questions —" He changed tack when I stood up. "Wait, wait! Don't go yet, we haven't decided what to do about Emily."

It was necessary for me to leave, though there was nowhere I had to be. Zep continued while I made my way to the door. "If I find out where she has lunch will you go there with me?" As I entered the corridor he shouted, "I'll call you when I find out!"

ZB Transcript 13

MARCIE, I GOTTA FIGURE OUT where Emily has lunch. Right this minute, that's my job. I'm not asking you to help, 'cause you're probably not gonna listen to this for a couple hours, and anyway if I thought there was something you could do right now I'd call you. I'm just talking here. Talking out loud. My old man used to do that. Which is probably not a good sign but whatever. All those odd jobs he used to do around the house, half the time he'd be yammering away at himself like he had three other people in his head.

Which is more friends than he had in the real world, so ... good for him, I guess.

Anyway, right now I'm just sitting here in the parking lot, trying to think. I guess I'll get back to you if anything comes to me.

OKAY, HERE'S WHAT I'M THINKING ... Fuck, it gets hot sitting in a car in the sunshine. Wait a second. Get some goddamn air in here.

So! Here's what I'm thinking. I can't call Em's parents. That's out. They fuckin' hate me for obvious reasons. I don't know any of her friends here, so I can't call any of them. And I already asked Pebbles and she doesn't know.

The only thing I got working for me is I know Em works at this event company, right? But if I call up her office and just ask, flat out — "Where does Emily Good go to lunch?" — nobody's gonna tell me shit. Why would they? I could be some psycho. And if I say hey, it's her ex-husband calling, they're *really* not going to tell me shit.

But I'm thinking about this job she has, doing events and weddings and that. Some of these are probably big special occasions, important to people, right? So if she does a good job — and that's totally Em, she's never been half-assed about anything — people are gonna be happy, right?

So here's the idea I had. Maybe brilliant, maybe fuckin' stupid. But …

[Voices, unintelligible]

No, sir. No, I wasn't talking to you … I'm dictating here. See? Dictating a letter.

[Unintelligible]

Huh? … Oh, your *kid*, sorry. Hi honey! I guess Daddy never swears, right? Yeah.

[Unintelligible]

Okay, sure. Yeah … Do I need to get out of the car? 'Cause … okay then. Good. You have a nice day.

Jesus Christ. Everybody's a tough guy when they've got their four-year-old with them.

Where was I? … Yeah, so people are gonna be happy when Em does a good job, right? So I'm thinking maybe it wouldn't be unusual if somebody wanted to do something nice for her. Not just a tip but, like, a present. Right? You see where I'm going with this, Marcie?

Okay, you know what? It's already past ten-thirty. I'm just gonna do it and report how it went later 'cause I'm running out of time.

Friday, April 24 (later)

I WAS IN THE BATHROOM when Zep called me, with my hand between my thighs. Why it seemed important to try again, it's difficult to say. Was there a chance the outcome might be different this time? Did the act of crossing the border cause a chemical flux that would obviate the need to make decisions? Would my presence in a new country strip me of responsibilities I'd acquired in a previous one?

Was this, in fact, why people travelled?

On the way back from the failed event in Emily's driveway, I'd passed a pharmacy and stopped. In the store, I looked for a brand I didn't recognize. A name that might conjure some wholly new consequence in a strip turned blue: Not only are you not pregnant, you are no longer you. All the shadows that crowded you are gone and everything is possible again.

Magical thinking is the last resort for luckless women. It's said the same is true for people who jump from the Golden Gate Bridge. And so, my phone rang with my hand buried. It was half past noon.

"I've got her!" said Zep. "She's at Lombardo's. It's a place on Hertel. Get here fast. I'll wait as long as I can. But if it looks like she's leaving, I'm going in."

I'd already returned the rental car so I needed to find a cab. It took me eight minutes to get to the lobby and hail one, and another fifteen to arrive at the restaurant. There was no missing it because its enormous sign, held aloft by large terra-cotta pillars, was visible blocks away. As we approached along Hertel Avenue I saw a car that looked like Zep's parked half a block from the entrance. He wasn't in it, which seemed to suggest he was inside the restaurant. But when the cab pulled into the small parking lot beside Lombardo's, I saw him standing there. He was partly hidden behind one of the sign's pillars, and by a low wall topped by shrubs that enclosed a patio in front of the restaurant. He had his hands in his pockets, the flaps of his suit jacket stirring in the cool breeze, and he was peering intently through the shrubs toward the restaurant's window.

When he saw me paying the cab driver, he waved me over. As I went toward him he pointed toward Emily's CR-V parked at the end of a bank of cars.

"She showed up just after noon. She's in there with a couple."

Somewhat later Zep told me, rather proudly, how he'd come to find Emily. Posing as a client, the husband of a couple recently married, he had called the company she works for and asked the receptionist if she would do him a favour. "I figure people like to be helpful," he said. "Especially if it's to do something nice."

He explained to the receptionist how thrilled he and his wife had been with the job Emily had done for them and wanted to thank her by buying her a gift certificate to her favourite restaurant. Was there a spot she went for lunch frequently?

The woman didn't hesitate: Lombardo's was the place. "Emily's always going there with clients. In fact, I'm surprised she didn't take you."

"Oh, yeah, she did," said Zep. "We just didn't know it was her favourite." He said goodbye quickly.

Now, behind the patio wall, he turned to me. "Since you're here I can go in, right?"

I shook my head. "Don't."

"She's halfway through her meal already." He thrust a finger into the shrubs. "I can see her!"

I told him to wait. I explained that if she was in a meeting right now, he'd be interrupting her. She wouldn't like it and it would set off a negative cascade from annoyance to rejection. Moreover, if she was with a client she would not be able to relax enough to laugh in the way that would advance us toward our objective. Zep, frowning hard, took a deep breath.

"When she's heading to her car," I said. "Go to her then."

WE WAITED FOR NEARLY FORTY minutes. Most of that time I spent in Zep's car, reviewing my notes and watching Zep pace the length of the wall. I'd also managed to find a spot where I could stand when the moment arrived and observe the area near Emily's car without being obvious.

And for some of the time, a few minutes, I stared at the test strip in my hands. At the indicators that had come to life in the darkness of my bag while I rode an elevator down. At the blue lines, come to slay the fragile magic in my mind.

Phase 2, Log B

(Notes: 1. Site for this event was the parking lot of Ristorante Lombardo, Hertel Avenue, Buffalo NY. 2. Observations were made with the naked eye from a distance of approximately 10 metres. 3. A digital stopwatch was used for all time measurements.)

1:22 p.m.: The subject, Emily Good, emerges from Ristorante Lombardo with a young couple. Emily is dressed in neutral-coloured business attire, suggesting this has in fact been a client meeting. In the restaurant's parking lot she speaks briefly with the couple, then shakes their hands goodbye. She is smiling; her mood seems buoyant.

1:24 p.m.: As Emily makes her way to her car, I signal to Zep that he should begin his approach. He does.

1:24 p.m.: Zep walks toward the front door of the restaurant and then stops, as agreed. Emily is now halfway to her car and Zep calls to her. She turns and he reacts as if surprised to see her. From my vantage point it is difficult to hear the words exchanged between them, but I have a clear view of Emily's face. She appears startled or confused.

1:25 p.m.: Zep advances toward Emily and stands within arm's reach. Emily appears calm and occasionally smiles as Zep speaks. Zep gestures toward the restaurant as he talks (discussing, per instructions, the coincidence of their coming to the same restaurant for lunch). Emily nods and speaks briefly. She checks her watch.

1:26 p.m.: Zep has now been speaking continuously for over one minute. His body language has become somewhat animated, indicating that he is in the midst of telling the story he has planned. Emily seems willing to listen. She nods and occasionally smiles, apparently in recognition.

1:27 p.m.: Emily laughs briefly, twice. Zep is now very animated in his body movements. This may mean he is coming to the end of his story and trying harder to elicit Duchenne laughter.

1:28 p.m.: Emily throws her head slightly backward and then quickly forward in a nodding motion, her mouth open, indicating the beginning of Duchenne laughter. It lasts for 5.7 seconds, stops for 2 seconds, then resumes and continues for 4.4 seconds, during which Emily places her arms across her stomach and closes her eyes, indicating the peak of this Duchenne period.

1:29 p.m.: Emily speaks briefly. She is smiling and appears relaxed. She checks her watch, touches Zep's arm and speaks again. Immediately she moves away from him toward her car, smiling. At her car she turns and waves, which Zep mirrors, then opens her car door and gets in. Zep does not move toward the restaurant at this point as instructed, but stands, smiling, and watches Emily back up in her car and then drive forward. As she passes him in the lot he waves again. Due to glare on the windshield it is impossible to see if she mirrors this movement, but as Zep's expression does not change it is a reasonable assumption.

EMILY'S CAR EXITED THE LOT and turned right, heading west along Hertel. The moment she was out of view, Zep raised his arms in triumph and whooped. He punched the air. I decided at that moment to go to his car. As Zep began bounding toward me his fists were clenched. He shouted, "Yeah! Whoo!" or sounds to that effect. He was a warrior in victory's thrall, clearly experiencing a rush of adrenaline, and I knew it was not the time to tell him of my concerns.

What I should not have done, I understand now, was get into his car. It had seemed at the time to be my best course, it had the allure of safety. Out on the sidewalk I was exposed while the car offered an enclosed space, a barrier to pass through, locks. It was a place I knew. These things registered subconsciously, instinctively, and directed me more than conscious thought. Any degree of cognitive clarity would have allowed me to see it was a mistake. But I had none. Because, of course, when I got in the car, Zep joined me. Of course he did. Even if I had had time or awareness enough to lock the doors, he had the keys. Being inside the car made no sense, but that's where I had put myself.

He came around the driver's side, opened the door and got in, and now his energy, his aggression, was inside with me, in that enclosed space.

"Fuck yeah!" Zep shouted. "Did you see that? Did you see?"

Zep pounded the steering wheel with the heels of his hands. He leaned on the horn of his car. "Whoo!" he shouted. His elation was an expanding balloon. A mushroom cloud. I began to fumble for the handle of the door I'd just closed.

"How long was that? Nine seconds? Ten? What are you doing?"

"I have to," I said. "I have to go." I couldn't breathe to speak. My hands were meat without bone.

"Wait! Wait! What the fuck? What's the problem? We did it!"

In the midst of all, the one clear thought that I had, the spidery vein of cognition in the white stone of reflex, was an understanding that the problem was his joy. If I could lessen his joy, said this thought, then the balloon that was flattening me, pressing the air from my lungs, might recede.

"Two seconds," I said. Coughed it out, or whispered it. Something in between. I meant the two-second interruption, the gap between the periods of Emily's laughter. She had laughed for a total of ten seconds, but less than six continuously. It meant we could not be sure that we'd achieved our objective. But at that time, in that place, I could not explain all this, and Zep misunderstood.

"Bullshit!" He shouted. "No fucking way. Two seconds? Were you even watching? It was eight seconds at least!" He was hammering the wheel of the car. Pounding on it. "Come on!" he shouted. "Come on!" He turned to me.

He lifted his hand. He raised his hand at me.

ZB Transcript 14

MARCIE, YOU EVER TALK to Lino? That guy, I dunno what's going on. Never called me back. You ever hear from him? Asshole never fuckin' called me back. One thing I was counting on, one thing I knew was going right, you know? Had that investor dude all lined up and then, just, nothing. I don't get it. I don't know if I should be worried about him or what. Think maybe something's happened to him?

Fuck, the whole world's going to piss here.

Weirdest goddamn day, Marcie. I dunno. Dunno what I'm doing anymore. You're supposed to know, right? You want something to happen you fuckin' make it happen. That's how I always did it anyway. You know what you want, you know what to do. Simple as that. Put everything in its fuckin' place, right? Like dominoes. You do your work, and you line everything up. And you start knocking 'em down, one by one. Bop, bop, bop, bop. And you're getting somewhere, right? It's all … and then some goddamn, I dunno, some goddamn wind comes, some goddamn tornado comes, and fuckin' whips all the pieces into the air and you're like … what? You know? What just happened?

Felt the same thing when I got sent down the first time in Cleveland. Coach comes up to me and says, "Manager wants to see you." And I'm like, great, 'cause I got three hits the day before. I figure he's gonna tell me I'm in, they're gonna put me in full time at third instead of the utility routine they had me going at. Third, second, third, out in left some games, all that bullshit. Whoever needs a night off, put Baker in there. I figure this is my shot, right? I'm twenty-six, getting better every game, it feels like. It's my time, it feels like. Three-knock night! You know? Only good things happen after a three-knock night. Full-time job, you're our third baseman. That's gotta be it.

Go into his office and he says, "Hollings is coming in to play third. We're sending you down."

They fucking traded for Hollings. Thirty years old. Guy never had a three-knock night his whole career. Craziest goddamn thing.

Whole world's crazy I think.

[Long silence]

I didn't do anything wrong, though. I know that.

[Long silence]

Sorry, Marcie. I'm just ... just thinking about shit, you know? Just lying out here in the goddamn Hyatt. The only part of me that's moving is what's in my head.

And this hand bringing this beer to my mouth.

I used to not think about stuff. Used to just do stuff. Just one gear, straight ahead. Never thought about a goddamn thing. Never thought about, did I want to play baseball? Just knew. You know? Just did it.

When I was going out with Emily, I never thought, did I want to marry this girl? Is it a good thing, us being together? Never thought about that. Never thought about, what if we have a kid? You know? What if I get her pregnant? What if we don't like the same stuff, what if she doesn't want me to be in baseball the rest of my life? What if she wants me to get a fuckin' job? What if she wants her parents to come live with us? What if after ten years she starts looking at me funny, like I'm some goddamn wart on her finger she wants to burn off? What if it turns out being married totally fucking sucks the life out of you, and makes you mean, or afraid? And makes you do shit you'd never imagined doing?

Never thought about any of that goddamn shit. You know what you want, you know what to do.

Here's a rock, Wilma. I love you and you're in my life now. We are man and fucking wife.

We went to Germany for our honeymoon. I ever tell you that, Marcie? Fuckin' Germany. I said they got these great resorts in Jamaica, let's go there. Let's go to, like, Hawaii, or Australia. Or someplace like, I dunno, Africa!

Germany.

She wants to see history. She wants to go to Berlin. She says the whole twentieth century happened in Berlin. I said it fucking happened everywhere else too!

She says don't be stupid.

We're married three days, she's telling me I'm stupid. I said don't call me stupid. She said I didn't say you were stupid I said *don't* be. I said, if I told you don't be green, that means you *are* green. She said I'm not talking about it anymore.

And I'm thinking in my head, I married this chick. Like that was the first time I thought about what being married meant. It meant I had to put up with *shit like this*. Going to the last goddamn place I'd ever want to go for my honeymoon, goddamn Germany, look at goddamn statues and stone buildings, because that's what my *wife* wants.

Funny thing, I actually didn't mind it. Some of the places were cool. I mean, I still think Hawaii would've been way better but we had a pretty good time. Drank a lot of beer. They got some weird beer in that country I'm telling you. Beer that tastes like bacon! I shit you not, Marcie. I think I gained ten pounds of beer fat in one week.

Anyway. I dunno how I got onto that.

Sometimes I think about the arguments we had, Emily and me, and I think, if I could go back and change one word, or one sentence, everything would be different. Or if I could go back and just say nothing. Like she's angry and hammering at me about something, and if I could just go and tell myself, Zep, don't fucking say a word right here. *Right here*! Shut the fuck up! Let her be mad. Maybe say something later but right now keep your mouth fuckin' zipped.

Instead of saying fuck you. Instead of saying leave. Instead of saying makes no difference to me. Instead of saying I don't care.

Which was a lie anyway. It was all lies.

My mouth can come up with some stupid fucking shit sometimes.

[Long silence]

Huh.

I just realized yesterday was a year since I stopped wearing my wedding ring. 'Cause I wore it for like six months after she left. Spent fifteen years getting used to how it felt holding a bat, catching a ball, washing up with this piece of metal on my hand. Couldn't take it off. The whole idea seemed nuts, like taking off a finger. Then it started to feel stupid, me still wearing it, but I told myself it would upset Pebbles if she saw me without it.

Then one day Pebbles asked me why I still had it on. She said, "Mom took hers off right away."

April 23rd. I must have looked at a paper or something. Don't know why I'd remember it otherwise.

I'm going for another beer. You want one, Marcie? Go ahead. I think there's some in the fridge in the office there. If there isn't, somebody's come in and grabbed it. Probably Lino. Fuckin' dickwad.

[Long silence]

Yeah, so, Marcie, I dunno. This weird thing happened today with Hope. I can't really figure it out, so if it makes sense to you, let me know, okay? Send me an email or something. I mean, the only other person I can talk to about it is Emily and that's not gonna happen, right? So ...

Anyway, so we were doing what we planned, right? I figured out where Em was having lunch. It was pretty cool how but, whatever. Doesn't matter. And we got there. I got there first, and I found Em, and I called Hope and she got there about twenty minutes later, and it was all good. And we talked about how to do it and when. And it was all set.

And then so we wait. And Hope goes and sits in the car and I stand there watching for Em to come out. And after a while she does and so I go for it, like we planned. And, you know, I did good. Fuck, I did good, Marcie.

I got her laughing like I was supposed to, like Hope told me to. I told her the whole story. I said, you know, I just remembered this thing that happened with us, and those drunk guys at the drive-in, remember? And I start telling it and she kinda had this vague look on her face like, I'm not sure, and then I could see in her eyes she remembered. That was cool. That moment, you know? That second, when she got there with me.

And then she was laughing. It was kind of a smile and a giggle at first and then pretty soon she was killing herself. Just like I hoped. I mean, I totally had her going. She practically had tears coming down her face. And man, it felt good, Marcie. To make her laugh like that? Felt really good.

Really good.

So then she had to go. She had a meeting or something. So she left. Kinda waved goodbye. Drove out, down Hertel. And I was like, woohoo, right? Totally pumped. Fuck, it was like grand-slam time. Like I needed to do it. It had to happen. And nothing was guaranteed. I could've totally whiffed but I didn't. I fucking slammed it.

And I run back to the car where Hope is. And right away. Right away, Marcie, something's weird. I don't know what. She's acting like I didn't do anything at all. Like everything was wrong. Strange look on her face, like she hated me or something. I mean, it just made no sense to me.

I'm like, what's going on? What's the problem? We fucking killed it here! Right? And she says some stupid shit like Em only laughed two seconds and that was crazy. That made no sense. So I'm like, trying to pump her up, like, come on! Get your head out of your papers, right? Come on! We did it! And I put my hand up, like high-five. Like we're a team here. *Come on*!

And she ... she screamed, Marcie. When I did that she screamed. Like she was afraid of me. Like I was going to hit her. I mean ... And she got the door open and she fell out onto the curb. And it was ... fuck, she hurt herself I think, she fell hard, and ... she's scrambling, like trying to get away from me. She spilled some of her papers. And her face ... God, I just ...

I got out of the car to run after her but she kept running, looking back at me like I was ... I dunno. I dunno what I looked like to her.

But she was afraid. And I don't ... seeing her look that way at me? Like I was bad? Like I was evil?

Never felt anything like that.

[Long silence]

So ... I picked up the pages she dropped. Had to chase a couple down 'cause the wind was blowing 'em. And now I dunno what's happening. I tried calling her. I left a message on her phone. So now I'm just waiting. I don't know what I should do.

Saturday, April 25

THE PTSD CHECKLIST IS seventeen items long. Each names a symptom that might be troubling the sufferer, and for each you are asked to select one of five levels to indicate how much — from "not at all" to "extremely" — you are bothered. Number 3, for example: "Suddenly acting or feeling as if a stressful experience were happening again (as if you were reliving it)." Or number 5: "Having physical reactions (e.g. heart pounding, trouble breathing, or sweating) when something reminded you of a stressful experience from the past."

There are two versions of the checklist, one for civilians and one for military personnel. The only difference between them is that the military version inserts the word *military* in front of every use of the word *experience*. That means for military personnel, the experiences being examined can only be military ones, as if any other would naturally pale in significance. As if an army corporal or a systems officer or a weapons tech could not still be haunted by something from her more distant past. A rape perhaps, or something else, some other dark thing, that occurred when she was young. I always thought that to preclude such a possibility betrayed a lack of imagination on the part of behavioural researchers.

Over the last ten years, since I was hospitalized at nineteen for my own protection, I have filled out the checklist at least a dozen times. On one occasion or another I have checked the fifth box of nearly every one of the seventeen "problems or complaints" itemized on the list. Complaints having to do with sleep, or concentration, or uncontrollable thoughts. Problems with fear, or anger, or avoidance. All in the extreme. (All but number 8: "Trouble remembering parts of a stressful experience from the past." Not remembering was never, for me, much of a problem.)

A counsellor once sat opposite me, across a small pool of blue carpet. He ran his eyes down my latest checklist, then set it on the table beside him and leaned forward, his forearms on his knees. "You know, for most people," he said, "life is a bloody hard trek through an endless forest. And in this forest there is always the chance of meeting a grizzly that will tear you apart. And so, for most people, life is learning how to avoid the grizzlies, and devising ways to keep them out of our tents, so that we can live without fear.

"But you see," he said, "for people like you, the grizzly is already in the tent. You can't avoid the grizzly. You must learn to live with him, for he will never leave."

And of course, this is a chemical matter. An experience of overwhelming terror, particularly if it happens to someone who is young, can alter the brain irreparably. It was a Yale psychiatrist, Dr. Dennis Charney, who said that victims of overwhelming terror "may never be the same biologically." The tiny locus ceruleus, a seed of barely twenty-five thousand neurons in the brain stem, becomes forever hyper-reactive, sending out norepinephrine at the slightest provocation. The hypothalamus churns out corticotropic hormone-releasing factor like a fire hose. The regulation of dopamine, serotonin, insulin, cortisol and noradrenaline are all affected.

And this is particularly true for one special sort of trauma victim — the one who must submit. All these chemicals relating to fear — many of which, incidentally, are also implicated in love — are meant to enable the body to fight or flee. The engine of the body begins to race. The heart pounds, blood pressure rises, breath quickens, senses become acute. And if, in the face of horror, the body can manage to act on one of the two saving impulses, the brain is not so terribly altered.

But if someone young has not the strength to fight or the means to escape, if she must face the inevitability of what will be done, if she can only surrender to the horror, as her engine continues to race and race and race, then she will never be the same. Her rational mind, her intellect, her clear-thinking self will always be the second-in-command, taking orders from the part of her that is broken.

ZEP HAD NO INTENTION of hurting me. I can write that sentence, see each of those words, know the thoughts behind them and admit that the statement is true. He is blameless. I know that here, in this park, on the grass under a still-leafless oak tree, with children climbing on a play structure in the distance, near a terrier that sees no joy in chasing the stick his owner keeps throwing. Here I can sit and breathe and feel no fear. But only here. And I can't stay here forever.

I called Lesley and told her what happened.

"I can be there in three hours," she said. "I just need to rent a car."

"There's nothing you can do here."

"You know that's not true."

She meant that she could keep me distracted, keep my thoughts away from the parlous territories they have been known to visit. It has been a long time since I've done anything that would alarm a watchful official, but it would be silly to deny the possibility.

But if she were to come I might as well go home. Her presence would interfere. There'd be no keeping her out of things, and once she was in things she would go at them like a termite, questioning and judging, and everything would disintegrate. Lesley is dear to me, but her instincts are protective, and protection is antithetical to investigation. She would keep me from knowing what I must know, for fear of where the knowledge would lead. She wants what's "best" for me, and the two of us would have very different ideas of what that is.

I knew, however, that she would come despite my protests unless she was presented with some other way to help, so I asked her to talk to Zep. Lesley knows how to communicate with people who aren't used to hearing certain things. She's patient with them in a way that I can never manage to be, insisting they hear, helping them to understand, but allowing them to do so at their own pace. Even my mother believes this to be true.

"Your friend talks very sensibly," she informed me once, sitting on the edge of my hospital bed. "She could do with a little more attention to her hair. When I look at her I can't help thinking of mice and I wonder what became of her hairbrush. But she does explain things quite clearly."

About Zep I have told Lesley almost nothing, except that he's a former athlete, that I'm using him in an investigation, and that while I find his particular brand of masculinity challenging I believe him to be essentially harmless. She will trust me on that; she knows my instincts are acute.

And I have asked her to respect his privacy when she calls him. She is not to ask him questions.

"What about your privacy?"

"I trust your judgment. Tell him ..."

"As little as possible."

"As much as you think he needs to hear."

The damp cold of the ground underneath me was beginning to seep through my clothes and I became conscious again of the bruise on my hip from landing like an idiot against the curb. I gave Lesley Zep's number and thanked her and said I'd talk to her soon. When she didn't respond immediately I waited.

"And how are you otherwise, Hope?"

I laid the palm of my hand against the grass. Felt the points of a hundred tiny blades press into my skin. Willed them to be strong. "Pregnant," I said.

"Still."

"Results have been confirmed."

"Okay, so … do you want me to talk to Adnan as well?"

"No."

"Hope, somebody has to. If you won't, I will."

"*No*, Lesley. That's not your job, it's *mine*. Stay out of it." I tugged at a clump of new grass by my leg, pinched off its tiny baby leaves.

"So do it, Hope. Do your job. Don't run away from it."

"I'm not."

"Remind me where you're calling from? Buffalo?"

"Shut up."

"You shut up."

I tried to suppress the grin but I couldn't, and we both sputtered into giggles.

"Thanks, Les."

"Love you."

ZB Transcript 15

MARCIE, IT'S SEVEN O'CLOCK here. I'm still in the hotel, haven't gone for dinner yet but I guess I'll do that soon. Ah, look, a lot of stuff's come up here so, I dunno. This whole thing might be off.

I got a call a couple of hours ago, from some woman named Lesley Gromen. Gramen. I dunno. Friend of Hope's. She said Hope asked her to talk to me. She couldn't do it herself.

She told me some stuff. I guess she was, like, bringing me up to speed or whatever. Because of what happened. "Help you understand," she said. She said that a few times.

It's a bit, ah, it's a bit … I dunno.

Fuck.

So I guess, what she said, Lesley said, she was telling me that, like … a bunch of years ago, fifteen or something, 'cause Hope was fourteen at the time, she was, uh, she was raped, I guess. Yeah, she was ... it was two men that did it. Two of them. So ...

This happened in her basement, where she lived. In her home, right? And I guess it ... they did some other stuff too, she said. This Lesley. Ah, she ... she didn't go into details about that. She just said they hurt her. They raped her and they hurt her and it ... I guess it ... she was like Pebbles' age, right? She was Pebbles' age, Marcie. And and she was ... sorry, just ...

One ... one second okay?

SO, YEAH ... ANYWAY IT LASTED a while, is what Lesley was saying, like a few hours or something and ... [Unintelligible]. And so now ... the deal is, Hope has this thing. Like a condition. It's the same as what some soldiers have, those ones coming back from Iraq. Like they hear a bang and they think they're being shot at, right? And I guess it can last a long time sometimes. You know, maybe the rest of her life. And so she gets freaked out about small things, that's what Lesley was saying. And so it's not my fault, is what she was saying, about what happened. I didn't do anything wrong. Which I knew, but still. I didn't do anything wrong. And that's what Hope said. That's what she told Lesley.

But she's saying that I gotta — if I want to work with Hope, I gotta be more ... she said "quieter." I have to be quieter.

And I'm thinking, like, yeah, okay. But how's that gonna work? How can I — like, it's no good being the way I am with her, I gotta be someone different? How's that possible? Like, I'm not an actor, right? I'm just me. Whatever I am, loud or whatever, that's just me. And I've always been like that. But ...

And why didn't she tell me? Why am I hearing this now? Right? Like shouldn't this have been like, item number one? By the way I have this thing? So, yeah, like let's work together and I can help you but just so you know I was raped when I was a kid so, like, don't fucking shout at me or whatever because that's not gonna fucking work for me.

Couldn't she have said that? Something like that? Just a heads-up, I mean. 'Cause fuck, I didn't want to make her freak out, Marcie. Make her remember all that shit? Jesus Christ! I didn't want to do that!

Let me ask you something, Marcie. Have I ever bothered you? Have you ever been upset around me? Because that's ... fuck, I don't want to hear that, you know? But like, tell me if you have. 'Cause I'm thinking maybe it's just worse for Hope, because of her ... because of what happened. And so maybe it's like, a version of that for you and that's ... like that's bullshit. If that's happening. I don't want that. So you gotta tell me, Marcie. Okay? Because ... you just gotta promise to tell me. I'm serious!

I dunno. I'm freaking myself out here I think.

My father keeps going through my head and I ...

So maybe this whole thing is off. Right? I don't see ... 'cause I gotta be, I gotta act different every second now. Every second I'm around her I'm gonna be thinking about this. About what they did to her and how ... like how she maybe looks at me, and what I'm doing. How I remind her of it. Not even knowing.

Fuck.

I gotta go think some more.

Saturday, April 25 /cont

THERE WAS A BOY in the park who made me think of someone. School must have let out because clumps of older children were suddenly marching along a path cut by feet in the grass. Two boys came toward me on bikes, racing each other, and perhaps the path was their finish line. Once they'd crossed it they dismounted and let their bikes crash to the ground. The nonchalance one of these boys exhibited, the way he let the momentum of his ride carry him on foot while his bike tumbled behind him, wheels rounding in the air, and the slump of his shoulders — maybe it was that most of all — before he bodied into his friend, it all brought Kevin Royceman to mind.

I couldn't think of his name at first, knew only that I recognized this boy, that he was of my life, some distant, forgotten, folded-away part of it. He was near enough that I could see the sweep of hair against his eyes and hear the ripple of his words though I couldn't make them out. Who, I thought, who? Who does he bring back to me? And then it came to me. Kevin. Kevin Royceman.

Kevin was twelve when I was eleven, and I don't remember how it began with us. Perhaps I threw a snowball at him one day in the schoolyard. Perhaps he was one of the boys my friend Corrine Mayley and I liked to torment, accusing them of grave inadequacies, being too short, being too tall, being red-haired or blond, too-well or poorly dressed or — the worst offence by far — being compelling in some way that confused and frightened us, in which case the boy would simply be "stupid" or riddled with "cooties." We would hurl these impeachments and then run away, giggling madly. Shrieking if they chased us. Batting at them and screaming if they got too close.

No one ever did more than knock us on the shoulder if they caught us. An arm might briefly encircle a waist, but only to slow us down.

Kevin was probably one of those boys. What I remember is not how he came to be a feature of my life, but that for a time he was. It was winter, with its crunchy, alien textures, its chafing and invigorating air that thinned all utterances into needles. Whether it was a coincidence that Kevin happened then, or whether it was because of winter, because we each felt safer, protected underneath the padding of our parkas and gloves, I don't know. But for two months we breathed as much of the same crisp air as we could.

Our school was single-storied and L-shaped, two wings enclosing a playing field bordered by trees on the far side. At recess he would wait for me at the end of the south wing, leaning against the rough brick wall. He wore a puffy, dark blue skiing jacket. I would emerge from the doors of the east wing and, seeing him, make my way to him as quickly as I could, skimming the wall and skirting pods of playing classmates, trying to be unnoticeable. It never occurred to me to go *through* the school, along one corridor and down the next, and come out of the door nearest him, the door he himself must have used.

There are lab rats smarter than I was then.

And yet it didn't matter, really. For a few days my friends called to me as I quick-stepped in snow boots toward the figure against the wall. But soon they seemed to accept this new routine. We were never bothered, or made objects of curiosity. This coupleness, it seemed, was too foreign a concept to generate interest. So we were allowed to be together.

I don't remember everything. Perhaps because we did nothing very memorable. We had no plan or goal in mind, we were not working toward something. We had none of the toxic awareness that children apparently have now. It seemed important to us only to be near each other. We would lean against the wall, sometimes facing each other, sometimes facing the field, and feel every nerve in our bodies sing. It was as if I could make out each synthetic thread in Kevin's jacket with the back of my cold, bare hand. I could hear the pulse in the invisible veins of his neck. I could see each molecule of moisture in his breath as it froze in the winter air. And though it could be that this was a phenomenon only I experienced, it *seemed* shared. Other boys were not quiet and still like this when they were around girls, and neither was Kevin, except when he stood with me.

He told me a secret once, in a voice that hung fragile as the frost crystals that flocked the tops of the windows. "I touch your coat," he said. Our school divided each grade into different home rooms, and we would shift locations for an hour or two every afternoon to take a class in French or Art. That meant I was sometimes in Kevin's home room, and he in mine. Our winter jackets hung from pegs at the back of our home rooms. And Kevin was saying to me that, as he entered or left my room, he would touch my coat as he passed.

"No one sees me," he said. He stared down as he said it, as if he were admitting something shameful. We were both looking down, into the narrow space between us, the crevasse of coats, that few inches of shared air. We could not look into each other's eyes, only into the space we made together. We were all alone as children played near us, children our age, though we felt vastly older. We were alone and together and I could feel the tickle of Kevin's hair against my forehead. I held so still.

Then Kevin lifted his hand, into the space we made. He stretched a surreptitious finger toward my coat and touched one of my toggle clasps. I watched as his finger curled around the clasp and he began to pull on it, not to draw me to him but harder, as if he meant to snap it off.

"You'll break it," I whispered. And I wanted him to. I remember that wanting ... wanting so that I could hardly breathe. Break it, I thought, watching his finger go white as he pulled against the clasp. *Please*, I thought, *please, please break it*.

I was so disappointed when he let go.

This boy in the park was not Kevin. Though he looked and moved so much like him, for a moment I could have sworn.

TONIGHT I WROTE ADNAN a new email. It was only one line.

"I think of you."

I wrote this, and then I hit *send*.

ZB Transcript 16

HEY, MARCIE ... IT'S, UH, it's close to eight and I'm going to get Pebbles right now. Have to apologize to her 'cause I was late picking her up yesterday at school — with the whole Hope thing, I almost forgot — and then she tried to show me this, some kind of map thing she made in class, and I was totally not paying attention to her so ... She actually said, "Why are you bothering? I thought you wanted to spend time with me."

Which is good, that she said that. And I'm gonna tell her that. 'Cause she's been so careful since her mom and I ... acting like she can't do anything wrong around me or even, you know, real. She thinks she has to be some perfect kid with me. She's not like that with Emily, just with me. Like she trusts her but I'm gonna fucking disappear if she gives me any hassle. So I'm gonna tell her. Hey, good for you for giving me shit. That's what I'm gonna say. Good for you, Pebs. Give me hell if I deserve it. Fucking right.

And then after that I'm gonna meet with Hope and talk about all this. I was thinking about it all night, going over what happened and what, you know, what we should do now. Didn't really get much sleep, which ... whatever. Stupid thing was I actually thought about calling my mom, 'cause she likes to give advice and she's pretty smart about stuff and, you know, she's sort of got experience. I mean, not the whole thing that Hope had because that's ...

Anyway, I decided it would just be weird for her, having to think about all that shit with Dad. Why do that to her, you know? And I figured she'd just tell me I was aces anyway and "Of course, you didn't mean anything" and "That poor girl must be very troubled," and all that bullshit. I mean, I can hear it all, 'cause she walked me through the whole thing with Emily like that. Totally on my side, pumping my tires the whole way. So, I figured that wasn't gonna be very, I dunno ... helpful.

The thing is, I gotta get her back on track. Hope, I mean. I don't want her bailing on me. 'Cause whatever happened with us, it still worked with Emily, right? We got her brain going in the right direction now, so I don't wanna lose that momentum. This is like playoff time. You can't have doubts. You can't be working against each other. Everybody's gotta be synced up on this thing. That's what I was thinking. You know, let's have it out. Let's get on the same page here. Tell me what I need to do! Right? Fucking right!

So, yeah, we'll meet and we'll get this thing fixed up.

And Marcie, I want the name and number of that investor dude that Lino was working on. Like, ASAP. Because I'm fucking through screwing around on that. None of this is gonna work if I don't have that whole part of it lined up.

So, that's the day right there. Pebbles, Hope, investor dude. Bam! Let's go!

Okay, that's it for now.

Sunday, April 26

ZEP SENT ME A TEXT this morning asking to meet as usual in our conference room, so I waited there for him, under the spastic fluorescent light. When he arrived he knocked on the door, which he had never done before, and entered. For a moment he stood near the door, his eyes on the table, his hands at his sides. He was carrying a folder. Then the flickering light drew his attention to the ceiling. He stared for a second or two.

"Excuse me," he said, and left.

Something told me to wait. And shortly Zep returned with a hotel employee. The two of them stood, looking at the flickering light as if receiving a signal. The employee nodded. "We'll deal with it right away," he said.

"Lunch," said Zep. "We're having a meeting right now."

When it was just the two of us again, Zep pulled out a chair across from me and sat. He laid the folder he was carrying on the table and slid it very slightly toward me. He moved slowly, and still had not looked directly at me. In the chair, he focused on the interlaced fingers of his hands on the table. Neither of us spoke for what seemed a long time.

The folder contained some loose pages which must have slipped out of my notebook when I fell.

"I'm very sorry."

Zep looked up at me with the eyes of someone who'd been slapped.

"What the hell are you talking about?" he said quietly. "Why should you be sorry? I'm the one. Jesus Christ." He smeared his hand over his face. His eyes were closed. "I'm the one," he said.

"It must have been upsetting for you," I said.

He held up the same hand. "You gotta stop," he said. "Okay? Stop talking like I'm the one hard done by here. It's fucking perverse."

The air seemed to go out of him then and he leaned forward on the table, rested his forehead against his folded hands. From the other side of the door came sounds of people calling. Someone named Terry was late, or missing. Had anyone seen him? Had Terry gone to the wrong room? No one knew.

The door jumped open and a woman in her forties, in a turquoise suit and large pearl earrings, leaned into the room. She took in the sight of a younger woman in dark clothes, across from her a large man in a suit laying his head on a conference table. Neither of these seemed to be the person she sought. Her eyes slid back to me and held for the briefest moment before she backed out. The door clumped shut.

Gradually the sounds from beyond subsided. Without moving, Zep began to speak into the table. I could feel the soft vibrations travelling across the wood into my hands.

"I probably seem like an asshole to you," he said. "That's okay, it seems that way to me too sometimes." He leaned back in his chair then, his forehead knuckled red.

"Lesley talked to you."

Zep nodded, staring into the table.

"I was taking Pebs to school this morning," he said. "I couldn't stop …" He shook his head, his voice gone hoarse. "She's the same age."

I said, "So if it's okay, and you understand, we'll just continue."

He turned toward me, his expression wondering.

"I was thinking I'd have to talk you into it."

"No. It's fine."

I opened up my notes.

EARLIER THIS MORNING, when I woke up, Adnan had replied to my email. I saw his name and felt heat in my ears.

Hope,

Thank you for send this email. It makes me happy that you are think of me. And also that you give me your email address so I may write to you. Thank you.

I am glad that you think of me Hope. I think of you every day. I have good thoughts that you are well where you are. And happy. You are a good woman and deserve to be happy. Maybe I say this word too much? I don't know. But it is what I hope for you.

It is very late here when I write this. I have been all night cook for some people in Forest Hill neighbourhood. It was a very nice home, with a good kitchen. All the homes are nice here, all the people are rich and have nice pans too cook with, but they are not too much used and the knives they have are no good. Its okay I bring my own.

One day maybe I will show you a good knife to buy. I can tell you these important things that even rich people and smart people like you don't know! I am joke now. My brother says I should tell people when I am joke because they are not funny.

One dish that I made for this party was the galette that we made, you and I, with apples and figs, and you were in my mind when I made it. I have not made it since our night, but I made it tonight. And then your email came! So I think it is not an accident. I made the galette, think of you, and you wrote to say you think of me. This is good. We are together connected. Yes?

I have tell my brother about you. One time I did. His name is Harout and he is younger but married and always joke at me about that I am not married like him. All the times he jokes at me I have nothing to say but one time when he joked I said but there is Hope. She is a wonderful woman. And he say no she is my imagination. She does not exist. And I say one day I hope you will meet her Harout, so then you will be quiet.

Now Hope, I must tell you some new thing. Which I am sorry to tell you but I must.

I thought it would not be hard, because you have not written to me, so I think maybe there is no worry. (And I think probably Harout will never meet you.) But now I don't know. So I just tell it because it is the truth.

There is a restaurant that needs a chef, and it wants me to be the chef. And I would like to be a chef in a restaurant. It is something I always wanted. Before I met you I went to see some restaurants and show how I cook, because I want to be a chef at a good restaurant, and now it can happen. They want me to start soon. In three weeks.

But Hope it is in Montreal. I would move to Montreal to be the chef at this restaurant. And I thought when they asked me that it was okay, it was good, because I did not think there was a chance to be with you. And so, okay, I can go and be a chef and it will help me not think of Hope. This is what I thought. But now you have told me that you think of me. So now I don't know. And Hope I must know because this is a good chance for me. To be a chef and make my future.

But Hope, if you think the chance is good for us, to be together, then I would not go to Montreal. I would stay and keep cook here and be more happy than ever, because we are together. And I would wait to be a chef here, because one day it could happen. And even if it does not happen it would be okay, because we are happy.

I am sorry to tell you this, Hope. I do not want to push, its not good I know. But if I had the chance I would choose to be with you, because you are such a good woman. And if there is no chance, please tell me, and do not worry that it hurts me, because I will go to Montreal.

Adnan

Phase 3 (preliminary)

Having mitigated to the extent possible the subject's previous negative attitudes toward Zep, and having established (if only temporarily) a foundation of goodwill and positive association, our focus now is to stimulate in her the symptoms of infatuation — quickened heartbeat, euphoria, obsessive thinking. We must induce the release of excitatory neurotransmitters in such a way that she associates the effects of these chemicals with Zep. We must activate the right ventral tegmental area of the brain to synthesize dopamine and release it into the accumbens, activating the reward system, causing Emily to perceive Zep as a source of pleasure. This increase in dopamine will in turn cause a drop in serotonin levels, triggering excess activity in the anterior cingulate gyrus, leading to anxiety and obsessive-compulsive thinking. If this is achieved in concert with positive sensations while in Zep's company, Emily should then perceive Zep as an answer to a need.

IT WOULD BE BETTER if we had more time. But we must do what we can do. Science does not always require absolute certainty, the confirmation of results, to spur its decisions or point it in purposeful directions. Sometimes a hunch is enough. We can devote the lives we have, and dispense with the lives we might wish for, on the basis of partial indicators. In this matter I won't need a solid blue line to know what I must do.

I told Zep that we needed to increase his access to Emily. It wasn't possible any longer to rely on "chance" meetings or fleeting encounters in her driveway. It was up to him to ensure that he had at least one daily interaction with her, lasting several minutes at a minimum. If possible, I told him, the encounter should occur at roughly the same time every day, and it should put the two of them in close proximity, preferably alone.

"So, what … you want me to lock us up in a closet together?"

"If you could do that every day for a week, that would be fine."

He tilted his head back. "Sorry, I just don't know exactly what … I mean, 'cause the lunch thing, picking up Pebbles, that's pretty much all my ideas, right there."

"Could you expand somehow on what you're already doing?"

His large hands lay flat on the table before him. "Expand," he said. "You mean what I'm doing with Pebbles?" I nodded, and he stared into space as he had before, but in a way that seemed less lost. His mind was engaged in a search, which brought focus to his gaze. Our bodies can't help but reflect the activity of our minds, no matter how much we might try to keep them separate. He reached over with his right hand and unclasped his fat wristwatch without looking, an act of the subconscious. He laid it on the table between his hands like a metallic toad and began to touch it lightly, running his fingers over the surface, nudging it, turning it, stimulating his peripheral nerves, prodding his brain to feel for a solution.

"Maybe I give them both a lift," he said, glancing at me. "Take Pebs to school, take Em to work."

"She has her own car though."

"Yeah." He continued to stare, to prod his toad. "Maybe if she has car trouble?"

"You could do that."

He nodded.

"But don't her parents have a car?"

Zep threw up his arms. "Fuck, I don't know. *Probably*?" He let his arms fall heavy on the table and then his eyes went wide and he hung his head. "Jesus. I'm sorry." He wiped a hand over his face and his chest rose and fell with a breath. "It's hard for me. I don't know why it's so hard."

"It's all right."

"No, it's not." He was shaking his head. "It's not right that you don't feel safe with me. I don't like it. It makes me feel like shit, honestly, if you want to know the truth."

"I can't —"

"Totally, Hope. I get it. Not saying it's your fault or you should do anything, right? But …" He exhaled, then gathered up his watch, began to slide it over the knuckles of his hand. "It's just probably, you know, maybe we were asking for trouble here. 'Cause I'm like how I am and you're like how you are, so …" He snapped his watch closed around his wrist.

"Please, don't —"

He glanced up, startled. "What? Am I being loud?"

"No, just …" He looked terrified. I think because I seemed to be crying. "Don't say it's over."

"I wasn't." The smallest voice. The gentlest man. "It's not, Hope. It's not."

ZB Transcript 17

MARCIE I GOT A LOT TO CATCH you up on so I'm gonna take it one thing at a time here. It's uh, it's six-thirty in the morning or ... six-forty, actually. Whatever. Too fucking early. I've had like two hours' sleep, if that, and I feel like I haven't had a proper crap in four days. I'm serious! Yeah, sorry, that's probably too much information for you but if you're wondering why this is sounding echoey it's 'cause I'm sitting on the toilet right now. This is the only time I have to do this thing with you and if I don't do it now it's all gonna get ahead of me and I'll forget to tell you stuff. So, that's just how it is.

I know you've dealt with worse, though, Marcie. I've seen what you feed Ramone.

Okay, first thing. So, Hope and I got all that stuff squared away, I think. You know, the reaction and how, how I caused it. We talked about the whole thing and it was ... I mean, it was more like me wanting to talk about it. She seemed to wanna move right past it, like it hardly happened. Which, you know, I don't know how I'm supposed to forget something like that but, it's like she's in a hurry all of a sudden. Like the clock's ticking on her. Maybe it's 'cause she needs to get back to work or maybe she just wants this whole business to be over? I dunno. Probably not that, though, because for a minute, while we were talking, she thought I was shutting things down and she got a little upset. I mean, there were tears in her eyes, so ... it's weird.

It's like she still wants to do it, *really* wants to do it, but she wants to do it fast.

She doesn't talk about herself though so, you know, I got no clue.

Second thing. Investor dude guy. What's his name — Hal Hempleman.

Fuck, so I called this guy yesterday after lunch, after you sent me his info, right? So get this. Get this, Marcie: Guy said no to the deal.

Okay? Yeah! Guy said no to the deal. He was in, and now he's fucking out. That happened like days ago! So you think maybe that's something Lino might want to tell me, right? So maybe we can move on, right? Find other prospects, 'cause he knows I wanna get this thing moving. But he doesn't do that, doesn't call me, doesn't *return* my calls. So why is that? That's a good question, right? Well, guess what? Guess what fucking what, Marcie. Turns out there's a good reason he doesn't do that. A very good reason. Are you ready for this? The reason he doesn't tell me investor dude Hal bailed is that it was *Lino who talked him out of it*!

Yeah. You believe that? My business manager, my best friend, who's supposed to be helping me fucking save this business plan, and who had a primo investor *on the hook*, fucking *talked him out of it*. Said my body wash was a "no-good investment." Said it was "unlikely to succeed."

Yeah. This Hempleman guy is reading me back his notes. The fucking notes he took when he was talking to my best friend Lino. Guy who was a goddamn usher at my wedding. Guy who comes to my house for dinner. Who's seen Pebbles so much the last thirteen years she fucking calls him "Uncle Lino."

Yeah.

Blew my fucking mind when I heard all this. Are you kidding? The only reason I can fucking sit down right now on this shitter, without kicking it out from under my own fucking ass, is because I found this out yesterday. You didn't want to talk to me yesterday, Marcie. No goddamn way you wanted to talk to me yesterday. And I made damn fucking sure to stay away from Hope the whole day. I mean, even *I* woulda run away from me yesterday if I could have.

I had the hotel guys up here, actually, 'cause I — *Hey*!

Sorry, Marcie, there's a stupid motion sensor thing in this bathroom here. You gotta keep moving or the fucking light shuts off.

So, yeah, hotel guys came because I somewhat messed up their little poncey desk in there. And the poncey lamp that was on it. I guess the maid was next door or something when I was kicking the shit out of it and called them so they came up — it was the manager and a security guy. They seemed a little worried. Which was fair. So I told them I got some bad family news. Which it is, in a way. It is in a way. And I said I'd pay whatever damages, no problem. I offered to hand 'em a cheque right there. So that calmed them down. They said, you know, another episode like that and I'd have to leave, which again — fair. So. Yeah. That was that.

They're gonna bring up a new desk this afternoon.

So now, you know, I'm out an investor, which fucking sucks. Hal seemed like a nice dude, too, except for the fact now he thinks I have leprosy or something. And I'm out, like, my best friend. Right? I mean, how can Lino be my friend now? Guy fucking stabbed me in the back. I still can't believe it. You know what? Don't trust assholes who never call you back. I mean, even before this he was slippery. He's been slippery for over a year now, I'm telling you.

After Emily left he was good for a while. He was good! We went out. We got drunk a few times. He helped get me laid a few times. Not that I needed help, but whatever. He was there for me. We talked about shit. I mean, he knew about the whole thing with the Allegheny money, when I started up in Lakeland and Valrico. He knew that was a screw-up. And when Em found out, he didn't say "I told you so" or anything. He knew why I did it.

But I dunno. Last year or so the guy hasn't been there as much. Just something different, I dunno what. Just a feel thing. Not around as much. Taking trips who knows where. Not calling me back as fast. That's been going on for months. That's why I didn't clue in sooner on this whole deal. It's like, okay, Lino's taking a few days to call me back, so what else is new?

And this whole investor thing. You know, I look back on that and it's like two and two don't add up. I mean, at first Lino was all for it. Like, "Yeah, man! Body wash — great idea! Extend your brand, man. It's perfect!" Like he got it, right?

Fuck off!

Goddamn light.

Anyway. He was on board. I just don't know why he went and found this guy and got him interested, and then he tells him forget it. Bad investment.

Makes no sense. Like, what changed?

Fuck this, I'm doing nothing here. I'm all like concrete. Just give me a minute here, I gotta concentrate.

OKAY SO, MARCIE, GOING DOWN the list, that's Hope and that's the investor dude and Lino and now this third thing, the last thing I gotta tell you right now ... it's kinda weird. You know ... I admit that. But this whole thing is weird, right? I mean, back when I told you I was doing this, you totally gave me the scrunchy eye, right? The Marcie scrunchy eye, man! That's serious shit — don't think I don't know it.

I dunno how Ramone deals with it. I see you giving him the scrunchy eye all the time. You should ease up on the dude,

Marcie. You know he loves you. Man, you think I was messed up after Em left me? Ramone, he'd be a puddle. Just a splash of dirty water on the floor.

Anyway, so here's the deal. A few hours ago, like around three in the morning, I went to where Emily's living, and I uh ... you know, I sabotaged her car.

Nothing serious. I mean, don't worry, she's not gonna get in an accident, okay? Like, I didn't mess with her brakes or anything. But, you know, she's not going anywhere. That's the point. Hope said I had to figure out how to be near her for more than a couple of minutes, and for a few days in a row, not just a one-off, right? So I figured this was the best option.

What I did, I drove over, and I parked like two blocks away. So I walked there. Pretty spooky, actually. All the houses dark and everybody sleeping, everything real quiet. Saw a couple of raccoons walking around like they owned the place. I guess I was lucky it wasn't garbage night.

Been a while since I was out real late like that. Kinda cool actually. The air had this nice fresh feel to it, and there's something, I dunno, there's something about being awake when everybody else is asleep. Makes you feel powerful or something. Makes you feel like you're in charge, like you've got the advantage. I mean, I kinda get why all the badasses come out at night, you know? It's not just a drinking thing, it's something else ... I was walking there, in the dark toward Em's house, and my heart's going 'cause of, you know, what I'm gonna do. And it was like, man, this is very cool. This is fun. I gotta do this more often!

Anyway, I got to Em's driveway and I had to look around. Make sure nobody was watching. Tried to see if there was anything moving in the windows. Totally paranoid, you know, I dunno why anybody'd be looking out at me just at that moment. Three in the morning, right? And then I was standing beside the car — and I'm wearing some dark stuff, some black pants and this dark blue sweatshirt I had to buy at the hotel gift shop 'cause I was getting on the ground, I didn't wanna mess up a jacket — and I'm thinking, like, get the fuck down! Right? Like, don't just be standing there like an idiot!

I went to the front of the car and it was only like three feet from the garage door. Anybody was listening they could've heard me breathing. But it was hard, 'cause that's the moment, right? When you get on the ground, that's when you go from being just a guy, to being a guy doing something he probably shouldn't be doing.

So my heart was jumping a bit. And I'm thinking, is this okay? Am I a bad guy? All that second-guessing shit. But then I did it. I got down, which wasn't easy 'cause of my knee. The thing's like rusted-up pig iron now. But I got down on my back under the front bumper. And now, like, every sound I make shifting around down there is *loud* to me, right? And I had this bag of stuff, I mean just a few tools, like a clothes hanger and a couple of wrenches I took from the Cadillac and a knife I picked up from this dollar store. And every time I move that it makes a sound and to me it's just so fucking loud, I don't know why there aren't sirens going, right? Like, *everybody* must be able to hear me.

I didn't really have a plan for what I was gonna do, because I didn't know what I could reach from under there. And it wasn't much. And I didn't want to turn on a light or anything. So basically I'm just under there as far as I can go, you know, wishing I was a hell of a lot thinner, just fishing around for stuff.

Like I said, Marcie, don't worry. I did not fuck with anything that could get her in trouble on the road. Jesus Christ, this is not some psycho revenge thing. I mean, fuck, I don't know why I'm even arguing with you about it. I just needed her to not be able to drive the car at all. So I figured my best options were like, starter or gas line. Probably starter. So I'm down there just jammed up against the wheel, trying to reach through past the suspension. I mean, the way cars are sealed up so much now it's hard to get at anything. It's almost impossible. And so at one point my arm's all jammed up in there but not close to anything I can grab and I'm like, "Fuck me," right?

Like, I said that out loud.

And then I realize and I just freeze. And I'm shouting at myself in my head, *you idiot what are you doing talking out loud you stupid dumb fuck*? I mean, I was really giving it to myself. And then I just listen, to see if I can hear anything in the house, any shifting around. Anybody getting up. I'm like Superman down there with super extreme hearing. Somebody coughs in a house a block away and I can hear that. Paper rustling on the street I can hear that. Squirrel on a branch. Breeze in the leaves. I can hear *everything*.

And it's okay. Nothing moving.

So I get going again. And it seems like I know where the starter is, 'cause I can feel the shape of it. But it's right at my fingertips and I can't reach the ignition wire. So I pull my arm out and I get the hanger. It's just a wire one from the dry cleaners, and I twist it into a shape that'll get in there. I need like another hand length, maybe a bit more. So I twist it up and make it into a hook and a handle. And I reach in again, and I have to be careful now 'cause every time the hook hits metal it makes a noise. I have to go slow. Really fucking slow.

And it gets caught on something. It gets hooked around the wrong thing when I'm up in there and I don't know what the hell I'm gonna do. For a minute I thought I'd have to leave it in there. Which is like, *no way*, right? And I'm thinking I'll just have to pull as hard as I can and get it free. And I want to jiggle the damn thing but I can't jiggle it. I want to force it but

I can't force it. And I can't swear. I can't shout. Basically I can't be me. Right at that moment, the worst person to be is me. Being me is just gonna ruin everything, right?

And I closed my eyes, Marcie, I'm telling you. I closed my eyes and I just said in my mind I said, easy. *Easy*. It got in there, must be a way to get it out. So I just breathed. Kept my eyes closed. Imagined how to get it out of there. Just made it up in my mind. Move this way ... and that way.

And it came free. Just like that. Fuckin' magic.

After that, it took me another two minutes. Got it hooked around the ignition wire and started pulling. Had to pull it slow but hard, like really hard. 'Cause Hondas aren't like goddamn Chevys where you blow on 'em they throw a valve. Basically I'm heaving on this thing. And when it finally pulled loose I hit my wrist on this bolt and holy shit the pain. Holy shit, Marcie. I had some fastballs hit me didn't hurt that bad. Every part of me wanted to shout but I had to eat it. I had to fucking eat that pain. For a minute I thought I was gonna pass out.

And that was it. That's all I had to do, except get out of there without anyone seeing me or hearing me. Which I did. I mean, that was the easy part. Got back to the car and sat there for a minute. My heart was going like anything, but not scared. Excited. Mission accomplished, you know? I mean ... a weird thing to do, maybe a bad thing, but it had to be done and I did it.

Monday, April 27

THERE IS NOTHING LEFT of Adnan's tarts. Even the foil that protected them has disintegrated. Each night I take the package from the refrigerator and peel it open, and another aluminum fragment tears away like sunburned skin. Inside, only shards of pastry and dried filling remain. I pluck away the infections of mould, break off the pieces that can't be saved, gather what's left. I scoop it up and press it together, hoping the warmth of my palms will knit this atomizing flesh, this unravelling memory. When I bring it to my nose now, it smells more of me than of him. He is apple and fig, tomato and onion, butter and flour, and he is dying in my hands.

THIS IS WHAT I BECOME now at two in the morning. It's a fairly new development, and as I look at this page, while sunlight at the window defines the edge of a new day, it's all I can do not to rip it out. Instead I leave it, and mark it. This Hope cannot be trusted. I will not leave important decisions to her.

Yesterday before lunch, Zep and I discussed in detail what he was to do before and during his next meeting with Emily. At the end he insisted he was clear on his instructions. He took notes, in fact, which he promised to study and memorize. I didn't follow up to remind him to do this, because he tends to bristle at what he calls "too much minding," and he made no contact with me for the rest of the day.

I spent the afternoon gathering supplies and making preparations.

Buffalo may not be a large city, but because several sports franchises make their home here I knew that even on a Sunday it wouldn't be difficult to find what I needed. By four o'clock I had passed a few twenty-dollar bills across two store counters and received small stapled bags in return.

Later at the hotel I called room service and ordered dinner, including what must have seemed a surprising amount of dessert for someone my size. The attendant on the other end of the line hesitated.

"Sorry, how many people in the room?"

"It's just me."

"So, one slice Boston cream pie."

"No, I said three."

"Three Boston cream pie for you."

"Yes."

He seemed unconvinced.

"I really like it," I added.

He chuckled, in a troubled sort of way, and declined further comment on the matter of the pie.

"So, you don't want the fresh strawberries."

"Yes, I want those as well. With whipped cream. And three chocolate croissants."

"Croissants. From the breakfast menu?"

"Yes."

"Three croissants also."

I asked if he had a small cardboard cake box that he could send up with dinner and I asked for an extra bowl.

"A bowl of what, ma'am?"

"Just an empty bowl."

After dinner, I knelt at the side of the bed, spread a white towel across its surface and assembled my materials. I scooped the Boston cream out of the slices of pie and mixed this with small, measured amounts from my stapled bags. I chopped most of the strawberries into finer pieces, added these to the cream mixture, and used the same knife to hollow out the centres of three croissants. Adnan, I thought, would have been pained by my technique. For a moment with my knees on the carpet I imagined him taking one of the croissants and gently entering it with his thumb, spreading open its inner leaves. Taking the cream and easing it in, showing me.

But in the end, my results were presentable enough. I set the box in the small fridge beside the resident foil package and tried to sleep.

At six a.m. Zep texted me — "Good to go" — which meant that during the night he'd managed to disable Emily's car. I will not feel guilty about that or anything else made necessary by circumstance. We have a lot to accomplish and not much time.

Before he left to get Pebbles, Zep came to my room as I'd reminded him to do. We went over the steps again to make sure he had it.

"Yeah, yeah," he said repeatedly. "Yeah, yeah." His eyes were pressed shut and I knew he was concentrating, visualizing the play.

"You'll do fine," I said. He gave me a tight smile. "Where's your phone going to be?" I had to monitor events in real time, and since I couldn't be there to observe, he'd agreed to call me and leave the line open so that I could listen.

He patted his right breast pocket.

"No," I said. "The sound will be too muffled. Hold it in your hand when you go to the door. Try not to move it around too much."

"Okay."

"In the car, maybe put it on the dash."

"There's a place between the seats."

I handed him the box of croissants. "Keep these hidden until you pick up Emily."

He held the box as if it were crystal.

"Because you don't know yet that she needs a ride."

"Right."

"Good luck." I patted him on the shoulder. "Nice tie, by the way."

He grinned like a boy praised by his teacher.

Phase 3 — Infatuation

This phase will stretch over the course of several days, during which we will use behavioural as well as chemical influences to induce the emotions we wish Emily to perceive.

By facilitating regular, repeated contact between Zep and Emily, we hope to instill in Emily a sense of expectation. We wish her to contemplate the prospect of seeing Zep. Over the course of several days we can achieve this by the simple mechanical requirements of Emily's daily transportation needs.

Our goal during this phase, however, is to turn Emily's expectation into *anticipation*, in the sense of her looking forward to seeing Zep with an element of pleasure. (Eventually, we hope anticipation will progress to *excitement*, although that may not occur until the final phase.)

This requires more manipulation. We will achieve *anticipation* by ensuring that her encounters with Zep are pleasurable to as many of her senses as possible. I have quizzed Zep on the sounds, scents, sights and tastes that Emily prefers, and compiled the list that follows:

Sounds: According to Zep, Emily likes a particular kind of contemporary cello music, often using it to relieve stress. He found this music hard to describe, but with effort we determined that it is generally ambient in nature and devoid of lyrics, and therefore not ideal for our purposes. We wish Emily to be happy and buoyed during her moments in Zep's car, not pensive. As an alternative, Zep suggested music by the band Oasis, citing the album *Be Here Now* as one of her favourites. He will have this playing in the car while Emily is with him.

On reflection, Zep suggested that, beyond music, the sound Emily most enjoys is the laughter of children. He described moments of joy in their household when their young daughter would laugh at a movie, or a game she was playing. There were times, such as during their daughter's birthday parties, when the house would be filled with laughing children, and Emily seemed to Zep profoundly happy. She explained to him that it is when she can hear the laughter of children that she feels most at ease. Unfortunately the nature of this sound makes it difficult to produce on demand in a manner congruent with normal circumstance, although Zep has been encouraged to take advantage of any opportunity that may arise.

Scent: Due to the experience-bound nature of olfaction and the connection between associative memory and the piriform cortex, we have narrowed our attention to scents closely associated with Zep and with a period of happiness in his marriage. Zep recalled that in the amorous, early stage of their lives together, when he was still playing for the Buffalo Bisons, Emily gave him a bottle of Bay Rum aftershave, which he used regularly. During his encounters with Emily in phase 3, Zep will be wearing this aftershave.

Sights: Here our focus is colour, because of its direct effect on the limbic system. We know that green is associated with positive emotion (Kuhbandner and Pekrun, 2013), and Zep has confirmed that yellow and green are two of Emily's preferred hues. For his meetings with Emily he will wear a series of shirts and ties in complementary shades of green and yellow.

Tastes: Zep indicates that in the food Emily eats purely for pleasure, she prefers sweet tastes over savoury; not unusual, given the abundance of hypothalamic glucose-sensitive receptors (Ren, et al, 2009). Boston cream is a particular favourite of Emily's, as well as certain berry flavours, including strawberry. She will also on occasion enjoy chocolate and mocha flavours. When Zep meets Emily, he will offer an array of confections featuring some or all of these flavours.

The multiplicity of the sensory triggers being employed may seem excessive. However, because Zep and Emily are likely to be together for only a short time during each encounter, it is our intention to bombard Emily's ventral tegmental area with pleasurable inputs in order to trigger a dopamine cascade into her nucleus accumbens, septum and amygdala. Dopamine is the significant neurotransmitter associated with a sensation of *want*. It is hoped that the effect of these brief, repeated "pleasure bombs" in Zep's presence will be to: 1. Direct Emily's mesolimbic dopamine system to associate Zep with reward; 2. Cause a corresponding drop in serotonin levels on the heels of their encounter, producing anxiety and a sense of *lack* associated with Zep's absence.

To enhance the effect of this induced infatuation, we will attempt to dose Emily with small but increasing amounts of phenylethylamine (PEA) via the sweet treats Zep offers her. The effect of this should be to enhance dopaminergic transmission, elevate Emily's heart rate and alertness, and produce in her a faint euphoria. The problems associated with ingesting PEA (1. That in order for PEA introduced through the digestive system to pass the blood-brain barrier, at least 500 mg must be consumed, and 2. That PEA has an unpleasant and bitter aftertaste) we hope to mitigate in two ways. The supplement hordenine has been added to the dose to inhibit the metabolization of PEA in the digestive system, allowing us to use less PEA than would otherwise be required. And strawberries have been added to the Boston cream vector, introducing a slight acidity to the compound that may offer a plausible explanation for any bitterness Emily perceives.

As well, because Zep Baker is overtly reactive to input and generally unable to hide or restrain his emotions, and because he therefore might betray the presence of an additive in the Boston cream (particularly if Emily notes an odd taste), he has not been informed of the presence of PEA or hordenine in the food he will offer Emily.

I'D TOLD ZEP TO CALL ME from the driveway as he was picking up Pebbles so I could hear his initial interaction with Emily. Her tone with him then would offer a baseline against which I could measure any future changes. I'd hoped he would call at seven-fifty. He needed to be early because whenever he arrived at eight, Pebbles tended to run out to the car before Zep could approach the house.

He called at 7:46. Zep was on his game.

"Hey. I'm here."

"Are you going to the door?"

"I just parked."

"Get to the door before Pebbles grabs her things."

"Yeah. I know. Getting out now."

"Don't hang up."

"I'm not an idiot!"

There was a beep.

"Zep?"

"Sorry, just hit a button. Don't stress out."

Phase 3, Stage A, Log A

(Note: the following transcript comprises audio from a transmission via cellphone. The descriptions of action are taken from follow-up interviews with participant Zep Baker.)

7:47 a.m.: Zep Baker walks up the driveway toward the residence of Joyce and Raymond Good, 126 Woodcrest Blvd., Buffalo, NY. He rings the doorbell.

7:48 a.m.: His ex-wife, Emily Good, answers the door.

Emily: "You're early."

Zep: "Yeah, you know, start of a new week."

Emily: "Okay. She's just finishing breakfast."

Zep: "Hey, Pebs!"

Pebbles: (from a distance) "I'll be there in a minute!"

Zep: "You're looking good. As usual." (According to Zep, his compliment was acknowledged with a small smile.)

Emily: "Did … you want to come in?"

Zep: "Your folks around?"

Emily: "Uh, they're here somewhere."

Zep: "Right. Out here's fine."

Emily: "Okay, well … she won't be long."

Zep: "Hey, listen, Em. Do you have my cell number?" (Zep holds up his phone.)

Emily: "Has it changed?"

Zep: "No, it's the 8708 number. Just wanted to make sure you had it in case, you know … just in case."

Emily: "Okay. I'll make sure."

(Note: Zep has successfully executed his first task, which was to refresh in Emily's mind the idea that he can be reached by cellphone. The hope is that within half an hour, when Emily needs to call someone for a ride to work, she will think of Zep first.)

7:49 a.m.: Emily closes the door and Zep waits on the front step.

7:56 a.m.: Pebbles emerges from the house.

Pebbles: “Why are you so early all of a sudden?”

Zep: “I dunno. Just wanted to be on time.”

Pebbles: “For *once*. Bye, Mom!”

Emily comes to the door.

Emily: “Do you have your music?”

Pebbles: “Yes, I have my stupid music!”

Emily: “Okay. Good thing you’re not cranky about it.”

Pebbles: “Yeah, yeah!”

Emily: “Bye!” (According to Zep, this “Bye” is directed strictly at Pebbles. It is as if to Emily he is no longer there. Zep lifts his hand, still holding the cellphone, in a wave, to which Emily responds with a small wave of her own as the door closes.)

7:57 a.m.: Pebbles goes to the front of Emily’s car. She bends and picks up something off the driveway.

Pebbles: “Here, Dad.”

Pebbles hands Zep several coins.

Zep: “What’s this?”

Pebbles: “They’re yours, aren’t they?”

On the way back to his car, Zep turns off his cellphone as instructed so as to be able to receive Emily’s call should it come.

(Initial assessment: All three goals for this stage of Phase 3 were achieved. Zep arrived early enough to make a direct encounter with Emily possible, and he successfully executed both the initial cellphone reminder and the follow-up visual reference. There were no unanticipated events or inputs that might have distracted Emily’s attention; she received their full benefit.

Throughout their interaction, Emily's tone toward Zep was cool and noncommittal. There was friendliness but little warmth. No apparent hostility. On a 1–10 scale — 1 being a complete absence of affection and 10 being romantic love — her demonstrated affection toward Zep was 3, the level of an acquaintance. Zep expressed some surprise at this result, given Emily's apparent enjoyment of their Phase 2 encounter. This might be a consequence of the failure to achieve a continuous eight seconds of Duchenne laughter in Phase 2, or some unknown factor.)

AFTER ZEP DROPPED PEBBLES at school, he called. This wasn't part of our plan, but he said he wanted to make sure I'd been able to hear everything. Mostly, though, he seemed to need reassurance that he'd done well. He sounded disappointed by Emily's behaviour toward him. He'd expected her to be warmer.

"It's almost like Friday didn't happen," he said. "I don't get it."

At the time, I had two primary concerns. One was to get Zep off the phone in case Emily called. The other was to build up his confidence so that he would relax and not try too hard in Phase 3/B. I know now that I was misreading him.

"She sounded good, Zep. Everything went fine."

"You don't know her. She was giving off this really strange vibe."

"You're doing great, though. Don't worry."

"Weird what happened with Pebbles too."

"What do you mean?"

"Didn't you hear? Some change must've fallen out of my pocket last night when I was working under Em's car. Pebs picked it up and gave it to me. Like she knew."

"We'll talk about it later. It's going really well. Call me after you hear from Emily."

Phase 3, Stage A, Log B

(Note: Descriptions in this log come only from follow-up interviews with participant Zep Baker as it was not possible to monitor audio.)

7:58 a.m.–8:14 a.m.: Zep drives Pebbles to school.
8:15 a.m.–8:25 a.m.: Zep drives to a location more proximal to 126 Woodcrest Blvd. and waits.
8:26 a.m.: Emily Good calls Zep. She sounds flustered. She apologizes for calling him and explains that her car won't start, and asks if it would be possible for him to give her a lift to work. Zep says he will be there right away.

IMMEDIATELY AFTER HE HUNG UP with Emily, Zep called me. He sounded even more agitated than before.

"It's her apologizing that gets me," he said. "It's like I'm some asshole from work. Some fucking stranger. Giving her a ride is some big burden."

"Zep."

"She doesn't understand that I *want* to see her."

"Zep, calm down. What are you doing now?"

"I'm driving over."

"How close are you?"

"Be there in two minutes."

"Stop. Pull over right now."

"What are you talking about?"

It would be suspicious if he arrived too quickly, and he was not in the right frame of mind. In his current state he might ruin everything. I begged him to pull over. My phone squeaked in my grip.

Zep pulled into a drugstore parking lot and I spent the next five minutes talking him down. I realized now that it wasn't confidence he'd lacked before, but perspective. He had already leaped ahead.

He wanted so badly to woo his ex-wife that a part of him thought he already had. I needed him to pull back from his expectations, his visualization of success. I needed him to leave assumption and return to hope. In hope he could find patience and humility, he could accept whatever might come, and in that state of mind he might at least have a chance.

As he listened he became subdued, stopped fighting the words I was giving him. I could almost sense him contracting, becoming cooler. "I hear you," he said finally. "I'm going too fast in my head."

"That's right," I said. "We're drawing Emily down a path. We have to encourage her; we can't force her. We need her to feel certain things."

I listened to him exhale.

Phase 3, Stage A, Log C

(Note: As in log A, the following transcript comprises audio from transmission via cellphone, and descriptions of action are taken from follow-up interviews with participant Zep Baker.)

8:34 a.m.: Zep arrives at 126 Woodcrest Blvd.

8:35 a.m.: Zep approaches the front door as Emily emerges and starts down the front steps. She is dressed for work, carrying her purse and a shoulder satchel, and seems rushed and somewhat on edge.

Emily: "Thanks for doing this, Zep. I never have trouble with this car, I don't know what's wrong."

Zep: "Did you want me to give it a try?"

Emily: "Dad tried it and thinks it's the starter. I just have to get to work."

Zep: "Sure."

8:36 a.m.: Raymond Good, Emily's elderly father, appears at

the front door. He steps out onto the porch and stands with his hands in his pockets.

Zep: “Morning, Ray.”

Raymond: “Zep. You’re a long way from home.”

Zep: “Just for a bit.”

Raymond: “Doing charity work, Emily says.”

Zep: “Uh, yeah, I guess.”

Raymond: “Different sort of a thing for you.”

Emily: “Dad, we have to go. I’m so sorry to leave you blocked in like that.”

Raymond: “Don’t worry about it. I just wish I could’ve given you a lift. We’re pulling Zep away from his good deeds.”

Emily moves toward Zep’s car, indicating to Zep her desire to leave.

Raymond: “I’ll call over to Fieldstaff’s and get them to tow you in for a look.”

Zep: “You know I could come by tonight and —”

Raymond: “All under control, don’t you worry.”

Emily: “Dad, I left the keys on the side table.”

Raymond: “That’s fine.”

8:37 a.m.: Zep opens the passenger door for Emily then walks to the driver’s side. Inside the car Zep starts the engine and puts the car in reverse, then stops.

Zep: “Shit.”

Emily: “What?”

Zep gets out and goes to the back of the car. He opens the trunk.

Emily: Zep, I’m really late.

8:38 a.m.: Zep retrieves the box of croissants and gets back in the car, handing the box to Emily.

Zep: “Almost forgot.”

Emily: “What’s this?”

Zep: "I know how much you like Boston cream."

Emily opens the box as Zep backs the car out of the driveway.

Emily: "Wow, where did you get these?"

Zep: "On the way over."

Emily: "Where?"

Zep: "Just, you know, some place. I don't even remember the name."

Emily: "You stopped for croissants after I called you in a panic?"

Zep. "Sure. Took two minutes."

Emily picks up one of the croissants and examines it.

Zep: "Go ahead. Have one."

8:39 a.m.: Zep now turns on the car's CD player.

Zep: "Where are we going, by the way?"

Emily: "It's out on Genesee. You can take the 290 … Is that Oasis?"

Zep: "Uh, I dunno, is it?"

Emily: "Oh, like you don't know *Be Here Now*. I thought you hated that album."

Zep: "Nah, I don't hate it. It's good. Turn it up if you want."

Emily turns up the music slightly. They proceed in silence for forty-two seconds.

Zep: "Bummer about your car."

Emily: "So weird that it just stopped working out of nowhere."

Zep: "Seriously, I don't mind taking a look at it."

Emily: "It's fine, Zep. Dad'll have it all fixed by the end of the day."

Zep: "So, are you going to eat those croissants? It's Boston cream, right? You love Boston cream."

Emily: "It's just that I had breakfast, so I'm not very hungry."

Zep: "Okay, well, whatever. I bought them for you."

Emily: "I know, I don't understand why you would do that."

Zep: "Just crazy, I guess. Nice thing to do."
Zep turns south onto Parkhurst Blvd.
Emily: "Why are you turning here?"
Zep: "Just figured we'd go down and hook up with Number 5."
Emily: "No, no, it's so much faster to stay on Sheridan to the highway."
Zep: "Traffic, though. Might be bad right now."
8:40 a.m.: Emily bites into her croissant.
Zep: "How is it?"
Emily: "Mmm."
Zep: "Good huh? Eat up."
Emily: "Actually, it's kind of weird Boston cream."
Zep: "How do you mean?"
Emily: "I don't know. There's an aftertaste."
Zep: "Well, don't finish it if you don't like it."
Emily: "No, it's fine."

She eats several more bites, approximately half of the croissant in total, before closing the box. (This should equate to a consumption of roughly 750 mg of PEA.)

Emily: "It was sweet of you, Zep. Thank you."
8:44 a.m.: Zep begins to slow the car, pulling it over to the curb.
Emily: "Why are we stopping?"
Zep: "I'm hot. I just want to take off my jacket."
As he stops, Zep presses the button to lower his and Emily's windows on the pretext of allowing air into the car. He turns down the music.

(Here Zep is executing a provisional plan. It had been predetermined that he would, if possible, divert down Parkhurst because it would take the car past a large elementary school. This would afford Zep the opportunity, given the right timing and circumstance, to stop and briefly allow Emily to hear the sound of children playing. In the moment, he has determined that the opportunity is good — there are children playing in the park adjacent to the school.)

Emily: "I'm going to miss my meeting."

Zep: "Just take a second."

Zep opens the driver's door and gets out. He takes off his jacket and goes to the rear of the car, opens the trunk and lays the jacket inside. (This has the added benefit, once he has returned to the driver's seat, of making the yellow and green of his shirt and tie more prominent.)

When Zep re-enters the car he notes Emily staring out her window, observing the children.

Zep: "Remember when Pebbles was that age?"

Emily: "Mmhmm."

Zep: "What was that game she used to play with her friends?"

Emily: "Jump rope?"

Zep: "No, the kissing one."

Emily: "Kiss tag."

Zep: "Kiss tag, that's it. Remember how she wanted us to do it? She had some friends over. She was all jazzed up."

Emily: "That was probably sugar."

Zep: "Hauling us out into the yard. 'You have to play too. You have to play too.' Giggling like crazy. She was six, I think."

Emily: "Did we?"

Zep: "Fuck yeah, we did. You don't remember?"

Emily: "Maybe."

Zep: "Chased you all around the yard. Jeez, I worked up a sweat, you were hard to catch. Pebs was like screaming the whole time."

Emily: "What were you doing home?"

Zep: "Must've been the off-season. November, probably."

8:46 a.m.: Seven seconds of silence here. Emily is looking out the window. She turns back.

Emily: "Zep, I really have to get to work."

Zep: "Sure, yup."

8:47 a.m.–8:53 a.m.: Zep continues to Emily's workplace. At a certain point he glances at Emily and notes that she is smiling. (Asked later if he observed an increase in her rate of breathing or blinking, Zep said possibly but he wasn't sure, so it is impossible to know with certainty whether Emily's smile reflected an early stage of mild PEA-induced euphoria.)

8:54 a.m.: Zep: "What are you thinking about?"

Emily: "Nothing."

Zep: "You were smiling."

Emily: "Was I? I don't know. It's strange being in this car with you."

Zep: "Just like before."

Emily: "Are you … are you wearing Bay Rum?"

Zep: "Yeah, I wear that sometimes."

Emily: "God, it's like the late nineties all over again … You know, I was thinking about —"

Zep: "So you *were* thinking."

Emily laughs. (This laughter seems free and marginally out of proportion to the cause, which does suggest PEA influence.)

Emily: "I was *thinking* about that *girl*."

Zep: "What girl?"

Emily: "Remember? What you were telling me at the restaurant. About the night at the drive-in."

Zep: "Oh! Bobby and Gabbers. Yeah, yeah. What girl though?"

Emily: "The girl in the front."

Zep: "The girl in … You mean the one with Rick?"

Emily: "Yes. I don't know what made me think of her. But you told that story — I mean, I hadn't thought about that night in years — and then later I had this image in my mind of that girl, sitting in the front seat. I don't think she ever turned around, or said a word to anyone, the whole time."

Zep: "Rick never had great taste in girls. Not like me!"

Emily: "I remember trying to talk to her … I didn't know whether she was just shy. She seemed … well, she didn't seem to be enjoying herself very much."

Zep: "Not like you."

Emily: "It *was* a bit crazy."

Zep: "Rick was a shitty driver too. She might've just been scared for her life."

Emily: "Mmm. Do you have any water?"

(Note: Due to PEA's effect on heart and breathing rates, excessive or unusual thirst can be considered a peripheral effect of PEA ingestion.)

Zep: "Shit, no. Sorry."

Emily: "That's all right, we're almost there."

8:56 a.m.–8:58 a.m.: Zep and Emily continue without further conversation until the car approaches Emily's workplace.

8:59 a.m.: Emily: "There it is, coming up. See it?"

Zep: "Got it."

Emily: "Oh, my God, I think I'm going to make my meeting."

Zep: "Told you not to worry."

Emily: (giggling) "Did you? I don't remember that." She begins searching for something at her feet. "Where's my … where's my … oh!" She puts a hand to her chest.

Zep: "You okay?"

Emily: "That was silly. I thought I'd lost my bag for a minute. Hoo! Okay, calm down. Thank you, Zep! I have to run. Thank you, thank you!"

Emily leans over and gives Zep a kiss on the cheek. She exits, shuts the door and continues up the path toward her workplace.

9:01 a.m.: Zep picks up his phone.

Zep: "You get all that? She kissed me on the cheek. First time in almost two years."

(Initial assessment: It is hard to gauge how much each sensory input contributed to the subject's emotional state during this phase, although it is likely all but taste had a small positive impact. The 750 mg of PEA consumed seems to have had the greatest effect, as Emily exhibited increased relaxation, in the form of mild giddiness and verbosity, beginning approximately thirteen minutes after consumption. Given there were no setbacks, and the encounter concluded with voluntary intimate contact, this phase may be deemed a success. On the 1–10 scale, her demonstrated affection toward the object, Zep, was 6, the level of a close friend.)

ZB Transcript 18

FUCK, MARCIE, I GOT SO MUCH to tell you. Jesus Christ, don't let anyone tell you making somebody fall in love with you again is a piece of cake. It's no goddamn such thing. I'm on my back here, just staring up at the ceiling. I'm worn out!

It's going pretty good, though. Hope says I'm halfway there. Got a big six on my test today. I gotta get all the way up to ten in just a few days — ten is love — and I don't know how the fuck that's supposed to happen. Hope says it's momentum. We got the momentum on our side now, she says.

The car thing worked perfect. I mean, it could not have been better. Picked up Pebbles and, you know, it's hard keeping the nerves off my face 'cause I know what's coming, right?

Anyway, get the call, she's all panicked. "My car won't start!" and I'm like, Yeah? Gee, that's bad. "Can you give me a lift?" And I'm like, "Uh, sure. Sure, I can do that. No problem."

Inside I'm going *Fuckin' yeah*! But I can't let any of that out, right? It's like acting. Seriously, I was totally doing some Tom Cruise shit there.

Then I get there and ol' Ray comes out. Her dad, you know? And you can tell I'm the last guy he wants to look at. Got all this judgment on his face, right? Every word he says to me, no matter what he says, I'm hearing "You're a piece of shit." Like, "Hello, piece of shit. Nice day, piece of shit. Taking my daughter to work, are you, piece of shit?"

I wish I could explain everything to him but … you know I tried writing him a letter once. Figured I owed him that and I thought maybe if I put it down on paper, what I was trying to do, he'd at least listen to me. I mean, he'd hear it, even if he didn't believe it.

And then sometimes I think, why wouldn't he believe it? He's her dad, right? If anyone should understand loving a woman enough to do something stupid it should be her dad. I mean, if ten years from now some asshole loves Pebbles so much that he robs a bank or something just to be with her, you know, fuck, I'd cut the guy a little slack!

Anyway I never sent that letter. Just seemed pointless. I never thought I'd be back here like this. Never thought I had a chance.

So, okay, back to this morning.

Everything went great, pretty much. Except Hope got these shitty croissants for Em that had this weird filling. Supposed to be Boston cream but it had strawberries in it and it was kinda … I dunno, kind of a confusing taste, not like any Boston cream I ever had. It wasn't *good*, that's for sure. Em only ate half of one and I took a bite after she got out of the car. Fuck. She was doing me a favour just to eat half of the thing.

I told Hope when we met up later. I said "I dunno where you got those croissants but you should get your goddamn money back." She just nodded and made notes.

Other than that, it went really smooth. And when Em was getting out of the car she gave me a kiss. I mean, it was on the cheek, but there she was, you know? Right there. Felt her cheek and I got a whiff of her, you know, that kinda soft smell. That smell from when she's had a bath the night before, and then the next morning she wakes up and goes. She doesn't shower, and so you can still smell her pillow on her. You can still smell sleep on her, like how it would be if you leaned over in bed and kissed her while her eyes were still closed.

That's gotta be the best smell ever. Which is weird, you know, because it's not even much of a smell. It's not like flowers, or pie in the oven. It's not even like sex. But it's a smell that means something. Fuck, I dunno how to explain what … It's a smell that says you know a person, you know what I mean? That she trusts you. She feels safe with you. It's like the smell of … everything's okay. It's that smell.

I was still thinking about it later when I went to pick up Pebbles after school. Things stay with you, you know? I get in the car and, bam, it's like I can feel Em's cheek again, I can still breathe in that smell.

Sorry, Marcie. I know this all sounds stupid. Fuck, I was like this for six months after she said it was over. You don't need to go through it again.

So, speaking of Pebbles — this is out of order but I'll tell it anyway — I picked her up at school and for the first couple of minutes she's real quiet. Staring straight ahead out the window. Then she says, "How'd it go this morning?"

And I don't know what she's talking about. Or, like, maybe I do, but I shouldn't. *She* shouldn't. I say, "How'd what go?"

She says, "I dunno."

So that's weird, right? You ask a question about something you don't know about? That makes no sense. I said, "Your mom had car trouble. So I gave her a lift."

She's still looking out the window. She says, "Oh yeah?"

I said, "Yeah. I said, You know anything about it?"

She says, "No." Like I'm offending her even suggesting it.

I just dropped it.

But now so listen. Marcie. I have to tell you what happened later. No, wait. I'm gonna take a leak first. I've been drinking water all goddamn night!

Monday, April 27 (evening)

WARREN GHIL HAS MOVED IN again. Warren and his friend, Cory Nickroe, forever smelling of bacon. Because he just had to eat breakfast.

It's hard to know what will trigger their arrival, but this is the month when something usually does.

For the first three years they never left. Not for one day. They were permanent residents who would occasionally skip out for an hour, sometimes when I was watching TV — *Saved by the Bell* reruns — but who mostly just hung around. Yeah, we're here. We're here. Still here. So that I assumed they would always be there, like a hole in a tooth I couldn't afford to get fixed. Something I just had to accept, the way my friends had to accept that I could do sleepovers but needed to leave early in the morning, before anyone gathered in the kitchen. Because when you're a guest, people want to make you feel welcome with food, and in the mornings that meant breakfast.

Moms asking, "Hope, would you like some of this bac— oh, dear. Are you ill, sweetheart? Come, the bathroom's this way."

Then for a while they did leave. Warren and Cory. They disappeared for a time and I still don't quite know why. Meaning, I don't know the medical explanation, which is annoying because it would be a useful thing to figure out. I can only speculate that they left because shortly after I turned seventeen I became unconscious. I went absent and so did they. Not entirely, but they stopped hanging around constantly. They went off and did something more constructive with their time. Perhaps I had become vacant enough to be boring.

Things changed again when I was nineteen. I took a large number of my mother's sleeping pills — she says twenty-six of them because it was near the beginning of a new prescription. I accept her word.

Although for a while I wondered if she said a specific number because she expected me to reimburse her.

Once I became conscious enough to want to harm myself, I must have become interesting again.

April in particular was set aside for Warren and Cory. They would visit briefly throughout the year but in April they settled in. It was like a tradition, although the start date changed, gradually becoming later each year. Lesley had something to do with that. She would sense them coming and become vigilant. The apartment would fill up with friends, days were given over to tasks. A week of April would slip by, two, and then they'd arrive and do what they did, sit just outside my peripheral vision so they could be felt but not seen. So that you'd think a quick glance to the left or right might reveal them, catch them unawares, though it never would. They were too quick.

So this year it's the 27th. Hello, Warren. Hi, Cory. No need to answer; I know you're there. Try not to make a mess of the place.

WHEN I WAS FOURTEEN, I came home from school one sloppy, late-winter day to a fresh peanut butter and blueberry jam sandwich, and the news that I was moving my things out of the basement. My mother had made me the sandwich to soften the blow.

She knew how infuriated I'd be — and a fourteen-year-old's fury can be a terrible thing — because I'd fought for three months to make the basement mine. To get away from her. My father had left the previous October and, in the rye-and-ginger fog that had prevailed since then, my mother had been rediscovering the pleasures of desolate, vengeful sex with a series of men behind her bedroom door. I don't know who they were, probably salesmen from the Saturn dealership where she handled the bookkeeping. Their visits seemed to be organized on a kind of rotation.

I rarely had to look at them. They'd accompany my mother

home late from wherever she spent her evenings and leave before I had to pee in the morning. But sound established their identities. We lived in a small, 1970s split-level with walls as thin as bread crusts. Inhabiting a room near my mother's was therefore not tenable. My choice was either a bedroom in the basement or The Smashing Pumpkins turned up to distortion level at three a.m. Our neighbours, and the police to whom they complained, preferred the former and my mother finally agreed.

The problem was the basement was only partly finished. There was an open storage area with a concrete floor, a laundry area with a toilet and shower, and a small rec room roughed-in with unpainted drywall, and plywood laid over the concrete. This rec room had once been a promised feature of our family's future, invoked like a vision of carbon-free transport. There would come a day, my parents said when we moved into the house, when we would gather in this room and watch movies, play air hockey. I would be able to invite friends over so that we could "chill."

Gradually, even while my father still lived with us, the rec room became a spillover storage zone. Luggage, boxes of old shoes, a stained ottoman, decommissioned computers and VHS players — all manner of worn-out things went there like old elephants to die. Bicycles roosted there for the winter. Leftover building materials from the roof and soffit repair landed there "temporarily," never to leave. And every added box or pile of detritus underlined the growing sense that the promised family future was a chimera. There was no will to make it come true.

For three months my mother resisted the notion of turning this space into my bedroom. Even when I said I would do all of the necessary hauling and painting, she refused. It was something about accepting the loss of that future, or admitting that she had never sufficiently believed in its possibility. And then late one night, as I was padding back from the kitchen with a slice of freezer cake, the man of that particular evening surprised me on his way to the bathroom, naked. And I screamed.

Suddenly a basement bedroom for Hope made perfect sense to my mother. She even paid for a junk hauler to relieve us of the bulkiest debris. I spent two weekends, and a week of evenings in between, cleaning, painting, hanging, laying mismatched carpet squares, turning that blank hull of a room into something livable. It was mine for five weeks. And then my mother, admiring the result, saw an opportunity to supplement the household income and decided to take in a boarder. The day she made me the peanut butter and blueberry jam sandwich, he had already signed a rental agreement.

MY MOTHER DID NOT THINK to do a background check on Warren Ghil. He was polite during the interview, she explained. He offered references, and she "liked his smile." During the tour of the house and the basement, he had noted the bedroom's girlish colour scheme, its peach-like meshing of pink and orange, but didn't seem to mind. In fact, told that it was the effort of a ponytailed fourteen-year-old, he was suitably impressed. "Good detailing," he said, according to my mother. And though she fussed at them during the showing, Mr. Ghil wasn't bothered by the short curtains this girl had sewed, which didn't quite stretch the full width of the window and left a narrow sliver of light against the wall that could be quite bright first thing in the morning. That suggested to my mother that he was "amenable."

He moved in with one suitcase, a brown, hard-shelled Samsonite that seemed to contain only khakis and collared shirts, and became integrated into our schedule. During the day he was mostly gone, attending community college, he said, in the city's east end. In the evenings he spent most of his time in his room, which was large enough to accommodate, in addition to my old bed and chest of drawers, an upholstered chair my mother and I hauled awkwardly down from the living room.

Occasionally he came up from the basement to watch television, which my mother had invited him to do. ("It's part of having a boarder," she said.) Whenever he did I left, went to my room, sat on my replacement bed, which was half as comfortable as the one I'd lost. My mother said I was being rude, but I didn't care. He had taken my bedroom from me, and my escape. And he made me uncomfortable, in a way that was impossible to explain.

He was too nice. "He's too nice?" my mother said. "How can a person be too nice?"

He moved strangely. Every gesture, every placement of limb seemed calculated. It was as though he *thought* about moving. "That doesn't seem strange at all," my mother said. "He's in a new house. He's getting used to things."

He looked at me too — I found this hard to articulate — too *deliberately*. He would turn his head to take me in, and linger on me, before turning away. "That just sounds like something you made up," said my mother. "You don't *want* to like him."

It was at mealtimes that I had no escape. Morning and evening, Mr. Ghil — this is what my mother expected me to call him, though he was no older than twenty-four — joined us at the table. He ate whatever was put in front of him. "Look, Hope," said my mother, as Mr. Ghil shovelled diced carrots into his mouth. "See? It is possible for a person to eat vegetables without complaining." (And up would come his eyes at me, as if to monitor my reaction, before slipping off me again like melting ice.)

He never initiated conversation — my mother had to work quite hard to keep silence from descending — but answered questions or responded to prompts with effusive pleasantries. The neighbourhood was "really great." The bus to his unnamed college was "extremely fast and direct." People he encountered "couldn't be nicer." The pancakes my mother made on weekends were "just the way I like them."

My mother once asked him what he thought of Mike Harris, the premier of Ontario.

"I don't follow politics very much," he said. "What do you think of him?"

"He's certainly doing a lot for business people," said my mother. "They just love him where I work."

"That's true," said Mr. Ghil, nodding deliberately. "Very good for business."

"He's an asshole," I said.

"Hope!"

"Look at all the hospitals he's closing!"

Mr. Ghil was apparently amazed that I could speak in his presence. The expression on his face, as he stared at me, seemed close to enchantment.

"Wow, I never thought of that," he said. He grinned. "You're quite the wild card."

After that, he began to treat me with a kind of amused reverence. Whenever a conversation topic surfaced that might be controversial in any way, he would look at me with mock fear, as if I might explode with another of my dramatic opinions.

It was both intensely irritating, and inexplicably appealing. At fourteen, I was suddenly notorious. I had a "reputation" in my house that involved more than being a child. Mr. Ghil had somehow ushered in for me a kind of personhood.

"I'm glad you're getting along with him better," said my mother one afternoon, when we were alone.

"He's all right, I guess."

"You see?" she said, lighting a Du Maurier. "I told you."

I DON'T USUALLY DWELL on how Warren Ghil came into my life. He just swells up at the back of my mind, he and Cory, like some ancient ophidian curling up to the water's surface to remind me he's still down there. Still potent. Something has brought him further into my thoughts this time. Something has pushed him up, out of the water.

ZB Transcript 19

OKAY, SO ...

Fuck, where'd I leave off ... Sorry, Marcie, my brain's going a thousand miles an hour here.

Okay, so, after the drive with Em I met up with Hope and we went over it all. Well, first I crashed. I came back to the hotel and I just flaked out 'cause I got *no sleep* last night and it was all pretty stressful.

I mean, making it all work, that was bad enough. 'Cause I knew I only had one shot, right? I had to nail it. But also just how I felt about the whole thing. 'Cause it was the first time this deal seemed, I dunno ... kinda shady. Kinda, just, slippery or something. I didn't want to think about it when I was doing it, but then when I dropped Em off she was really nice, you know? Like I'd totally helped her out. Gave me a kiss on the cheek. Had this crazy look in her eyes like maybe she actually, you know, liked me or something.

It was just weird ... I mean, I was happy about it but it gave me this bad feeling, too, sorta like when I was doing the deal with that Allegheny money. When it looked like, you know ... like it might work out. And I still felt like a fuckin' asshole.

So anyway, after that, after I woke up, I went down and met Hope and she asked me a bunch of questions. Walked me through the whole thing again, top to bottom, so I could tell her *exactly* what was happening when Em said whatever and *exactly* what the look on her face was and ... fuck. I thought I was taking a goddamn exam! And I told her that too. And I said, "You know, pretty soon I'm gonna need a drink here."

She looked at me and I said, "Okay, not a drink. But come on, let's loosen up the chains here a little. You know? Let's go have some fun!"

I said, "Hope, we have not, for one minute since we got here, acted like normal people. We're just working, sitting in this fucking blank room, or out driving around in a car, doing something that probably most people would say is crazy. And then every day we go to our own fucking rooms and then we don't talk to each other. And we have not relaxed once since we've been here. And it's not like we don't deserve to relax."

I mean, I didn't bring up the whole ... what happened ... but I said, you know, "Let's just go have dinner." I said to her, "I bet you eat in your room every fucking night."

And she didn't deny it.

And I said, "Okay. There's this nice Italian place up on Bryant, let me take you to dinner. Let me buy you some tagliatelle, or some gnocchi, or whatever you want."

She said, "We have nothing to celebrate yet."

And I told her, "We don't have to celebrate. We just have to have a nice time. How's that sound?" And I said, and this was kind of mean of me. I said, "Can you do that, Hope? Can you *have* a nice time? Is that even possible for you? Does that, you know, *compute*?"

Like I said, mean. And she didn't answer the question. But she was quiet for a second, looking down at her papers, and then she said, "We can go to dinner." And right away she looked up at me with this stone face, all serious, and she said, "But this is not any kind of date, Zep. Do you understand? I have *no interest* in you."

I'm not gonna say that didn't sting a bit. 'Cause I do have *some* ego. But whatever. I told her I said, "Hope, I'm all about Em right now. You could be a Victoria's Secret model for all I care."

And way back, I mean way, way back behind her eyes, there was maybe a hint of a smile. At least she relaxed a little.

So we went to dinner.

Driving to the place, I was actually worried. I was thinking it might be closed, 'cause a lot of the better joints shut down on Mondays. Shoulda called ahead, you fuckin' idiot. That's what I was saying to myself. 'Cause I was thinking, like, we need this. Team-building or whatever. Honestly, Marcie, at the time I didn't know why it was important to me, it just was, and I knew Hope was gonna bail for the least reason, right?

But anyway, it wasn't a problem. We got there and it was like half of Buffalo was eating at this place. Looked bad for getting a table at first but I gave the girl at the front twenty bucks and a few minutes later we had a table up against a red wall, smelling the bread and the roasted garlic like everyone else.

I could tell Hope was nervous. You know, looking down at her plate, shifting her knife and her fork around, glancing sideways like she was looking for the fastest way out. Maybe because she thought I was lying before about not being into her, which, you know, is fair because any other time I would've been for sure. Or maybe she thought I was gonna drink and do something that might freak her out. I dunno.

I was thinking when the waiter came for drinks I'd order some Pellegrino to help her chill out. Wine for her, Pellegrino for me. But while that was going through my head I kinda had this brain flash. It was like, man, I have never in my life spent so much time thinking about what a woman might be worried about.

Seriously ... it's like there's a ... like a stone or something in my back pocket and I'm sitting on this fuckin' stone All. The. Time.

And I said to her, "You know, I think about what's going on in your mind more than I ever did with my wife." And she said, "Maybe that was the problem."

Like, bam. Honest to God, Marcie, nobody's ever talked so straight-on to me like Hope. Not even you. And I know it's 'cause you got your job to worry about and that's fair. But I'm just telling you, it's a helluva thing. You can do it if you want, I won't mind. I know you got it in you.

Anyway, I told her she was probably right. I said — and it was funny, 'cause I kinda leaned forward like I was telling this big secret — I said, meaning Em, I said, "I never thought about what she thought about, except for what she thought about me."

And Hope was looking at me and the corners of her eyes kind of crinkled and she told me, "Zep, I think that's the smartest thing you've ever said."

So I lifted my empty water glass to her — because the fuckin' waiter still hadn't showed up — and I said, "Here's to you, for making me smarter." And she looked at me like I was playing her, and I said, "No, seriously." I had this kinda wave come crashing down on me or something. It was weird, Marcie. I just ... suddenly I knew why this whole deal, going to the restaurant, was important to me. I just felt like I had to say something, I dunno ... *big*. So I looked at her and I said, "Seriously, Hope, nobody has ever worked so hard to help me get something I want. Not my mom, sure as hell not my dad. Not any coach either. Nobody. So, seriously ... thank you."

She looked real uncomfortable and she said, "I told you, it's premature. We have nothing to celebrate yet."

And I said, "Hope, are you hearing me? Can you hear *thank you?*"

She seemed to think about that for a second. Looked down at her plate again and nodded. And then she said, "I'm not doing it just for you."

Okay? "I'm not doing it just for you." Right?

So that kinda bounced around in the ol' batting cage for a minute. Like what the hell does that mean? And of course, that's when the waiter came. Fuckin' master of timing. So I told him to bring a glass of Chianti for the lady and a bottle of Pellegrino for me. And when he was gone I tried to get her to tell me. "What do you mean *not just for me?*"

But she totally clammed up. She said if she told me anything more it could affect the results. "You might behave differently," she said.

So for a few minutes we just stared at our menus. Pappardelle, tagliatelle, pollo Milanese, all kinds of pizza. But right then it's all just words to me. I'm trying to focus but everything's just swimming. 'Cause I had no idea what all this meant, but I knew it meant *something*.

I said, "So ... if you're not just doing this for me, that means you're doing it for somebody else too. I mean, I'm no master scientist, but that much is pretty obvious."

She didn't say anything.

I said, "So who else knows about this?"

She said, "No one."

"Not even your friend Lesley?"

"No."

So, I said, "Okay. That means the other person is you." I said, "That's why you were almost crying the other day, when you thought I was pulling out. You've got something riding on this."

She said, "It's not what you think."

I said, "I dunno what I think."

"Please let's drop it," she said. She was looking at me, Marcie, and I'm telling you she was almost shaking. "Please let's not talk about it anymore. For the sake of the results. *Please.*"

I just sat back in my chair. And she was all upset. It looked like she was trying to find ten ways to cross her arms at once. She said, "I shouldn't have said anything. This is part of the reason I didn't want any extra contact. But it doesn't matter why I'm doing it. It doesn't change what I'm doing for you."

"Okay," I said. "Whatever. Let's eat."

So ... we didn't talk about it for the rest of the night. But mainly that was because of something else that happened.

For a while we were just quiet. The food came — she got the pappardelle piemonte with the mushrooms and I got the short ribs and fuck, it doesn't even matter what we ate, I don't know why I'm talking about that. The point is, we were just kinda coasting through the rest of the evening as if nothing was gonna change.

And that's what's so funny, Marcie. 'Cause things can change fast and you don't even fuckin' know it's coming. I mean, that's what's so *goddamn weird about life*!

[Ringing sound]

Wait, Marcie, that's my phone.

Shit, I gotta take this. You're never gonna guess who this is.

—

Monday, April 27 (evening) /cont

I HAVE NO FAITH. Certainly none that a church would recognize. So I have never understood why, in the face of fear, Christians reach for Psalm 23:4.

Yea, though I walk through the valley of the shadow of death, I will fear no evil: for thou art with me; Thy rod and thy staff, they comfort me.

At the hospital there was a woman in my ward named Kathleen who would recite this verse under her breath, over and over, whenever she became overwhelmed. It was an indicator of a bad day for her, and the nurses would become even more watchful. But that verse has always seemed to me a rather passive response to the threat of danger. Were I faith inclined, I think I would choose something more retributive, such as Psalm 27:2.

When evil men advance against me to devour my flesh, when my enemies and my foes attack me, they will stumble and fall.

The promise of such a consequence seems much more comforting to me. Although it's true there is no empirical way to measure comfort, and there are limits to its absolute value.

THERE WAS AN APRIL AFTERNOON, marshy with rain, when Warren Ghil came home from wherever it was he spent his days — it turned out he was not enrolled in any school — and brought a companion with him.

I was in my bedroom when the two of them entered the house.

I could hear the thrum of male voices. My mother was still at work. They came first into the kitchen, because Warren had a habit of going to the refrigerator immediately and pouring himself a glass of chocolate milk. This time he poured two. Then he called my name.

From the dark upstairs hallway I asked what he wanted.

"Where's the butter?"

"In the cupboard," I called back. "Like always."

"Can't find it. Come help me look."

It seemed important to stay upstairs. To not do as he asked. To refuse to enter the part of our home that had now, somehow, become public. But my mother had insisted I be reasonable where the boarder was concerned. Refusing to help him locate the butter would not have been reasonable.

When I entered the kitchen I kept my eyes down and went straight to the cupboard. Warren was leaning against the refrigerator with his thumbs hooked in his pockets. I could feel the presence of someone besides Warren, but I didn't acknowledge it. The butter was exactly where I knew it would be.

"Here." I set it on the counter. As I left, I couldn't help adding, "You didn't look very hard."

"Hey, don't be rude," he said.

I stopped and waved at the cupboard. "It was right there."

"I mean, don't ignore my friend." He nodded toward the other presence at the opposite end of the room, which forced me to look. I saw a man about the same age as Warren, slightly shorter, but wider at the shoulders, wearing a forest-green hockey jacket with scuffed, white-leather arms. His hands were shoved deep into his jacket pockets, pulling the jacket outward and making it appear that the pockets were stuffed with rocks. He wore jeans that were too short at the heels, and on his feet were cheap, black penny loafers that had tracked watery mud across the floor from the side entrance. Standing where he was now, near the kitchen's second door, the one leading to the dining area, he was more fully inside the house than either Warren or I.

"Say hi," said Warren.

To my fourteen-year-old eyes this person, who was Cory Nickroe, was somewhat better looking than Warren. Warren was soft-focus, pinkish, with grey eyes and thinning sandy hair. This friend was high-contrast, with dark eyes and thick black hair, wet from the rain, set against a canvas of pale skin. He had a small nose and small ears, like a child's. I looked at him and he looked at me, and neither of us said a word.

"When's your mom getting back?" said Warren.

"Soon," I lied. "She just called." I was proud of myself for thinking to add some support for the lie, to make it more credible. This was further evidence, I thought, of my becoming more adult, although I suspected an adult wouldn't have felt the fear I did in that moment. As I turned to leave I pointed at the mud on the floor. "You should clean that up before she gets here."

"Aren't you the maid of the house?" he said, but he was speaking to my back since I was already out of the room. Upstairs I sat on the floor at the end of the dark hall, balled against my door, trying to decipher murmurs until I heard the side door open and close.

FOR THE NEXT SIX OR SEVEN DAYS, Warren Ghil was an especially model tenant. He wiped the counter after he made himself a snack. He moved our garbage to the curb on garbage night. Twice after dinner he did the dishes, which allowed my mother to leave early for dates. Since Warren had moved in and I'd been forced back into my bedroom, she had not brought a man home for an overnight stay. But she stayed out late once or twice a week. I spent those evenings at the homes of either Tara Klewe or Allison Sevish, the two friends I could call on short notice. I'd return only after she called to say she was home.

I didn't tell my mother about Warren's friend because I knew there was no point. "Warren is allowed to have friends here," she would say. If I mentioned feeling afraid she would ask, "Did he do anything? Did he *say* anything?" The answer would have to be no and then she would shake her head at what she'd taken to calling my "campaign of hostility." It seemed to me that I had one or two bullets of complaint about Warren left before I was stripped of all credibility and disarmed. I had to save them for something big.

Warren rendered all of that moot the night he established beyond doubt his bona fides as a person to trust. It was about two-thirty in the morning when he started banging on our bedroom doors to wake us up.

"There's a fire!" he shouted. "Fire!"

As my mother and I rushed out into the hall, Warren had our coats ready. Downstairs our boots were set out near the side door. There was smoke visible in the basement. My mother grabbed the phone to dial the fire department when Warren yelled, "Wait!" and began heading down the stairs with a dishtowel held to his face.

"Where are you going?" she shouted.

"It's in the dryer," he called back. "I think I can put it out."

She started to go after him. "Warren, don't!"

"Stay there!" he shouted, and my mother obeyed.

Below us we heard coughing, banging, the sound of something heavy being shifted on the concrete floor. A moment later Warren appeared at the bottom of the basement stairs.

"I think I got it," he said. "It's out."

We went downstairs to investigate. It seemed there'd been a lint fire. Through the smoke and the smell that lingered we could see that Warren had pulled the dryer away from the wall and yanked out the exhaust hose. Where it had attached to the dryer the hose was melted and charred, and scorch marks blackened the dryer itself around the vent. There was relatively little damage overall, and not a great deal of smoke. A small cloud hung near the bare lightbulb in the laundry area. Nevertheless, my mother was impressed.

"You probably saved our lives," she said. "You're a hero!"

"Who," I had to ask, "was doing laundry at two in the morning?"

"It doesn't matter," said my mother.

"That was me," Warren admitted. He wiped at a smudge of soot on his cheek, making it bigger. "I couldn't sleep and I thought I might as well, but … I'm really sorry."

"Don't be," my mother said. "I'm just thankful it happened when you were here."

WARREN GHIL'S NEWLY MINTED STATUS as the ultimate trustworthy tenant dovetailed conveniently for my mother with her desire to continue her sexual hopscotching. She mentioned someone named Jim once or twice, flinging his name into conversations like a playing card. "Oh, Jim was talking about that today," she might say. Or, while listening to the radio, "Jim loves this song."

One afternoon, just a few days after our lint-fire drama, my mother took an opportunity to speak to me alone, appearing at the door to my room while I worked on algebra problems.

"Jim has invited me for dinner tonight," she said, twisting a sock in her hand.

"Okay …"

"I think I might stay over."

"No."

"He wants me to."

I turned away from my homework and pleaded with her. There was nothing to wait for now. I told her that she couldn't leave me at home with Warren. She just couldn't. It wasn't right. It wasn't safe. I told her he was not what she thought he was. I couldn't prove it but I knew it. I didn't believe there had been a lint fire. It wasn't real. He'd set it up. I told her she was my mother. Which now, this last, seems an odd thing to have felt the need to say, but I did.

"It's hateful the way you treat him," she said.

"I don't care."

"You should care. You should want to be kind."

She suggested that I have a friend stay over, but I refused. She told me to ask if I could spend the night at Allison's, and I told her Allison had missed school for three days and might have mono. "What about Tara?" she said.

"Maybe," I said.

"Well, try."

Tara said yes to a sleepover that night. A relief. But there was a complication. A month before, she had gotten slightly drunk with a friend on her father's vodka while her parents were out. New rules were now in place — she couldn't have anyone over unless there was at least one parent at home. The night I called her, the night of my mother's big date with Jim, Tara said her parents weren't going to be home until seven p.m. My mother was leaving for Jim's at six-thirty.

"Can't you wait?" I asked my mother.

She couldn't. Jim had something special planned.

"But I need you to drive me."

Tara's parents would be happy to pick me up, she was sure. Hadn't she done it once or twice for Tara? Parents did favours like this for each other all the time; it wouldn't be a problem.

There was a strip mall about a twenty-minute walk from my house. I thought maybe Tara's father could pick me up there. But it wasn't on the route he would normally take so I needed to be able to give directions to Tara, and I couldn't remember the name of the street it was on.

My mother was in her bedroom, standing in front of an open dresser drawer, looking at underwear.

"Mom, what corner is the strip mall on? The one with the Indian food place."

"Why?"

"I want Tara's dad to pick me up there."

"Hope, that's ridiculous. That's —"

"I'm not staying here."

"You've been in the house alone with Warren plenty of times."

"Not at night."

"We're talking about *half an hour.*"

She shoved the drawer closed and looked at me with a sudden intense curiosity.

"When did you become such a scaredy-cat?"

"I wonder," I said as I walked out of her room.

ARRANGEMENTS WERE FINALIZED with Tara, who was excited that I could come and help her with her biology homework. She couldn't reach her parents before they got home, but the minute they did she would tell them about picking me up, and it would only be another twenty minutes or so after that. Half an hour at the most. Meekly, I agreed to this, for what choice did I have?

"That makes it almost an *hour*," I said to my mother, as Warren came in the side door. He hesitated at the top of the stairs, apparently interested in the emotional display. This prompted my mother to make a bold decision.

"Warren," she said, taking her cigarettes out of her purse. "I'd like to speak to you for a second."

"Mom, *don't.*"

My mother struck a match to light her cigarette as Warren took off his shoes. She blew a stream of smoke sideways and waited while he set his shoes by the door and entered the kitchen in his sock feet with an air of pleasant curiosity.

"Warren, I have to go out tonight, and Hope is going out too.

Someone is picking her up. You'll have the place to yourself."

"That's fine," he said. "Till when?"

"Mom, *no*."

"Till the morning." She grinned. "If everything goes the way it's supposed to."

"Okay."

She glanced over at me where I was dying.

"But Hope has to be here for an hour after I leave, and she's worried about that. So, that concerns me and I want to know from you, Warren, if she has any reason to be worried."

Warren's head jumped back.

"No. Absolutely not." He chuckled as though confused, astonished, by this remarkable question. "I don't know why that's even an issue." He looked at me. "I thought we were really getting along."

My mother drew on her cigarette while she waited for me to answer and when I didn't she blew out a sharp stream. "Well, I don't care if you two get along or not. But I want everyone being respectful."

Warren smiled. "Of course."

I STOOD AT THE SIDE LANDING as my mother prepared to leave. At her feet sat her large tan purse, big enough to accommodate her overnight necessities. She was tying a filmy scarf at her neck, a swirl of greens and blues like something pulled from the sea.

"Don't stay up late tonight," she said. "You and Tara have school tomorrow."

"I wish you had a cellphone."

"Does anyone really need one of those things? Maybe salesmen, I guess. How's my lipstick?"

"Fine."

She leaned forward for a hug, turning her face away to discourage a lip-smearing kiss. Her neck smelled of Calvin Klein's Eternity.

"Now, be sure to thank Mr. Klewe for picking you up, okay?"

"Okay." My voice trembled slightly in spite of my effort to control it. Tears came to my eyes.

"Oh, Hope," my mother said. "Honestly."

AS SHE BACKED HER PONTIAC SUNFIRE out of the driveway, I went to the front closet, my heart banging, and began to put on my shoes. I felt for a draft slipping in around the front door because the weather-stripping there had corroded; it was an easy way to know how heavy a coat to wear. My plan was to wait for Tara's dad on the porch.

I had my hand on the doorknob, intending to ease the door open, when I remembered my homework. Tara would pout if I didn't at least bring my biology notebooks with me. I hesitated, anxious about going back upstairs, but then I decided it would be okay. Warren was in the basement. I could sneak up the stairs, get my homework, come back down and go straight out the front door. I released the doorknob, letting the spring twist it closed in my hand.

The process of memory is still largely mysterious. We don't know exactly how the impressions our minds store are sorted and prioritized during consolidation, why the brain attaches significance to some details and not to others. But regardless of why, I do recall that, as I hurried back from my room along the upstairs hall, something seemed different about the light coming up from the base of the stairs. There was a change in tone, a slight dimming. The reason for this difference, at least, is easy to understand. The walls at the base of the stairs were painted cream, and so the light reflected off them easily. Warren, however, was wearing a dark sweater over his collared shirt, and so it absorbed some of the light as he stood waiting.

He was smiling as he looked up at me. So although I froze at the top of the stairs, dizzy from the pounding in my ears, I didn't run or scream.

"Hey, I have a question," Warren said amiably. He nodded for me to come down and I shook my head. "See, that's what I'm wondering about." He leaned back against the wall, his hands in his pockets.

"You've picked up something from me," he said. "Right from the beginning. Some weird signal that made you think I was dangerous. Something I've said or done. I really want to know what it is. Can you tell me?"

I shook my head. My hand on the railing was numb. It was all I could do not to topple forward. Warren sighed and shrugged.

"I was hoping you could tell me so I wouldn't do it next time." Then he bounded up the stairs.

THE PAINT IN MY BASEMENT ROOM, the space I had made, was still girlish, nothing had changed. On the orange-tinted wall under the window trim, below the edge of the little curtains I'd sewn, a tiny streak of pink showed. I hadn't noticed it before, this amateurish flaw, the work of a stray brush hair. What a child I'd been when I painted this room, three months before.

A smell hovered around my face like a bumblebee, no matter how I turned my head. Heavy and sweet, it was the remnants of what I came to know as an inhalational anesthetic called Halothane. Lab techs use it occasionally to euthanize lab animals, when the carbon dioxide tanks run low.

Voices filtered down to me from the floor above. Tara's dad, Mr. Klewe … he was conferring with Warren at the front door. They were commiserating about young teenage girls, their capriciousness, their unreliability. I had decided to go off with my mother, Warren was explaining. I hadn't called Tara about the change of plans? Typical.

Of course, I tried to let Mr. Klewe know that I hadn't changed my mind. I was still here, still very much wanted to go with him to see Tara, to help Tara with her biology homework. I wasn't unreliable, really. But the sounds I made didn't leave my mouth. Something dense and fibrous, some kind of batting stuffed in against my tongue and cheeks, kept my avowals from being heard. And my arms, like my legs, were secured with electrical cord. So Mr. Klewe could not help but form a poor opinion of me, which I knew he would soon share with Tara.

This was the first thing I cried about. Because I was still naive. I didn't know what the future held. Or the past, for that matter. I didn't know, in fact, that I had already been raped, until I looked down toward my feet, over the bare skin of my chest and hips, past the confusing pain, past the wire at my ankles to the end of the room and saw Cory Nickroe, still nameless to me then, sitting on a chair by the dresser with his pants off. He noticed me looking at him.

"About time you woke up," he said. "You're missing all the fun."

So that was the beginning. The beginning of everything, really. From these moments forward it no longer mattered what had happened before. Whether my grandparents had spoiled me with secret chocolates. How long my mother had fed me from her breasts. How often my father had lifted me above his head and spun me around until the room swirled, or how well he had taught me about looking left and right before stepping into the street. It made no difference whether I had played with dinosaurs or dolls, or built sofa cushion forts with friends. Whether I had loved The Spice Girls when I was nine and hated them by the time I'd turned twelve. Whether I had worn braces, or stolen cigarettes, or daydreamed about skating with a boy. The minute I awoke, bound, in my basement room that night, the life I'd had till then was disappeared. All that mattered, for now and forever, were the next thirteen hours.

There were practicalities. Warren and his friend had done this before — they spoke of others like me, in other cities — but never had they faced the prospect of so much uninterrupted time. It was partly a matter of pacing, they decided, trying not to do too much, too soon.

They took turns, naturally. A young fourteen and not overly developed, I wasn't enough body for two men at once, and each needed time to recover from his exertions. The occasional pill, washed down with chocolate milk, allowed them to keep going after other men might have surrendered to fatigue. Even so, blood is not a good lubricant, and after several hours, they began to talk of soreness — such repeated use of sensitive body parts was unusual, even for them. It was an inconvenience they hadn't considered and it made them angry. For a time, afterward, it was difficult to see for the swelling around my eyes.

And then there was the matter of boredom. Assuming you intend to keep the surrounding body alive, there is only so much you can do with a vagina. It accepts things or it doesn't. And the action, regardless of the implement, is always a version of the same plunging and prodding routine. At a certain point, interest demands innovation.

They quit for a while. Left me to go upstairs. By then I was dissociative and fading in and out of consciousness. I had long ago stopped my muffled screaming. And, as I now understand, my body was becoming adaptive to extreme levels of cortisol, dopamine, and catecholamines such as epinephrine, norepinephrine. Excessive secretions from the adrenal medulla were rewiring me. PACAP receptors had begun mutating to establish new normals. Then I became aware of Warren and his friend upstairs, rooting among the kitchen utensils and, fearing the worst, I had another surge.

But they were only making themselves something to eat. An early breakfast. I heard pans scraping across the stovetop, plates clattering on the table. For a strange, psychotic moment as I listened, I worried that they would leave a mess in the kitchen, and that my mother would blame me. When she came home, it would be the first thing she'd see.

The other thought that came to me, wafted through me, while the two of them were upstairs, was that they might be done, or that at least the worst might be over. During the trudge of hours their mood, almost festive when they'd begun, had turned cheerless. Raping me in the various ways they'd tried had become something of a chore, the way a family gathering can start with a giddy bang and then grind toward a tired, sullen conclusion. They might leave, I thought. They might kill me and leave. Either possibility registered as good news.

When they finally returned, they seemed refreshed. They both smelled of bacon, Cory most of all. And Cory had had an idea.

"My friend," said Warren, "thinks he's in love with you."

Standing beside the bed, Cory gave a sheepish smile and shrugged. He was no match, it seemed, for the inexplicable, undeniable force of his emotion.

"But he's worried," said Warren. "Tell her what you're worried about."

"Naw, man. I'm shy."

"Tell her. Go on."

Cory heaved with a sigh. He looked down at me. "I'm worried … you're gonna forget me."

Warren shook his head. "Stupid, right?" He turned to Cory. "She's not gonna forget you. You're worried about nothing."

Cory shrugged. "Can't help it."

"Anyway." Warren leaned down and patted my leg, ignoring my spastic flinch. "The good news is, we've got a solution."

It was for this they'd been rooting through the cutlery drawer. Although nothing there, it seemed — none of the brilliant metal edges — had captured their interest. Something else did. Something that better fit Warren's apparent predilection.

"Your mom must've got a deal, huh?" said Warren. He held up a carton of matches and shook it. "There's gotta be thousands in here."

"How long?" said Cory.

"Long. You mean till Mom comes home?" He glanced at the bedside clock on my left. "Six hours?"

"So let's get going!"

Here, finally, was something they could do together. Positioned on either side of me, they could work without getting in each other's way. Cory started precipitously, striking a match and pressing it into the skin above my small left breast before they'd finalized their plans. In chastising him, Warren reminded him that there was a reason he was holding a pen.

The design he sketched out over my chest was inspired, Warren explained, by a cartoon he'd once seen — was it *Bugs Bunny*? *The Flintstones*? *Scooby-Doo*? He couldn't remember. But some animated someone had carved a heart, with an arrow through it, into the bark of a tree. It proclaimed to the world that someone loved and someone was loved. He'd suggested this to Cory, and Cory had said yes. And as he sat beside me on the bed, he explained that it would be a good thing for me. It would be a sign for people that I was special. It would say to the world, "I have been loved."

Once he was finished, the outlines of the heart stretched the length of my sternum from top to bottom, while the two wings of the cartoon heart curved outward against the insides of my pale breasts. I had thought, briefly, that my nipples might be spared. But when Warren drew the arrow he positioned the pointed head atop my left areola, and while the matches were being struck, this was where Cory spent much of his time.

So they began, and the sharp fetor of sulfur conjoined with the smell of charred meat, and sweat too, theirs and mine. There are no true equivalences for the sensation of an igniting match pressed to tender skin. Each was a small, focused fury tearing a piece of me away. They learned to work quickly once each match was struck, while the head was still boiling and the wood was strong enough to withstand the pressure applied. While I was conscious, an hour or more, I longed for the relief of a knife. I lived, I think, only because I had no food in my stomach to vomit into my sealed mouth. Letting my eyes close as they wanted to, I saw ravaging teeth, dogs ripping me into strands. When I forced my eyes open, I looked not down, at what these men were doing, but upward, toward the wall above my head. I remembered, from the few days I'd slept here, that morning showed there first, in a bright, narrow strip of sunlight that snuck past the end of my poorly measured curtains. So while the smoke and stink rose from my chest, I watched for that strip of sun.

I SHOULD DIE, MY MOTHER SAID when I awoke to her face. We were in a hospital and it was afternoon, the room was oiled with the light of early May. At the wall, beyond the foot of my bed, sat a female police officer, crisp and blue. Above me stood a nurse. My father was there too, holding someone's hand. Mine.

I should die, my mother repeated in a whisper.

She meant herself.

ZB Transcript 20

SO MARCIE, YOU WANNA KNOW who that was on the phone? You're not going to believe it. Fucking Lino. That's right.

I gotta back up though.

Okay, we're at the restaurant, me and Hope. Having a pretty good meal. Talking a bit about tomorrow but not too much, because she seemed a little shaky. I asked her about, you know, why. But she didn't want to talk about it. Fair enough. I wasn't gonna make her get into it if she didn't want to.

So right then, I look up and guess who I see walking in the door? Fucking Lino! Ha. That's his name now as far as I'm concerned. Fucking Lino.

Anyway. I see him and it takes, like, a second for my brain to compute it, and I say "Holy shit" and I stand up right away, shove my chair back and start walking toward him. And I can hear Hope behind me saying, "What, Zep? What is it?"

He doesn't see me yet. He's just looking around the restaurant, like to see if there's any tables free, figure out if it's worth his time to wait 'cause he's probably got some chick in the car, right? And I'm heading straight for him and I'm gonna fucking clock him one. That's my plan. I don't care it's dirty to coldcock a guy, I'm just gonna hit him as hard as I can. All I can think about, my fist hitting his face, that's it. That's all there is.

So he sees me. Turns my way and his face just kinda pops. His eyes go big and his mouth drops open and it's the funniest fucking thing I ever saw. Right then if I wasn't so angry I'd've just killed myself laughing. 'Cause he didn't know I was here! I never told him I was in Buffalo! So I'm the last guy on Earth he's expecting to see.

I mean, Buffalo's pretty much the last place I expected to see him too. But I'm not thinking about any of that. Man, I'm just balling up my fist. And I know it's gonna be a scene, and I'll probably get thrown out of the restaurant and maybe I'll be heading to jail and right then, Marcie, I'm telling you I didn't give a fuck.

But then, behind me, I hear Hope. I hear her voice. Don't know what she's saying, really, something like *No, Zep*, or *Please* or ... I can't really make out her words, just the sound. It's all high and panicky and I look back at her and I see her face, and she's confused, I can tell, but mostly she's afraid. Afraid of ... I dunno, what I'm gonna do, like maybe I'm gonna ruin everything. Or maybe bring all that other stuff back like I did before.

And I'm close to Lino now, like a step and a half, and he's saying, "Not here. Not here." And I can reach him, Marcie, I can reach him from here and I want to hit this guy *so bad* ...

But I can't do it. Can't do it. 'Cause I know if I do it's just ... I mean, I can't do that to her again.

So I'm standing there in the middle of the restaurant between the tables like an idiot. And people are looking at me, waiters are trying to get around me, and Lino says, "I'll call you. I'll call you tonight." He's backing out the door and I let him go. Just watch him. And my body's all seized up so it takes me a second to kinda move again. Even breathe. For a few seconds I'm just like a big piece of stone.

And this is how things change, Marcie. How everything can change in a second ... because when I get moving again, I turn around and start heading back to the table where Hope is, and out of nowhere this guy at the other end of the restaurant starts waving at me. He calls out my name, "Zep! Hey, Zep! Zep Baker!" And I'm thinking, oh fuck, great, some goddamn Bisons fan wants my fucking autograph. Stick a broomstick up my ass, that's how much I need this right now.

But that wasn't it. I turn to get a look at this guy and it's Rick Kelsoe. It's fucking Rick Kelsoe! From way back! You know, the guy — it was his car we took to the drive-in that night, with the two assholes in the trunk, Gabbers and Bobby Mercin. It's him and he's calling me over. I can see he's there with some woman, I figure it's his wife, and sure enough it is. Her name's Tammy. He introduces me and I tell him I'm here with Hope and ... so anyway we ended up sitting together. Hope didn't want to come over at first but I nudged her into it.

I mean, shit's so weird. The guy wouldn't have even seen me if Lino hadn't walked through the door. Or I hadn't gotten up to pound him.

But now, it's not just that Kelsoe's there and it's nice to see him and meet his wife and all. I mean, she's okay. Sorta pretty but quiet. I mean, once Kelsoe gets going it's hard to shut him up so I guess that makes sense. She was pretty much just watching it all happen at the table. One of those people that's there but isn't there almost. I don't even know what that means. Fuck, what time is it?

Anyway, that's not why I'm talking about change. Turns out Kelsoe's in construction now. I guess he never left Buffalo. He got dumped by the Indians pretty soon after they traded me to the Expos. The Bisons were with the Indians then, so, we were all Indians property ... So anyway, they cut him. Didn't demote him down to Double-A or wherever. Just cut him loose. Which is weird because he was going pretty good when I was there.

He skipped over all that, talking about it. I mean, nobody wants to talk about that stuff. He mainly just talked about his business. Marcie, listen to this: He's got like the third biggest construction company in this part of New York State! I'm not kidding — the guy's building fucking strip malls! He's making more money now than he ever could've made in baseball.

Still looks good too. He was always a big guy, but he keeps himself in okay shape. Hasn't gone all paunchy like so many guys do when they go into business.

Anyway, so I'm listening to him, and you know what I start thinking? I'm thinking it's fate. I'm thinking there's a reason I got up to pancake Lino and it's this guy who sees me. It's like some fucking, I dunno, chessboard move in the sky.

I had to hold off because Hope wanted to leave. She kinda leaned over and told me she wasn't feeling well but that was probably an excuse. I don't really blame her, I mean, she didn't come there to listen to Rick Kelsoe spout off about this fucking parcel of city land and that fucking four-storey development. And this Tammy woman beside her wasn't doing much more than look at her. But she understood I wanted to stay. So I gave her some money for a cab and she went back to the hotel.

And then after she went I started telling Kelsoe about my car wash business and how I was looking to extend the brand. And I said, you know, I'm working on this body wash product. I'm trying to tell him all about the whole Stay Clean idea.

I'm leading up to talking about investing, right? It took a little while 'cause after Hope left he was more interested in talking about her. Wanting to know if I was dating her, which, I guess he'd heard about me and Emily. So I told him no, no we're just working together.

"Nice-looking girl," he says. "Has something special." And I said yeah. I mean she does, no question. I didn't want to fucking dwell on it because his goddamn wife was right there. I mean, seemed kinda rude to me but, you know, maybe she's used to it.

Anyway, so, I got him back on the beam and I start telling him about lining up investors. I figured that was a good way to put it — "lining up" — and he says, "How much?"

And I told him, I said I had an investor who was thinking of coming in for about a million and a half.

He pounced on that real quick. He said, "Had? Not Have? Did it fall through?"

And I said, you know, we're still talking.

He nods for a second, looks at his wife, and he says, "Sounds promising." He says, "Why don't you come by the house on Wednesday night? We're having some people over. We can talk about it." He says, "Who knows, some of the people who'll be there have a bit of money. Maybe you can put a few of us together to replace that two million you lost."

I mean, fuck, this guy's a real businessman now. He totally read me. So I said sure, that sounds good.

He said, "Bring Hope along. Tammy'll make her feel right at home."

I said, "You know, I'll definitely ask her but it's hard to tell with Hope. She might be busy that night or she might not be up to it."

He says, "No, you should bring her. She makes a good impression. And with certain people you're trying to impress, that could be important."

So I said, "Yeah, I'll definitely try."

Then his wife, like pretty much the only time she said anything for two hours, she puts her hand on mine and she smiles and says, "Try."

And I'm like, okay people, message received!

So that's it, Marcie. That's the whole story for now. I guess we'll see where it goes.

HEY, MARCIE, I WAS BRUSHING MY TEETH like a good boy and I remembered I forgot to tell you about the call from Lino. I dunno, trying to put it out of my mind I guess. Fuckin' asshole says he wants to meet with me. He says he's got stuff to tell me, which I said yes you sure as fuck *do*, motherfucker.

I told him the only reason I didn't kick his ass in the restaurant is I was with a lady and she wouldn't've liked it. He said, "That's good to hear."

I said "Yeah, I'll bet it is."

Anyway, whatever he has to tell me he says he doesn't want to do it over the phone. Says it's not right, whatever that means. I guess what it means is he's willing to risk getting his face pushed in, which suits me, so we're gonna meet up in a couple of days. Probably Thursday sometime. And you know what I'm gonna do? I'm gonna take this baby with me and I'm gonna put it out there in the open and record everything the asshole says to me. Get it all on the record how he tried to screw me. See how he likes that.

Okay. That's it. I gotta get some sleep.

Tuesday, April 28

I HAVE PURCHASED FREESIAS.

Four large bouquets in white and butter yellow, which I had delivered last night, now command the spare bed in my room like a silent chorus. They won't be here long, and it's just as well. I could begin to imagine them judging me harshly.

Three days ago when I was interviewing Zep about Emily's favourites, I asked him specifically about flowers. After a few fumbling seconds he mentioned roses. It took very little time, however, to gather that "rose" was the only flower name he could recall, so this suggestion was unreliable. For that reason, I'd put aside any thoughts of including flowers among the sensory triggers we would use with Emily during Phase 3.

Unfortunately, the use of Zep's Bay Rum aftershave during the first stage produced disappointing results. Emily noticed it but failed to react in a way that Zep could characterize as positive. Given how powerful scent can be in emotional memory retrieval, it was important to find a viable alternate scent candidate.

Freesias seemed the most promising. Not only are they highly fragrant, they're also a popular wedding flower. There's no way of knowing with certainty that freesias were used in Emily's own bridal bouquet, or in Zep's boutonniere, when the two of them married, but it's probable. And it's beyond question that Emily has at some point encountered freesias at the weddings of relatives or friends, giving her strong positive associations with the fragrance. In the coming stage, those positive associations should accrue to Zep.

I've informed Zep about the freesias, and he will come for them shortly, before he heads to the house on Woodcrest to pick up Pebbles. I have also instructed him on a new component of today's plan of investigation, in the event Emily asks him for a ride to work as we hope. He was hesitant at first, but he accepted my guidance.

And the freesias will stand in judgment until they leave.

Phase 3, Stage B

Preliminary Notes:

Given our logistical constraints and the progress made to date, the success of this investigation requires that Emily Good soon experience stronger emotions than she has so far acknowledged. Put simply, for the hypothesis to be supported in Phase 4, she must, at some point during this phase, perceive the onset of love.

To prompt this result we will again, as in Phase 3, Stage A, bombard the subject with pleasurable sensory input. Aural and visual stimulation will be used here as before, but scent will be the chief component, as it has been underutilized and may offer an incrementally disproportionate effect.

Having thus re-established Zep as a source of "good feelings," we will then link him in the subject's mind to an experience of euphoria, and immediately thereafter to feelings of safety and comfort.

Note that the induced euphoric effect must be greater than that previously achieved. For the subject, Emily, to perceive the onset of love, she must understand her emotions to be increasing. The induced euphoria must spike higher and crash lower than in Phase 3, Stage A. In a controlled environment this would call for an increased dosage of artificial phenylethylamine, however, delivery of this dosage via food is not available to us, given Emily's demonstrated sensitivity to the taste. We will therefore employ other means to trigger the rapid release of cortisol and catecholamines. (For more details please refer to the notes contained in Log B.)

Phase 3, Stage B, Log A

(Note: as before, the following transcript comprises audio from a transmission via cellphone. The descriptions of action are taken from follow-up interviews with participant Zep Baker.)

7:51 a.m.: When Zep arrives at 126 Woodcrest Blvd., Buffalo, NY, Emily's Honda CR-V is parked as before in front of the driveway. Zep parks and, with his cellphone in hand, walks up the driveway.

7:52 a.m.: Pebbles Baker greets Zep at the door.

Pebbles: "Hey, Dad."

Zep: "Hey, Pebs. Ready to go?"

Pebbles: "I just have to get my music."

Zep: "Sure. Where's uh, where's your mom?"

Pebbles: "I dunno." (She leaves Zep holding the door open while she walks down the hallway toward a set of stairs leading to the basement.)

Zep: "I dunno?"

Pebbles: "She's around somewhere I just don't know where."

Zep: "Any chance I could talk to her?"

Pebbles: (She shrugs.) "Maybe."

Zep: "Come on, Pebs, help me out here."

Pebbles: "I am!"

Zep: "Oh … Sorry, I missed that because of how you weren't doing anything."

Pebbles: "You don't know everything!"

(Pebbles disappears down the stairs. Zep continues to hold the door open for a moment, then sees Emily's father, Raymond, entering the hall from the kitchen and lets the door close. He waits on the front steps. Raymond comes to the front door and pushes it open.)

Raymond: "Emily won't need a lift from you this morning."

Zep: "No?"

Raymond: "No."

Zep: "Any chance I could talk to her about it?"

Raymond: "We had her car fixed yesterday. Would you like to know what was wrong with it?"

Zep: "You figured it was the starter you said."

Raymond: "Nothing wrong with the starter."

Zep: "Huh."

Raymond: "That's right. Turns out it was the wire from the starter to the ignition. Just pulled clean out, like somebody yanked on it."

Zep: "So … can I talk to Emily?"

Raymond: "No, Zep. I don't really think so."

Zep: "Why's that?"

Raymond: "She's busy. She's —"

Emily: "Dad?" (Emily has approached her father from behind and now is trying to get around him.) "Thanks, Dad. I'll take —"

Raymond: "You don't have to talk to him."

Emily: "That's okay, Dad. Thanks. You go back to your breakfast."

(Emily moves aside to allow her father to leave then waits until he has entered the kitchen.)

Emily: "Sorry."

Zep: "That guy's never going to forgive me."

Emily: "Well …"

Zep: "Yeah … so, you got your car fixed?"

Emily: "Mmhmm, something to do with the wiring. Dad has conspiracy theories."

Zep: "So you don't need a ride then."

Emily: "No, but thanks."

Zep: "Sure. Hey, do you mind coming out to the car for a minute anyway?"

(As Emily does not require a ride, Zep is following his instructions to execute a secondary plan. He must get her to interact with the flowers in order to achieve the minimum goal of emphasizing him as a source of positive feelings.)

Emily: "Oh, well" (she looks down at her feet, which are bare), "I don't have any shoes on."

Zep: "Just take a minute."

Emily: "Why, though?"

Zep: "Something out there I want you to see."

(Emily bends down and puts her hand to her eyes to peer out toward Zep's car.)

Emily: "Are they flowers?"

Zep: "Come out and have a look. Put some shoes on."

Emily: "Oh …"

Zep: "Or I can carry you! Ha!"

Emily: "Zep, I'm just rushing around here trying to get ready. I'm sure they're lovely. Are they for … I mean, are you …"

Zep: "Am I what?"

Emily: "Are you seeing someone?"

Zep: "No! What? No, not at all. No way! No those —"

Emily: "Oh. I thought —"

Zep: "They're for the hospital. I'm taking them to the hospital."

Emily: "Right. You're still doing that."

Zep: "That's why I'm here."

(Pebbles appears beside her mother.)

Pebbles: "Are we going?"

Zep: "Yeah. Sure. Positive you don't want to come out to —?"

Emily: "I really don't have time."

Zep: "Okay."

Emily: "Good to see you again, though."

Zep: "Yeah. Good to … good to see you too."

Pebbles: "Let's go!"

(Pebbles runs out to the driveway and Emily closes the door. Zep leaves the front steps and walks to his car.)

Pebbles: "What are all the flowers for?"

Zep: "Never mind. Get in."

(Zep and Pebbles enter the car and close their doors.)
Zep: "Fuck."
Pebbles: "You shouldn't swear."
Zep: "Put your seatbelt on."
Pebbles: "It stinks in here!"
Zep: "Whatever. Why are you grinning?"
Pebbles: "No reason."
7:58 a.m.: (Zep ends the connection.)

(Initial assessment: This is a disappointing outcome. Because the subject did not require a ride, Zep was compelled to abandon the primary scenario and attempt to execute a secondary plan designed to maintain his chemical status quo in the subject's reward centre. However, as none of his attempts worked to get the subject to engage with the flowers and their scent, he was unsuccessful even in this.

It is a concern as well that the interaction demonstrated a reversal or lessening of the subject's level of affection toward the object. Emily exhibited some warmth but also reluctance and resistance to Zep's suggestions. This may be a result of negative influence from her father or some other factor. On the 1–10 scale the subject's affection would be rated a 4 at most.)

THE FRUSTRATION AND DISAPPOINTMENT rippled through Zep's voice, and I understood. I shared his disappointment. All of this seemed an insurmountable setback. Completing the next stage of this phase had depended on Emily requesting a ride from Zep and that now seemed impossible.

About twenty minutes later, after I'd put away my notes, I reached for my cellphone. Arrangements had to be made to return the car I'd rented for the second part of this stage, but as I was punching in that number the phone rang in my hand. It was Zep.

"Hope, we're on! We're on!" he said. "How far away are you?"

I made him stop and explain.

"Em called me. She said she can't find her keys! Not her main set or her backup set, so she's stranded. She wants me to come get her now."

As he talked I pulled my notes out again.

"It was Pebbles," he said.

"Hold it, what?"

"Pebbles. She stole Em's keys! All the time Em was on the phone, Pebs was giggling in the seat beside me. When I hung up I made her tell me what was going on. She admitted it! She had the keys in her bag the whole time. I wondered what she was —"

"Wait a minute," I said. "Let me think about this."

"Think about what? You gotta get into position."

The immediate impulse was to take the opportunity Pebbles had given us, but was this the best option? Or was there more to gain by having Zep come clean, by revealing to Emily what her daughter had done and giving her back the keys? If trust remained an issue between Emily and Zep, then in openly passing up his opportunity, perhaps Zep might rebuild that trust. But was trust the key? Would its effect be stronger than what we had already planned?

Trust or euphoria, which was the better path to love?

"Zep, do you have the keys with you? Did you take them from Pebbles?"

"I couldn't. She has to put them back where she found them."

He would be able to confess Pebbles' actions and still give Emily a lift, with the possible benefits that entailed. But he might seem underhanded for having allowed Pebbles to keep the keys, so the trust might be impaired. And what other questions might arise?

"Hope, come on! What are we doing?"

"Original plan. Go with the original plan."

"Then get a move on. I can't delay much at this end."

I turned the key in my car's ignition.

Phase 3, Stage B, Log B

(As before the following transcript comprises audio from a transmission via cellphone. However, the timing notations and quotes within this transcript were assembled from memory and should be considered approximate as the principal investigator was also a participant during portions of this stage. Descriptions of action are taken from follow-up interviews as well as, where noted, direct observation.)

8:43 a.m.: Zep pulls into the driveway at 126 Woodcrest Blvd. The subject, Emily Good, is waiting for him on the front steps. She immediately hurries toward his car and gets in as he comes to a stop.

Emily: "Oh, God, I'm so late! Why did it take you so long?"

Zep: "Got here quick as I could. I was on my way to the hospital with these flowers."

Emily: "Okay, well, thanks. Thanks for doing this again. It's so stupid I couldn't find my keys."

Zep: "Yeah, but good for me, 'cause I get to spend more time with you. Hey, you want some tunes?"

Emily: "You know what? I think it was Pebbles."

Zep: "Oh? Why do you say that?"

(Zep turns on his stereo to play Oasis music.)

Emily: "All last night she was sneaking around like a little spy. Every time I turned around she seemed to be flitting out of the room. And then this morning she was in a crazy good mood. She's never —"

Zep: "Turn here, by the way? I'm guessing you want me to take the 290."

Emily: "Oh, I wasn't watch— Why are you going up Parker? It's so much better if you just keep going on Sheridan. It's so much more direct."

Zep: "Tell you what. Ogden's coming up so I'll just turn right there and head back down to Sheridan, how's that?"

Emily: (sighing) "Well, now that you're here, you might as well just keep going up Parker."

Zep: "No, this is good. I'll go east on Ogden. It'll be fine."

Emily: (Covering her face with her hands.) "Fine, whatever. I'm going to be so late it hardly matters. I'm going to kill that girl."

Zep: "You don't know it was her, though."

Emily: "I'm pretty sure. She likes that you've been around."

Zep: "I bet they turn up. What do you think of the flowers, by the way?"

Emily: "Well, there's a lot of them. What are they, freesias?"

Zep: "That's what I'm told. You like that smell?"

Emily: "Mmm."

Zep: "Have a good sniff. Breathe it in … That's it, good. Okay, I'm turning onto Ogden now."

Emily: "I see that."

Zep: "Never been on Ogden Road before. Decent-looking neighbourhood. Crossing Springfield here … And what's this? Melody? Nice name."

Emily: "You're in an odd mood."

Zep: "I should probably step on it, though. Don't want you to be —"

Emily: "Zep watch … watch that car! *Watch out*!"

Zep: "Jesus Christ!"

(Zep slams on the brakes to narrowly avoid being hit by a blue sedan coming from a side street on the left.)

Emily: "She … she just pulled out in front of you!"

Zep: "I know! Are you okay?"

Emily: (Slightly flushed and displaying an elevated rate of breathing.) "Fine, I'm fine … So now she's just stopped. Why is she just sitting there?"

Zep: "I don't know."

Emily: "Should you check on her? Maybe she's an old lady and she had a heart attack."

Zep: "Um. Yeah, I guess. But she could be nuts, right?"

Emily: "Well, can you go around her?"

Zep: "Yeah. I'll just back up a bit." (Zep turns in his seat to look out the back window.)

Emily: (screaming) "Zep! Look out! She's coming! She's got —"

Zep: "Holy fuck!"

(The driver of the blue sedan runs toward the subject in the car, holding above her head a wooden baseball bat. The driver swings the bat against the car, hitting the windshield on the passenger side.)

Emily: (Screaming, crouching in her seat.) "Ahhh! Oh God! What's she doing? Go, Zep! Go! Get us out of here!"

(The woman brings the bat down again, harder, to cause a crack in the windshield. As Zep turns to go around the car blocking their path, the driver swings the bat again, hitting the passenger-side window as the car passes.)

Emily: "Zep! She's trying to kill us! Go!"

(The subject is panicked, leaning toward Zep, protecting her head with her arms. Zep speeds the car forward, around the blue sedan and away from the scene. Beside him the subject displays every visual confirmation of fear response: her eyes are wide, her nostrils flared. Her face is flushed and she is hyperventilating.)

Emily: "Oh my God, my God! She was crazy. She could've killed us!" (She looks back at the blue sedan now behind them.)

Zep: "Holy shit that was wild. You're okay though, right?"

Emily: "I can't catch my breath. I can't —"

Zep: "You're okay, Emily. She didn't hurt you. She didn't even — it's just a crack in the window. You're safe."

Emily: "She was insane, that woman. Why was … why was she …"

Zep: "I'm gonna pull over."

Emily: "No! No! Don't stop! She might be following us. What if she has a gun?"

Zep: "Em! It's okay. Em! She's not gonna follow us. She's *not* gonna follow us. I'm just gonna stop for a second."

(Zep steers to the side of the road and stops. He turns to the subject and pulls her toward him. She clutches his shoulder and begins to weep. After a moment, Zep touches the subject's cheek with his hand. She lifts her head and they make eye contact. Zep attempts to hold this eye contact for five seconds as instructed to facilitate bonding but is unsure if this duration was attained. Before he reaches a count of five, the subject kisses him fully on the mouth. This kiss lasts several seconds and, from Zep's description, indicates sexual attraction on the part of the subject, as would be expected from the elevated levels of catecholamines in the adrenal gland and dopamine activation in the ventral tegmental area.)

Emily: "Zep, get us away from here, please."

Zep: "Sure, Em. Don't worry, okay? Don't worry."

8:52 a.m.: (Zep ends the connection.)

(Initial assessment: A positive outcome. It is reasonable to assume, from the subject's extreme fear response during this stage, that unusually high levels of corticotropin-releasing factor flooded her pituitary gland. The release of adrenocorticotropic hormone from the pituitary, acting on the adrenal gland, would have caused the release of stress hormones in the hippocampus during the aversive event. We anticipate this will positively affect long-term memory retention both of the trauma and the person (Zep) most associated with it.

Given the high levels of catecholamine compounds likely expressed by the subject's adrenal medulla, her emotional response to the object (Zep) in the wake of the event is consistent with past findings (2005, Aron, et al.) and represents an achievement of the stated goal of Phase 3, Stage B of this investigation.

On the 1-10 scale, the subject's demonstrated level of affection toward the object was 8, the level of intense infatuation, suggesting the onset of love.)

ZB Transcript 21

MARCIE, DID I EVER TELL YOU what a great job you do for me? All this, I mean, I know it's a lot of extra work. And you took it on with no fuckin' issues, or anything, and that's even despite all the other shit you have to deal with at the shops because I'm up here, not down there where I should be. I mean, Julio's a job all by himself, right? Total pain in the ass that guy, I don't know why I ever hired him. And ... anyway, I just wanted to say that it's pretty awesome, the job you do, and I appreciate it. And probably I should give you a raise when I get back, hey? Good idea? Yeah, I will, don't worry. And maybe an extra week for your Vegas trip too, how's that? I shoulda thought of that before. And be sure to type this up along with everything else so it's real, right? Like on the record or whatever. Hold me to it!

And you tell Ramone he's married to a star, okay? I just wanted to say that. Make sure he appreciates you like I do or I'll kick his ass when I get home.

So ... just a second ...

Thanks, man. [Unintelligible] That's okay, keep the change. Hey, could you throw this out for me?... And this ... Yeah, thanks.

So ... let me just get on the road here ...

Yeah, um, I dunno ... I guess it's sorta weird up here for me right now 'cause ... on the one hand, it was a good day. I mean, really good. We pretty much did everything the way we wanted to, and everything worked out, I would say, perfectly — just the way Hope drew it up. I think that's probably why she went home early from the restaurant last night. She needed time to think it all through. I don't know that for sure, I'm just ... I'm just the meat that carries out the orders up here.

But this morning it all went sugar-smooth, like my mom likes to say. I mean, I think it's working. I'm not gonna get into the whole thing that happened right now which ... I know I should be saying everything here. I mean what's the fuckin' point otherwise but I guess it ... I guess it was a little *different* from how I imagined. I'm still trying to, I dunno ... sort a few things out in my head.

Not like Hope didn't set me up right for it. I mean, she walked me through it all first thing this morning when I went to her room. I had to get these flowers she'd ordered. Whole goddamn roomful of flowers, it seemed like. Soon as I got 'em into the car it smelled like I was inside a bar of soap.

Just dropped those off at the hospital, actually. Which is funny 'cause that was the story I told Em, why I had the flowers, and then I actually did it. At first I was just gonna find a dumpster but then I thought fuck that. Let 'em do some good, right?

Reception person at the hospital didn't know what to do. "Who are these for?" she said. I said, "I dunno. *Everybody.*"

So I guess that means I'm not a total asshole, right?

Anyway, so ... so this morning Hope laid it all out. She said, Zep, here's what has to happen. And here's what you have to do. She put the whole thing down on paper, like a schematic, and it all made sense. This comes here, this happens here, the whole thing.

She said she had to scare Emily. I mean, I wasn't ... she said she had to get her heart rate up, like way up, and get these fear chemicals flowing around because in the brain they work just the same way as love, or pretty close, right? Or something like that. I don't really know what the fuck I'm talking about.

But so she put this plan together and it was gonna be simple and it was gonna be fast and she promised that at the end of it we'd get some real progress. She said Em would really feel differently when she looked at me. And she did, Marcie. I mean, that's the amazing thing. She really did. I mean she ... she kissed me on the mouth.

And it was a deep one, right? Just like back when we were dating. I mean it was ... it was great. I mean, fuck. It was like all of her, every part of her was right there. Right there in her lips. And I was kissing her and she was giving me everything she had. *Everything.*

So ... yeah. It was amazing.

But ... right before then ... see, Marcie, right before then ... um ... sorry, I think I might have to ... just ... see because see right before then I was looking into her eyes the way Hope told me to. I was looking into her eyes, Marcie, I was looking into her eyes and she she she looked so scared. She looked so goddamn scared. And I couldn't ... I mean that is *not what I wanted!* Never. I *never* wanted that. I didn't understand. I mean, fuck ... I can't ...

[Unintelligible, possibly coughing]

I'm sorry ... wait now, I gotta ... I gotta pull over. I'm sorry ... Just give me a minute.

[Unintelligible]

Um. Fuck, where's the ... jeez, why the fuck did I throw that out, that was stupid! ... Uh, okay. Just ... get it together, asshole.

I mean, I was looking at her and ... she looked like a little girl. In her face Marcie she looked like Pebbles, like when she woke up from a nightmare. Big eyes looking at me and I mean they're the same eyes. I mean Pebbles, she gets her eyes from Em so ... it was just like that.

But ... the other thing she looked like, and I know, fuck, I know this is weird, but I keep thinking about it, I keep thinking about it … last few hours I've been … she looked like my mom! When my dad was hitting her! Comin' down on her with all that … I mean, that look in Em's eyes, that fear. It was the same as my mom …

And all I can think about is I caused it. I fucking caused it! I mean, it was Hope's idea, whatever, I said yes. I said okay. And we're only here because of me. Only in this city because of me. Because I wanted it … So I did it, right? Me. And so I'm no better than my fucking dad. Fucking piece of shit dad.

I'm no better.

[Unintelligible]

Sorry, Marcie.

Sorry for all this … Not what you signed up for, right? I know. Fuck. So, probably … I think I'm gonna … that's it for now.

Tuesday, April 28 (evening)

LESLEY SENT ME A MESSAGE this afternoon. Its subject line said, "Adnan goodbye?"

When I opened it, I expected a long and heartfelt denunciation of my treatment of this blameless man, and a directive to put an end to whatever it was I was doing with or to him. Or I half expected it and fully wished for it, the way a child wishes secretly to be told what to do, because the weight of choice and possibility can be unendurable.

The only thing that gave me pause about the contents of the email was that question mark. That wasn't like Lesley, because Lesley doesn't traffic in doubt. She is clarity and certainty when you need it most. She is the staying hand on your wrist.

It wasn't, however, a set of commandments or an excoriation. It was a picture. It showed a small white box, tied with kitchen string.

Lesley prefaced the picture with a simple message: "A tall, sad man left this for you. I'm to keep it cold until you return."

There is nothing left of the tarts I brought with me. I couldn't throw out the last few crumbs of pastry and filling that had evaded the mould. So I gathered and pressed them together into something the size of a truffle and placed it in my mouth. There was no taste left, except a trace of salt from my hands, but it was another small thing he'd made, inside me.

BEFORE I RECEIVED THE EMAIL from Lesley, Zep came to my room. It had been a few hours since he'd sped off down Cleveland Avenue. His face was red and his tie was loose at the neck, but he didn't appear to have been drinking. He stood in the hallway and told me he'd taken the flowers to a hospital and he hoped that was okay.

It's fine, I told him. We don't need them anymore.

He hesitated for a moment, looking at his shoes, and then off toward the elevators, and seemed to have something else he wanted to say. We were scheduled to meet in the conference room after lunch, but I let him enter. He came in trailing the faint smell of freesias.

At the end of the first bed he sat, stared at the dead TV screen and said he'd been thinking about what we'd done and he was ashamed. He couldn't live with himself if anything like that happened again because of him.

"She was still shaking when I dropped her at work," he said. "And she kept thanking me. She kept fucking thanking me, like I was some big hero instead of a son of a bitch."

It was my fault, I told him. I should have been clearer about what to expect.

"No," he said. "You explained it fine. I just didn't let it sink in." He leaned on his knees and buried his chin in his chest. "I wanted this so bad I thought anything that helped make it happen was okay." And he added, "It's not the first time, either."

I asked him what he meant.

He cleared his throat and swallowed, and looked up at me as if he thought my opinion of him was about to change.

"Back when I figured out something was wrong between me and Em, when it seemed like she might leave me any time, I got a little desperate."

Zep convinced himself that it wasn't him that Emily had grown tired of, but his failure. His playing career had never amounted to what it should have. He'd had a couple of good years and tried to act like a success, but it was hard to do that at thirty-three, riding a bus from Scranton to Pawtucket.

The summer I had interviewed him for the study, in 2006, was his final season in baseball. His final chance ended when the Blue Jays gave him his unconditional release. He tried minor league coaching for a while but didn't seem to take to that.

"I'm not much of a talker," he said.

Then one of his friends in Tampa suggested he buy a small business, and he thought a car wash might work. With the name "Get Clean" he could play off his reputation as a former steroid user. And that had gone well enough that in 2008 he expanded to two locations.

The financial crisis was a blow. By the end of 2009 he had to remortgage his house to keep the business going, and after that it was a struggle. Within a couple of years Emily gave every sign of being a woman who was fed up. Zep thought the next time he walked in the door would be the time she'd tell him they were through. And when a former baseball player is down to his last chance, he can think of only one thing to do that will solve everything.

"I had to hit a home run," he said.

So he launched two more locations, in another part of Tampa. He put money down to double the size of Get Clean Car Wash overnight.

But it wasn't what he bought, or where he bought it, or that the new locations quickly failed. It was the money he used. A few years before, Emily's parents, Joyce and Raymond, had sold a property and made a gift to Pebbles, putting $257,000 toward her education. Raymond had gone to Allegheny University and hoped one day Pebbles would too.

"I took that money," said Zep, his voice gone hoarse. "I stole my daughter's future."

Neither of us said anything for a moment. I heard maids in the hall knocking on doors to determine which rooms they could clean, so I got up silently and moved past Zep to put out the Do Not Disturb sign. When I came back into the room, Zep was walking toward the window.

"I meant to take you up to Beaver Island Park while we were here," he said. "Show you where Em and I used to hang out on my off days when we were just starting out. She said she liked going to the beach. I told her only somebody who'd never lived in Florida could call this a beach. She told me she didn't need perfect."

He was quiet for a moment, then heaved with the sigh of someone just waking up.

"Zep," I said, "what does all this mean? Why are you telling me this now?"

He glanced over at me and shook his head.

"I just don't know what made me think this would work."

"But it is working. This morning went well. We haven't reviewed everything yet, but I saw how she reacted, and I was listening when you drove off. Whatever you think about what happened, I know it got you closer to where you want to be."

Zep said nothing.

"You had a moment together, I heard that. Did you kiss?"

Zep nodded.

"See? You're so close, Zep."

He took another deep breath, turned his face toward the window's light.

"I never … I never told you about this idea I had. It's a personal grooming product. Those are big — you know, high-margin. You understand 'high-margin'?"

"Yes."

"I wanna call it Stay Clean Body Wash. The whole idea …"

With a hesitant but growing enthusiasm, Zep proceeded to explain his concept, and the hope he'd had of finalizing an investment deal to fund development before we arrived here. He'd wanted to be able to show Emily the contract, present her with the proof that he was going to pay back Pebbles' money. He'd thought that was the only way his plan, to make her love him again, really stood a chance. And then it had all crumbled when his friend and business manager Lino had stabbed him in the back.

"Remember that guy in the restaurant?" said Zep. "That was him. Don't ask me what the fuck he's doing here."

I was confused. I asked if he meant the man who had invited us to sit with him and his quiet wife, and Zep said no, that was Rick Kelsoe. Rick had actually offered to help.

"He's throwing a party tomorrow night. He said there might be some investor potential there. He said I should go. And I should bring you."

One of Lesley's mantras to me, when I came to live with her, was always to listen to my body. It communicates in the language of tension, she said. Your body will tell you what you want, and what you don't. It will tell you what interests you, what pleases you, and what makes you uncomfortable or afraid. When Zep told me that the man we had dined with wanted me to come to his party, my body stiffened in a way that made it very clear: I had to say no.

Whatever my face betrayed, Zep noticed it.

"That's okay," he said. "There's no point anyway. I've been kidding myself about this whole thing." He shoved his hands in his pockets and began to move away from the window. "I can drive you back to Toronto tomorrow if you want."

In my mind an image came to me; it was the same one that had played behind my eyes since I'd opened Lesley's email. Adnan was bent at the counter of his kitchen. He was labouring on some small, sweet thing. And this image held the knowledge that soon he would slip his treasure with care into a clean, white box and deliver it to my door, hoping that it would make me understand what somehow, inexplicably, had so far eluded me: the full scope, the wholeness, of how much I meant to him. As if that understanding was all I needed to be convinced to love him in return. As if, in answer to all my questions, that was the proof I required.

But it wasn't. I needed something more conclusive. I needed to know beyond doubt whether real love was manifest, unmistakable, if I was to know whether it mattered at all.

"We haven't finished," I said.

Zep shrugged, defeated. "I just … I can't keep playing games with her."

I was thankful the freesias were no longer here to judge me.

"It's because you're afraid."

His head jumped back. "No. Why —"

"You're afraid that you'll get funding for your idea, and give back your daughter's money, and Emily still won't love you. And then —"

"No."

"— and then you'll know for certain the reason for her leaving was you. It wasn't your failure. It wasn't the money. It was living with you she couldn't bear. You're afraid that's true."

He was shaking his head. I was nodding in return.

"I understand fear," I said. "I understand."

Wednesday, April 29

I KNOW I AM CRUEL. I have come to accept that I am not the daughter a mother would wish to raise. No one has been helped by me. No living thing knows a better life because of me. Those who think I have done them good have been fooled.

My own interest is all that matters, and if I must kill a thing to look inside it, I will. I hold minds in my hands like half-peeled oranges. Emotions are measurable compounds; passion and panic are needles that move. I don't create, I consume. I take what I need, use what I need, leave behind nothing of value. I am larval. Depredatory. God, what kind of mother would I be?

Zep believes because of me, and he will believe for as long as I need. After that, it won't matter.

But while he believes, I cannot distract him. Nothing must get in the way. So things will happen, events will occur, whether I want them to or not. I will go to his party, and I will be, and do, and endure whatever I must, as well as I can.

ZB Transcript 22

MARCIE, I WANT TO ... that was bad what happened yesterday. I mean it wasn't — I wasn't really thinking when I started talking and ... well I suppose you could say that most of the time, right? I guess that's why they tried to keep me away from the mics back when I was playing.

Yeah.

Anyway. Sorry for all that. I'll try to …

Listen, I talked to Hope yesterday and she made me feel a little better about everything. I went in there thinking I was gonna shut it down, the whole business, 'cause I was feeling like … well you know. I pretty much told you.

But, so, she said what's done is done, right? And if we stop now then all that stuff was for nothing. Everything that we've done, everything that happened yesterday with Em. That scare we gave her and the … the memories she's gonna have from that. That'd all just be wasted and pointless. That'd just be mean, is what Hope said, and then I'd feel even worse. And she's probably right.

And she asked me, she said, do I think I'm the right man for Emily? Do I think I'd be good for her? And I said yeah.

You know, I'm a better guy than I used to be, definitely. I've thought a lot about stuff. About being a good husband and a good person and I know — the big thing is I know how easy it is to lose everything, if you're not careful. I mean, it's like love is this thing that's alive, right? And if you don't keep feeding it then it'll die. And that's what happened before. Em and I had love between us and she fed it as much as she could, but I didn't feed it at all. Never even thought about it. And it died. And so that's on me and I know that now. I learned my lesson. And I know there's a lot of guys out there that are still like I was. And she could end up with one of them and go through the whole thing all over again.

But if she's with me then … there'd be a better chance at least.

So Hope said then let's try and finish it. Let's give it another day. Let's do one last thing to see if she'll love me again. And I said okay.

It's not gonna work, me giving Em a lift in the morning anymore. After what we did ... Hope said it has to be something else. Some other reason for us to be together. I said, fuck, I got no idea other than, like, asking her for a date. And then I thought, why not, right? I mean, she kissed me. And like I told you yesterday, it wasn't just a friend kiss. So why don't I ask her for a date?

But, uh, Hope said no. She said it can't be that 'cause Em can't be thinking about it ahead of time. It'll bring up doubts and cause resistance. Hope said the feeling has to sneak up on her. It has to grab her before she's ready for it. Like what happened before, in the car. Just more so.

I couldn't think of anything so she said sleep on it. And that was a stretch because I didn't sleep at all last night. I mean, for a bunch of reasons.

But anyway, Marcie, it's all gonna be okay. Somebody's smiling on me I think. 'Cause, like, I needed something to break right for me and it totally did!

What happened was, this morning, when I was taking Pebbles to school, she said she has a music thing she wants me to come to. She's in the school orchestra and she plays some kind of horn. Basso? Bosno? ... She told me what it was ... Bonsoo? There's an 'n' in there somewhere ... Anyway, some goddamn thing. Maybe it'll come to me.

Point is they're having a show tomorrow night, like a concert, for parents. And she wants me to come ... Bassoon? ... Bassoon ... Yeah I think that's it. So, she asked Em if it was okay and Em said sure, so it's happening. I'm gonna meet them there. I offered to take them myself but Em said no 'cause Pebbles has to get there early.

So this morning, after I got back, I went up to Hope's room. Which I probably shouldn't've done because she fuckin' hates it.

But I did it yesterday, right? So I wasn't really thinking.

Anyway, she opened the door and I said, "Hey! Guess what?"

And she just waited. She didn't play along with me. Which, okay, fine, it was stupid. So I told her about the concert and going to see Pebbles.

She was all business, like usual. She said, "Will you be sitting with Emily?"

And I said, I guess so. That's the point, right? I mean, I'm pretty sure that's why Pebbles wants me there. She admitted to her mom that she took the keys 'cause she was trying to put us together. And they had a big talk. And she seemed to be in a good mood about it, so that's a good sign.

I don't think Em told Pebs anything about what happened yesterday, on the ride to work. Pebs would've just felt guilty, so luckily I didn't have to get into any of that with her.

Uh, what else? ... Hope asked me a couple of other questions, like about timing, when the show's gonna start, when Pebbles has to be there, where it's happening in the school. She thought about it for a second and then she nodded. Said, "Good." And started closing the door.

I said, "Wait! Like, what's the plan?" And she said she had to think about it. And then I asked her about the party tonight at Rick Kelsoe's. I said, "Hope, this is my chance. I mean, if I can tell Em at the concert that I'm gonna be able to pay back Peb's money, that might be the capper. That might be the last piece I need. Everything could come together."

So I basically pleaded with her. I said, "Will you come? Will you come to the party?" I said, "I know it's not what you want to do" — because she didn't look happy about it at all — "but Rick and Tammy, they really like you. They really want you there and if I walk in and you're not with me ... it's not gonna be good. In business, you don't want to start off by disappointing people, right? You want people in a good mood."

She asked me what she'd have to do. And I said, "I dunno, what, you've never been to a party? Just be nice. Be friendly. Talk to people who want to talk to you. Have a drink. Loosen up. Have a good time for once!"

She looked off into space for a minute with this face that looked like somebody'd just told her she was dying. And then she said okay. I said, "I'll pick you up at eight." And she closed the door.

I dunno. Should I feel bad about that, Marcie? I mean, "Go to a party with me." I don't think that's asking too much, is it? And we're both trying for the same thing, right?

Fuck. I never met anybody more complicated.

OKAY SO, THIS IS A BIT different, Marcie. I've got Hope with me in the car and we're heading to the party.

Woman's voice: Should you be doing that while you're driving?

Yeah, it's fine. I do it all the time.

Anyway, Marcie, I told Hope about this whole dictation-transcribing thing we've been doing and she's okay with it. Right?

No, don't just nod. Say it so she can hear you.

Hope: Yes.

Right, because you've been doing your own notes and stuff too. So it's like we've got these two sides to it, which is kinda cool. And you're even taking your notebook with you to the party. So, does that mean you're going to spend all your time at the party writing stuff?

Say it so —

Hope: Possibly.

Right. Possibly you're going to be writing stuff all during the party. Which sounds like a hell of a good time to me. But, whatever. Whatever works for you.

So ... anyway, Marcie, I just thought since I've talked a lot about Hope — you don't mind that, do you? No, she doesn't mind — uh, I thought you should get a chance to hear her voice on this.

You wanna say anything more for Marcie?

No, she's done talking for now. You're not in a very good mood are you? Like, worse than normal.

Yeah, she's usually a little more talkative, Marcie. But, anyway, we've got her on the record now. Not that that matters I guess — *Jesus Christ*! Stomp on the brakes for no reason why don't you.

You see that guy? I swear the drivers here are worse than Tampa.

Okay, that's it for now, Marcie.

And see? I just hit this "send" button and it's gone. You should —

Wednesday, April 29 (evening)

I AM SURROUNDED by eyes.

This is no place for me, but I cannot leave. The way to survive, the way to get through, is to keep my head down and my pen on the page. If I look up, I become too aware of my role here as an object of curiosity. And I encourage them, these people, these men. Give them hope. These men, whoever they are, who want to know me.

Zep is in the kitchen, which is even more crowded than this corner of the living room, at the end of this white leather sofa. I can hear his voice rising above the music, the brawl of noise. I try to focus on his voice. He's excited, selling his idea: "clean" I hear, "clean," over and over, "wash" and "body" and "clean ... clean" like the pealing of a bell. His voice is a church. For me, for now, his voice is salvation and in my mind I beg him to keep talking. While these men stare at me. Come at me. Shout at me.

"What's your name?"

"What are you writing?"

"How do you know Rick and Tammy?"

They shout their identities at me. They are letters and syllables and words with faces. Faces and eyes and mouths.

"What's your name!"

There are women here but they don't care about me. It's the men who approach. Want to get me drinks. Something to eat. I don't look up. I don't respond.

"Who are you?"

"What's your name?"

"What are you drinking?"

"What can I get you?"

"What are you writing?"

"Why are you here?"

They sit next to me. Lean into me. Jar my writing hand. My pen slips on the page.

"Hey! I'm —"

"Hey! What's your name? I'm —"

"I'm —"

"I'm —"

"Hey, beautiful!"

"Hey, gorgeous!"

"Hey, who —"

"Hey, what —"

"Hey!"

When I don't respond they leave perplexed. They leave angry. They leave but they come back in different forms, with different syllables. Different smells. Some of them smoke. All of them sweat. They want to know me. They come in waves. There are lulls. They come back. They try again.

"Do you smoke? You want a cigarette?"

"You have a cigarette?"

"You have a match?"

"Look at this. Got this in Peru."

"See this tattoo? Got this in Texas."

"You got any ink? Is that why you're all covered up?"

"Hey, what's your name!"

"Hey, what's your problem!"

I listen for the peal of Zep's voice. Clean … Clean … Clean.

"How are you doing, sweetheart?"

Where is Zep? Is Zep still talking? I close my eyes and try to hear.

"Are you all right? Are you okay?"

This voice is different. Soft and concerned. This is Tammy. Tammy is here. She is perfumed. She has a tight skirt, a miniature smile. Her eyes are on me and somewhere far away.

"Do you want to get out of this room?"

Tammy takes my hand.

BETTER. IT'S BETTER HERE. Quieter. I am able to breathe. Tammy brought me here, taking my hand and pulling me across the room, through the eyes and mouths, down a hallway. Into a bedroom.

In the wave of relief, I immediately thought, I can wait for Zep here.

Tammy sat with me for a while. She's gone now, but for the time she was here, she sat near me on the bed and she talked. So strange since she had hardly spoken before. Not even when Zep and I arrived, when he dived into the crowd shaking hands and I was devoured by the noise and faces. Or perhaps she did speak and I don't remember. I don't seem to be thinking too clearly.

But now she has unburdened herself of things she seemed to need to communicate to me. Tammy understood me. Insisted she did. And she didn't mind when I sometimes failed to respond.

"The truth is, Hope ...," she said. "The truth is I don't like parties very much. Because I'm quiet like you. I could tell right away when I met you, you're just like me. We're the same. We're sisters, in a way. That's what I think."

Tammy breathed deeply. She encouraged me to breathe. She put her hand on my back to comfort me.

"Is this better? Are you feeling better now?" Her voice was so soft it seemed to emanate from something airborne, too light to bend grass. The skin at the back of my neck tingled as she spoke and I shut my eyes to let it happen. "It's quieter here. It's better here. I could tell you were upset. I looked over at you and I said to myself, she needs me. Hope needs me. So I came over. I came to you. Parties can be hard for women like us, Hope. They can be very hard. Half of these people I don't know. They're Rick's friends. I don't know them. Some of them are nice. Some of them ... But Rick likes these parties, so I do it for him.

"Excuse me for just a moment. Don't worry, I'll be back."

Tammy went out of the room. The sounds of the party swelled with the open door and shrank when it closed and only emptiness remained. Just one small light on a table beside the bed. Pictures on the wall that would take effort to stand and see. When Tammy came back she had two glasses of wine, one for her and one for me. She sat beside me again and spoke to me and I shut my eyes.

"Oh yes," she said. "It's so much better in here." Then Tammy began to talk, in her wafting, tingling voice, about forgiveness.

"Would you like to hear a confession, Hope? This is a confession. I want to tell you. I shouldn't drink so much wine. That's my confession. I drink too much for someone my size. Much too much. I'm as thin as you, and I'm smaller. But I love wine, Hope. I just do. And Rick is good about it. He doesn't criticize me. He knows it's what I want, it's my vice and he accepts it, you see? He accepts and forgives. Isn't that kind?

"That's the key to marriage, I think. Forgiveness. You accept people for who they are. You don't try to change them. Because people can't change, not really. So if you don't like something at first, if you don't understand something, then you must either leave or you must try to understand. And that's the key to marriage. It's the key to love. Understanding and accepting someone for who he is, and what he wants.

"And you give him what he wants. Do you see? Do you see, Hope? You must give him what he wants, if you love him. Love isn't about denial and saying no, it's about saying yes. If you love someone, you say yes. That's what I believe. You say yes, Hope. You say yes. You give him what he wants, Hope. You must do everything you can to help him. You must, and so you say yes."

Tammy looked at me with her faraway eyes and smiled.

"You're so beautiful," she said. She leaned over and kissed me on the temple. Then she pressed my hand and rose.

"There's a bathroom there, if you need it," she said, pointing. "And if you feel like sleeping, it's okay. Just lie back. I'll make sure Zep knows where you are when it's time to go."

Tammy left the quiet and emptiness behind. It's mine now and I wait. I wait and shut my eyes.

ZB Transcript 23

MARCIE IT'S, UH, IT'S A LITTLE after one in the morning and I'm just in the room here and I'm trying to think. I'm trying to think because it's, uh, I'm just a bit worried. I'm a bit worried here. I should probably call you. Fuck this thing I should probably just call you. But it's late, so I don't want to wake you up because maybe I'm worried for no reason. I dunno ... I dunno. Maybe I'm nuts, I dunno.

We went to the party, right? And it was okay. Big place. I mean, Rick … the guy's doing really well, obviously. And it was packed. Bunch of guys from Rick's work, you know construction guys and developer guys. A lot of guys with money, it seemed like. A few restaurant owners. I dunno who else. Some guys who used to play for sure. I knew a couple of them.

A few of them had their wives with them or their girlfriends. Rick had some working girls there too, I think. Just a guess. I wasn't paying much attention, but seemed to me there were a few girls who didn't have partners, you know? They were looking. Good place to look, I guess, all the money in that house. Drugs too. Fuck, a lot of drugs. I haven't seen that in a while. And I live in Florida so that's saying something.

Rick was right too. You know, about it being a good chance for me. I talked up my idea. Rick kept introducing me to guys. I mean, I fucking talked myself hoarse after a few hours. Place was really loud. I dunno why they had to have the music turned up so goddamn loud, but anyway, there were some guys who seemed really interested. I got some numbers to follow up on. I'll send those to you maybe tomorrow. Maybe tomorrow I'll do that. Uh, remind me if I forget okay? Right now I'm just … I dunno I'm just …

I feel like I should do something. I feel like I'm supposed to do something here but I … I don't know what.

There were these two guys I got talking to. They played for the Bisons around the same time I did. Joe Cornwall was one of them and Pete … Pete somebody. Anyway, it doesn't matter.

We got talking, right? Trading stories. I mean, by this point I was happy to talk about anything besides fucking body wash. I mean, I was done selling. Absolutely done. I don't know how guys make a living that way.

So anyway, we're talking and one thing leads to another

and I start telling that story about the guys in the trunk, right? Mercin and Gabbers, piss all over them and all that. And they're laughing. They're laughing these guys. But not, like, as much as they should be, right? 'Cause it's a funny story and they're giving it the haw, haw, right? Like, half-hearted, kind of. And I'm thinking maybe they already heard this story before. 'Cause they played here. Maybe they heard it from somebody else. I mean, it's been almost twenty years. Maybe Rick told them, I dunno.

So I say, like, "I guess you heard this story already." And they kind of nod and look at each other.

And one of them, Pete I think, says to me, "So, were you around for the end of that?"

I say, "What do you mean, 'the end'?"

And he says, "I dunno I just heard it got a little weird."

"What do you mean 'weird?'" I say. "What are you talking about?"

And he starts backing off right away. "Nothing. Nothing."

So I look at the other guy, Joe. I say, "You know what he's talking about?"

He sort of shrugs. Looks over at Pete. "Yeah," he says. "I heard the same thing."

And it's loud, right? So all this is like shouting. We're shouting at each other. And I'm thinking maybe these guys don't want to shout what they know. So I say, "Come with me outside."

And they're like, "Naw, man. Forget it. Forget it."

And I say, "Fucking come with me outside."

I guess they see I'm serious so they kind of mope along behind me while I start pushing through to this door at the back. And I keep checking behind me to make sure they're still coming and they are, and we get outside.

It's a big fenced-in area. Some grass, a lot of stone. There's a pool but it has a big cover over it. Couple of guys out there smoking cigarettes or whatever, so I walk these guys around the pool so we're away from the house.

"Okay, tell me," I say. "Tell me the end."

Pete says, "So, like, you weren't there?"

I say, "No, I was not fucking there. I was with my wife. Or, girlfriend then. They dropped us off on the way back."

Pete starts nodding, saying something about how he thought maybe I was just checking to see what people knew.

Joe says, "So you never heard anything?"

"Fuck," I say. "No. We weren't talking about it. We didn't want to get those guys in trouble. And then it was like a month later I got called up."

So they're both nodding now. Like it's all adding up for them. But I'm still in the fucking dark! And then Joe takes this deep breath and says, "Gabbers said something to me."

"Yeah," says Pete. "It was Gabbers. He was a bit freaked out, I think."

And now, Marcie, it starts coming to me. And I don't know whether it's just my mind working, like figuring out what they're gonna say. Or whether it's bits of things I might have heard over the years kind of coming together. I don't know, honestly. But right then I start getting this idea. Like a door cracking open in my head.

I say, "Something about the girl?"

Pete just nods.

"What?" I say. "What happened?" But I already know. I already fucking know.

"Rick," says Joe. "Rick and that other guy. The big guy."

"Ham Tacada," I say.

They nod.

"What about Mercin?" I say.

Pete shakes his head. He says, "They kept those two guys in the trunk. Kept 'em locked up there while they did it."

"But they listened," says Joe. "They could hear."

"Gabbers said they tried to get out," says Pete. "They tried to kick the trunk open. He was pretty freaked out."

Joe's nodding. "He was."

I say, "Did he ever go to the cops?" They just shake their heads. "And not Mercin either?"

Joe says, "Rick told them to keep their mouths shut or he'd put it on them. 'Cause they were already in trouble, those guys. No matter what happened, they'd have gotten booted off the team."

I say, "But Rick got released, right? Was that about this?"

Pete shrugs. "Might've been. Or something else, maybe."

So I ask these guys when they heard about it. When Gabbers told them the story. They think it was like eight or nine years ago.

I say, "So what the fuck are you doing here?" They stare at me like I got three eyeballs, like they have no clue what I'm talking about. I say, "What the fuck are you doing *in his house*?"

Joe shrugs. Says, "He throws a good party."

And then so Marcie I'm turning away from them, right? 'Cause if I don't I think I might fucking lose it. And my mind's right back to that night. I've got all these images in my head, like of that girl in the front seat. But I can't really see her that well 'cause I didn't really pay much attention to her. I can see the back of her. I can see her sitting there in the front seat. And I'm thinking were there any signs, any warning signals that I should've clued in to?

But back then I was only thinking about Emily. I wasn't thinking about anything else. And then I'm just walking back to the house and I think, I should get Hope, because I wanna get the fuck out of here.

And then I think ... *Hope*. When was the last time I saw Hope? I haven't seen her for maybe two hours!

So I start moving. I run into the house and push my way through this crowd, all these people, searching for her. Last time I saw her she was against the wall in the living room but she's not there. She's nowhere in there. And my mind's racing. It's all over the place. I'm thinking about how much Rick and Tammy wanted me to bring her. Like, why was that? Why did they want her here? And I'm thinking about how she didn't want to come. I made her. She's only here because of me. And where the fuck is she?

I'm asking people, "Do you remember that girl I came with? Did you see her? Did you see where she went?" Nobody knows! Nobody knows anything!

And then I spot Tammy. She's at the end of a hallway. She's standing there minding her own business. Like maybe she's waiting for the bathroom or maybe something else. Some other reason. And when she sees me coming she knocks on this door.

"Where's Hope?" I say. I go down the hall past a bunch of doors. I go right up to her. "Where's Hope? Is she in there?" I go to reach for the handle but she blocks me.

"She's sleeping," she says. "Let her be. She's had a hard night."

I say, "What do you mean she's had a hard night? What the fuck does that mean? Let me see her, I want to see her!"

So I push past her and go in. It's dark in there, it's a bedroom. Hope's on the bed. Middle of the bed just lying there. I go to her and she seems half asleep. Groggy, you know? I say, "Hope, are you okay?" I'm standing there like an idiot. I don't know what to do. She's blinking up at me. I bend down a bit closer and I say, "How are you feeling, Hope? Are you okay? Anything happen to you?"

And then Rick comes up behind me. I don't know where the fuck he came from but he's there. He says, "What's going on?"

I turn on him and I say, "You fucking tell me. Did you do anything? Did you do anything to her?"

He's all like what? What are you talking about? Like he's the most innocent person on earth. He says, "What does that mean, Did I do anything to her?"

"Why's she in here?" I say. "Why's she acting like that?"

"She was sleeping!" says Tammy.

Rick starts acting all fucking offended and making big man noises. "You can't come in here and accuse me," and "I think you should leave," and all that bullshit.

So I push him. I shove him up against his closet. Tammy gives this little scream but I'm just on Rick and I say, "I know what you did. I know what you did, you fucking asshole, you fucking scumbag."

He says, "I didn't do anything! What are you talking about? I didn't do anything!"

And I'm going to wail on him. I swear to God, Marcie, I'm going to give him everything I've got. And there are people there now, like in the hallway, watching. They've heard the shouting or something so there's maybe six, eight? I dunno. Doesn't matter. They're starting to edge in but I'm not thinking about them or anything else, just this asshole and making him fucking hurt and then … and then Hope, behind me, Hope says, "Zep." This small voice she says, "Zep."

She's sitting up on the bed. She's giving me this look like she really doesn't know what's happening. Like a little kid. And she's taking big slow breaths like people do when they're waking up.

She puts out her hand to me and says, "Let's go, okay?"

So I just put my arm around her and get her to her feet. And I pick up her notebook and if Rick or Tammy or anybody else is saying anything I don't hear them.

And we just ... we just got out of there. That's all we did.

I got her in the car and drove back here. And she didn't say anything the whole way. We got to the hotel and rode up the elevator and she was just quiet, staring ahead like she was, I dunno, half asleep or half dead.

I walked her to her room and stood there while she was trying to go in. She was fumbling with her key card. You know, not putting it in the right way, like she hasn't done it a thousand times. So I took it out of her hands and I put it in and got her door open.

She was going in, still hadn't said a word. I said, "Hope, what happened? Are you okay?"

She just looked up at me and gave me this kinda sad smile and said, "I have to go to sleep. Good night." And she shut the door.

So now, Marcie ... I dunno. What should I do? I'm kinda locked up here. You know? Like I can't ... I can't figure out what to do. If you think of anything, you know, when you hear this, call me or email me or something. No, call me.

Okay.

Thursday, April 30

THE NATURE OF INVESTIGATION is extrinsic. It can have nothing to do with the investigator; it is impersonal. The moment bias enters, or wishful thinking, the moment a scientist in the act of inquiry is beset by anger, or fear, or hope, the investigation is rendered useless. Nothing can be believed. No finding is left pure.

On a day of work, in the midst of study, the investigator is inviolate, untouchable. Logic can only be cold.

Zep is confused and concerned. I have no place for his concerns. Nowhere to put them. He comes to me with his questions, his anxieties, his earnest desire to help, and I let them fall off me like shavings. Today, this is the only way it can be.

Phase 4 — Attachment

(Preliminary notes)
The primary goal of this investigation has been a) to resuscitate or reforge the "love" of the subject, Emily Good, for the object, Zep Baker, by stimulating appropriate neurochemical responses, and b) to do so in such a way that the subject perceives her emotions to have arisen spontaneously, without outside interference, and to represent her true feelings.

To the extent that previous phases of this investigation have successfully induced in the subject feelings of warmth, affection and infatuation (however transient), the objective of this final phase is to expand and anchor these emotions with the perception of a special bond between the subject and object. In the clinical expression we call this the "attachment" phase.

Based on our research, we believe that the primary requirement for attachment (assuming the precondition of infatuation) is a shared interest or concern. Further, to induce the strength of bond required for this final phase, within the compressed time frame available to us, we believe that this shared concern must be extreme in nature.

While past experiments, such as those with prairie voles (Carter, 2004), show oxytocin to be a chief neurochemical component of attachment, oxytocin alone drives feelings of comfort and nurturing, the sort of love one feels for a child. Added components are necessary to elevate this feeling to the level of a romantic bond.

We propose to intensify the subject's attachment to the object by activating release of catecholamines simultaneously with the attachment chemical oxytocin. By triggering the fear/excitement chemicals involved during the infatuation phase — epinephrine, norepinephrine, phenylethylamine — in concert with the compounds associated with nurturing, we intend to precipitate in the mind of the subject a profound emotional connection with the object.

To achieve this we must therefore cause both Emily and Zep to perceive a threat or feel fear in connection to a shared concern, which in this case will be their daughter, Pebbles.

ZB Transcript 24

MARCIE, THANKS AGAIN FOR CALLING this morning. Sorry if Ramone got upset with me for dragging you away from making breakfast and all that. The guy's gotta learn how to shove some bread in the fuckin' toaster, you know?

Anyway, I've been thinking a lot about what you said … about letting Hope kind of take — what did you call it? — take the lead on this whole thing. Like take charge, I guess. She's the one who knows what she needs on this — I mean, if anything happened. So I gotta wait for her to tell me. I know that's what you're saying.

Trouble is though, she's not telling me shit. I called her this morning, after I got off the phone with you, and she said she couldn't talk to me. And then I went up to her room and knocked on her door, and she just slid a card under telling me, basically, have a nice day.

I'm serious! I'm looking at this thing right now. "Have a good time with Emily and Pebbles." That's all it says.

What the fuck is that?

I dunno, I'm really worried. I just think, if you've got bad stuff to deal with you gotta deal with it. You can't, like, pretend it didn't happen. I'm worried that's what she's doing. And I'm worried that just means it's gonna, like, get worse for her. Eat at her insides or something and make her crazy or make her … I dunno.

I mean, people do things, right?

Part of me, I mean … part of me *really* wants to go back to Kelsoe's and put him face down in his fucking pool until he tells me what he did to her. But I know I can't do that either. Like you said, whether he did anything or not, that's an assault charge for me either way. So, yeah. That's out for now.

No promises if I hear that asshole did do something, though.

So, the rest of the day I'm just basically gonna hang out here in case Hope needs me. And then when it's time I'll head over to the school for Peb's concert. I don't know what Hope has planned. We haven't gone over anything so maybe she's not gonna be involved. Maybe it's all up to me now.

Last night, before the party, Hope was saying that Emily's probably been thinking about me a lot since that thing in the car. Thinking about the scare, mostly, but thinking about me, too. And about the kiss we had. She said it'd be on a loop in her mind, all night probably. "Obsessive thinking," she called that. One of the chemicals I guess.

So now maybe all I have to do is pay off on that. Maybe this card is all the instructions I'm getting: "Have a nice time."

Guess we'll see.

Thursday, April 30 (later)

I HAVE SPENT TWO HOURS SHOPPING for the clothes of someone opposite to me. Bright colour has never lain comfortably on my skin. It suggests a wish to be seen, to be picked out in the crowd. Sunny blues, pinks and yellows come as naturally to me as they would to a field mouse waiting for a hawk's shadow to pass. But when one has a well-established preference for dressing neck-to-ankle as a pall, colour can function effectively as camouflage.

It also helps to catch the eye of a young girl.

Phase 4, Log A

(Note: This log is a record of findings involving two subjects: Emily Good and Zep Baker. Whereas previously Zep Baker was

a knowing participant as the object of Emily Good's attention, for this phase he was excluded from preparations and had no foreknowledge. This was done to allow the greatest potential for attachment by ensuring that the reactions of Emily Good and Zep Baker would be equally spontaneous, and equally strong.

Descriptions of events in this log were taken from direct observation. The investigator was stationed nearby the subjects, moving as they moved, close enough to discern facial expressions but for the most part too far to hear words exchanged. At no time was the presence of the investigator detected by the subjects.)

4:35 p.m.: Driving her Honda CR-V, the subject Emily Good arrives at City Honors School accompanied by her daughter, Pebbles, and parks in the lot behind the main building.

4:36 p.m.: Emily and Pebbles exit the vehicle and quickly enter the school. Halfway to the auditorium, Emily and Pebbles hug and part. Emily proceeds to the auditorium while Pebbles makes her way down a different corridor toward the classroom where she is expected to assemble with other participating students prior to the concert.

(Note that the investigator was, for approximately ten minutes from this point, unable to observe the subject, Emily Good. However, it is reasonable to assume she remained in the auditorium. Observation resumed at the moment she was joined by Zep Baker.)

4:47 p.m.: Driving his rented Cadillac, the subject Zep Baker arrives at City Honors School and parks in the lot several car spaces away from Emily's Honda.

4:48 p.m.: Zep enters the school and makes his way to the auditorium along with other parents just arrived.

4:49 p.m.: Zep enters the auditorium and scans the audience

already assembled, which takes up approximately a third of the seating. On stage a group of approximately thirty empty folding chairs and music stands await the arrival of the student orchestra.

4:50 p.m.: Zep spots Emily, sitting in the fourth row of seats. He walks quickly toward her, weaving his way through the other arriving audience members.

4:51 p.m.: Emily sees Zep approaching. She seems pleased to see Zep, as if she has been anticipating his arrival. This would be consistent with depressed levels of serotonin caused by a surge of dopamine released in the wake of the previous day's traumatic event.

4:52 p.m.: Emily and Zep greet each other with affection, hugging lightly and kissing on the cheek. Zep takes the seat to the right of Emily and engages in conversation with her. He leans toward her with an expression of concern, which suggests he is asking questions regarding the shock of the previous day. Emily responds seriously at first, pausing occasionally as if the discussion is difficult, but then smiles briefly. There is intermittent eye contact between them.

4:54 p.m.: After several minutes of discussion, the subjects both seem more relaxed, even buoyant. This suggests a decision to put the dark memory of the previous day aside in anticipation of their daughter's appearance on stage sometime within the next few minutes. (The concert is scheduled to begin at 5 p.m.)

4:56 p.m.: A middle-aged adult male in a grey suit, probably a teacher, appears on stage at the side, next to the open curtain, and looks out toward the seats, scanning the crowd. After a moment he leaves the stage.

4:57 p.m.: This same teacher enters the seating area through a door beside the stage and continues up the aisle to the fourth row, where he waves to someone seated in the row. This appears to be Emily as when the teacher catches her eye, he waves her toward him. She speaks briefly to Zep, then stands and makes her way to the end of the row, past the seated parents.

4:58 p.m.: The teacher engages in a brief conversation with Emily. He speaks quickly and seriously. At one point Emily shakes her head. The teacher nods and briefly smiles, touching Emily's arm in what appears to be a gesture of reassurance. He leaves and she returns to her seat.

4:59 p.m.: Emily's face shows concern as she speaks with Zep, who immediately stands and turns, looking over the crowd. He stands like this for three minutes, scanning doorways and the seating area.

5:08 p.m.: An adult female appears on stage and announces a delay in the start of the concert. "We hope to get underway very shortly." This appears to trigger a moment of excited conversation between Zep and Emily. Emily makes agitated gestures, indicating an elevated heart rate. Zep seems to make an effort at calming her.

5:09 p.m.: The teacher who spoke to Emily earlier appears again in the doorway next to the stage and waves her toward him. This time both Emily and Zep make their way past the seated parents. When they join the teacher, Emily makes a gesture toward Zep, perhaps indicating that his presence is necessary or welcome.

5:10 p.m.: Emily and Zep accompany this teacher through the doorway and enter a backstage area.

(Further observation was impossible for the next two minutes.)

5:12 p.m.: Emily and Zep reappear in a school corridor to the rear of the stage, accompanied by the unidentified teacher.

(Note: observation at this time was conducted from a vantage point that prevented continuous visual contact, however, the investigator was able to overhear much of the conversation that occurred.)

Emily Good: (Voice elevated in pitch, indicating stress.) "… just don't understand. When I left her she was going down the hallway to the meeting room."

Teacher: "But you didn't see her enter."

Emily: "I went to get seats. But it was fifty feet. How she could just go missing?"

Teacher: "We don't know that yet. But I want to assure you we are taking this seriously."

Zep Baker: "You better be taking it —"

Teacher: "Sir, we are. I understand you're concerned. We have a protocol in situations like this and we are following it."

Zep: "What is it? What are you doing?"

Teacher: "We have staff on call who are being contacted now. They will arrive shortly and will help to conduct a search of the school and the grounds."

Zep: "What about an announcement? Why don't you make an announcement?"

Teacher: "We will. To this point we haven't wanted to cause alarm but we will do that shortly."

Emily: "What should we be doing?"

Teacher: "You said she doesn't have a phone?"

Emily: "No, I didn't want — stupid."

Teacher: "Do you have a picture of her on your phone?"

Emily: "Um, yes!"

Teacher: "If you could send that to me … This is my number."

Zep: "I'm gonna go look for her."

Teacher: "Mr. Baker, I really recommend that you stay here."

Zep: "— can't just fucking do nothing."

Teacher: "Please, stay with your wife so that we can keep you informed."

Zep: "We're not —"

Emily: "Zep, it doesn't matter."

Zep: "What about the police?"

Teacher: "We will be contacting them shortly."

5:14 p.m.: Emily emits a gasp and begins to cry.

Zep: "Hey, hey, it's okay. She's gonna be fine. Don't worry."

Emily: "But *where is she*? She's been missing for more than half an hour! I can't —"

Zep: "Em, we're gonna find her. We will."

Teacher: "What I'd like you both to do now is come with me to the office. We can get you a coffee or water —"

Emily: "I don't want —"

Teacher: "We'll make you comfortable. This way, please."

5:15 p.m.: Emily and Zep follow the teacher down a corridor and enter a glass-doored office.

(Note: Observation of the subjects was impossible for approximately two minutes until another vantage point was located that allowed visual contact through the glass door.)

5:18 p.m.: Emily and Zep sit together on chairs against the wall of the office waiting area. The teacher brings two bottles of water. Zep takes one, which he opens and drinks. Emily accepts the other but holds it without opening it. Emily appears distraught, her eyes closed, her face damp. Zep comforts her with an arm around her shoulders.

5:19 p.m.: An announcement is made over the public address system: "If anyone knows the whereabouts of Patricia

Baker, thirteen years old, please contact the principal's office immediately. Thank you."

5:21 p.m.: An unidentified male in a dark suit enters the office. He speaks briefly to Emily and Zep. Emily nods. This man leaves the office.

5:23 p.m.: A female teacher — the same who had appeared on stage earlier — appears in the corridor from the direction of the auditorium. She is hurrying, and she is holding the hand of Pebbles Baker. The teacher opens the door to the office and allows Pebbles to enter first.

5:23 p.m.: Emily and Zep see Pebbles and jump to their feet.

Emily: "Oh my God!"

Emily and Zep appear joyous. Each in turn pulls Pebbles into a tight embrace. Emily repeatedly kisses her daughter's forehead and holds Pebbles' face to her cheek. Zep holds Pebbles' hand throughout. Both subjects are laughing and crying. Pebbles appears confused by this attention.

5:26 p.m.: The male teacher speaks to Pebbles, appearing to ask her several questions, which she answers, occasionally nodding. Pebbles shows the teacher something in her hand. She shrugs and gestures as if she is unable to answer one or more of the questions.

5:29 p.m.: A discussion occurs between the two teachers, male and female. The female teacher then addresses Pebbles and the two subjects. Pebbles nods, as does Emily. The teacher addresses Zep and he nods in agreement.

5:30 p.m.: The female teacher leaves the office, accompanied by Pebbles and her parents, who walk on either side of her holding her hands. They walk in the direction of the auditorium.

5:33 p.m.: The concert is proceeding. Zep and Emily take their seats. For the next several minutes they respond to apparent questions from people sitting nearby. They laugh and appear relieved.

5:37 p.m.: The students emerge onto the stage and take their seats. The female teacher speaks into the stage microphone, apologizing for the delay. She begins to explain the program.

5:39 p.m.: Zep and Emily turn their attention to the performance about to begin. As the house lights dim, Emily leans into Zep, and tilts her head so that it rests against his shoulder. She closes her eyes for a moment and appears to cry briefly. She lifts a hand to wipe away tears.

5:40 p.m.: Emily reaches her hand up to Zep's cheek and gently pulls his face toward hers. The two subjects stare at each other for a moment, then Emily speaks briefly to Zep. She appears to say the words, "I love you." Her facial expression supports this observation. Her eyes are wide and filled with emotion, and her demeanour suggests that, for her, this is a profound moment. Zep says something in return that is unclear. Emily then leans closer to Zep and kisses him deeply for six seconds.

5:41 p.m.: As the performance begins, Emily and Zep sit tightly together, their arms entwined. Zep lifts Emily's hand and kisses it. Emily smiles.

5:42 p.m.: Observation ends.

(Initial assessment: The goal of this phase appears to have been achieved. An emotional attachment was observed to form between the subjects.

The primary goal of this investigation — to create in the subject Emily the perception of romantic love for the object, Zep — also appears to have been achieved. On the 1–10 scale, Emily's demonstrated affection toward the object during this phase was 9, the level of romantic companion. Only an expression of love during sexual intercourse would achieve a higher rating, but as this cannot be observed, 9 is the highest possible level.)

I HAD A STORY PREPARED to draw Pebbles out of the meeting room, a small and admittedly frail fiction about a surprise visit by a cousin from Rochester. But it was quickly apparent that I wouldn't need it.

After Emily said goodbye to Pebbles and continued to the auditorium, Pebbles stopped for a drink at a water fountain. I waited as long as I could so that Emily would be out of earshot. But it was necessary to act while Pebbles and I were alone in the hall.

I gave a little whimpering cry. And as Pebbles turned toward the sound, I fell back weakly against the wall.

"Are you okay?"

"Please," I whispered, holding out my hand to her. Of course, as a caring child, she came close.

"I'm severely diabetic," I gasped, sliding toward the floor. "I'm having an insulin attack. Can you help me?"

"I'll get a teacher!" she said.

"No!" I said. "No, please, I need a certain kind of sugar. Please! It's the only thing that will save my life. You must help me!"

"What should I do?"

I pulled out a ten dollar bill and handed it to her. "There's a store," I said, "at the corner of Delaware and Tupper. It's the only one that has what I need. Go there, and ask for glucose tablets. Can you remember that? Glucose tablets."

"Glucose tablets."

"That's right. That's it. Go now, please. Delaware and Tupper."

She looked toward the meeting room. "I have to be in a concert."

I added a wheezing quality to my breathing. "I'll die," I said. "You're the only one who can help me. If someone comes I'll tell them where you are. Go, please. Don't stop or talk to anyone. I only have a few minutes. Just run!"

She ran.

I knew that if Pebbles ran all the way it would take her thirteen minutes to get from the school to the corner of Delaware and Tupper, because I had timed it myself. She would find no store there, so she would spend a few minutes looking, thinking she had somehow gotten the directions wrong. In stealing Emily's keys she had already proved herself to be resourceful, so she wouldn't immediately give up. She would spend more precious minutes trying to find another store, where she could buy a chocolate bar or a bag of candy, just in case. The run back to the school would take her a little longer because the passage of time would make adrenaline less of a factor.

Altogether, once she had sped off on her mission of mercy, I knew Pebbles would be "missing" for more than half an hour. Forty-seven minutes was longer than I expected. It was more than enough time for a mother's worst fears to light fire to her adrenal-cortical system and trigger everything that followed.

While Pebbles was gone I imagined her running, pounding along the sidewalks, her legs and lungs burning, trying to save a woman she didn't know. I could feel her astonishment at how things could change so quickly, and how promises and expectations that had seemed important could suddenly cease to matter. I would have told her, if I could, that there are worse ways to learn.

ZB Transcript 25

HOLY SHIT, MARCIE, WHAT A FUCKIN' day. Oh my God you wouldn't believe ...

I don't even know where to start here. Uh ... I'm just at Emily's place now. I said I had to make a few calls so I'm out in the car.

They're having me over for dinner. Even Ray seems to be okay with it. Emily told him what happened and so ... But you don't even know — so, okay.

You remember I told you about the concert at Pebbles' school, right? So we were there in the auditorium, Em and me. And then this teacher comes up and tells Em that Pebbles wasn't where she was supposed to be and, you know, did Em know where she was? And Em said no, she'd dropped her off at the room. So where the hell was she?

Anyway, it got a bit crazy. Concert didn't start, didn't start. And then they took us back to the office to wait. It was like, past a half an hour that she was gone and nobody knew where she was. They started calling teachers to come in and do a search. Em's freaking out. They made an announcement that Pebbles was missing and they were gonna call the cops. I mean, shit, it was bad. It was a bad, bad scene. 'Cause there are some fucking nut jobs in this world, so anything coulda happened. I mean, look at Hope, right? Fuck, don't think that wasn't going through my mind the whole time.

I mean, I didn't want to let on to Em, but ... I was scared, Marcie. Really scared.

Anyway, obviously 'cause I'm telling you all this it worked out okay. Pebbles showed up finally with a goddamn Mars bar in her hand. She had this story about some woman having an insulin attack and giving her ten bucks to get candy. And then she came back and the woman was gone. It was the weirdest fucking thing.

I said, "Jesus Christ, if you needed candy, why the hell didn't you just go to the vending machine in the cafeteria?" She said she didn't think of it. Fucking kids, man. They'll crack your heart like walnuts, I'm telling you.

Part of me though, I mean, I dunno ... there was a minute

where I had this crazy idea that this insulin woman was Hope. But the way Pebs described her it couldn't've been so … I guess not.

But the thing is, it worked out somehow. Emily was so freaked out and then when Pebs came back she was so relieved it … it was like this tap got turned on inside her. It was exactly like after the thing in the car, but ten times more. It's almost like Hope couldn't've designed it any better.

But what a thing to do, right? I mean … so I don't know.

I tried calling her but she won't answer her phone.

It's good though … Em and I, we feel close right now. And that's what I wanted, right? I mean, this is what I came here for. This is what I asked for, so … however it happened I guess. As long as she's happy.

Anyway, Marcie, I gotta get back. Em's mom — you know, Joyce. She did a big meatloaf for us so … can't let it get cold..

Friday, May 1

Dear Adnan,

I am sorry. Which is pitiful, of course. You won't understand why I have done all this, and I'm not sure that I can explain. But you are so good, and I have taken so much from you, I want to try to give you something in return.

So, let me tell you what I remember.

I remember not wanting to go to the dinner where we met, and then wishing I was anywhere else but there. And I remember that all of those thoughts dissolved from my mind the moment you came out of the kitchen and set your tiny amuse-bouche in front of me. You must understand, Adnan, that I am someone who would never want to be singled out. So my first reaction was mild horror. But you were so earnest, and so quiet, as if you wished no one could see this act but me, that I hurt for you more than I did for myself. And after you vanished through that door, I remember hoping you would come out again and realizing that you were the first man, in all my life, that I had ever wanted to see.

I remember your reticence all that night, your obvious fear of intruding, of forcing yourself upon me or giving me the impression that you might. And your bravery for making yourself known to me despite all that. You seemed to know something about me that even I was only vaguely aware of — that I was afraid, yes. But also that I was angry with my fear, wishing to be free of it, waiting for something to tell me finally it was time.

I remember your eyes, how dark and full of want they were, when you looked at me. When you had not yet seen me fully, and then later (amazing to me!) even when you had.

Adnan, I remember watching you in the market that day, and noticing how sad you looked, like a man condemned to a lifelong punishment for some unknown crime. And then how pained your face became when you saw me, as if I had the power to make your punishment even worse. (I suppose I have.)

We were surrounded by people, and I remember you breaking apart that butter tart in your hands, because you were dissatisfied with the crust. It was such a strange thing to see, savage and at the same time absurd. And almost magical to me, that someone could be so passionate about a piece of food. And so funny that you hadn't thought about what to do about all the syrup you'd released. Or maybe you had and it was irrelevant to you, the mess and stickiness. You accepted it as a natural consequence. I know I'm overthinking it now, but I wasn't then. I wasn't thinking at all. And because of that, when we were outside, and my thumb stuck to you where the syrup spilled, I did something I couldn't remember ever doing before. I gave myself to a moment freely. I decided to let something happen.

And I remember what came then.

You opened the door to your van apologetically, and drove us through the city. I don't know if you were thrilled that I was with you, or worried. You seemed to concentrate only on the task, almost as if I wasn't there. And that was good for me, Adnan, whether you meant it for me or not. It gave me time to catch up with what I'd done, to be okay with the decision I'd made.

I took in everything. The smell of oil coming from the engine, the damp cool from the produce in the back. The way sunlight collected in the dirty corners of the windshield. The empty paper coffee cups, the clutter of old plastic bags on the floor. The way your hands gripped and moved on the wheel. And at intersections, the way you watched for people and other cars, and seemed to be in no hurry. You behaved like someone content to be in his landscape, and not only to move through it. Every minute of that drive I felt as though I was being taken further from my known world, and the person I had been.

At your kitchen, you wouldn't let me help you unload your produce, so I was able to wander around, to peek into things, to draw my fingers over the gleaming steel tables and equipment, to sniff your bunches of drying herbs and touch the pots hanging overhead. I opened doors, found the pantry where you kept your dry goods, and the huge cold closet where you kept meat. I found a room with enormous rolls of parchment paper and foil, and boxes of unused food containers. And I found where you slept, a small room with an unmade bed, a heap of white laundry in the corner and a small table piled with books written in Arabic.

A bedroom: this was something of a shock. I wasn't expecting to glimpse into so personal a space, and for a moment it made me anxious. I pulled the door closed and, when I felt my heart beginning to race, I shut my eyes and leaned against the wall. In that moment, Adnan, I fought an urge to run toward the sunlight, to find an open door and flee. But I knew if that happened I would always be disappointed in myself. So I kept my eyes closed instead, and tried to breathe.

Which is how you found me.

"Hope," you said, "are you hungry?" And when I opened my eyes you were crouched down (How did you know it might startle me to open my eyes and see you at your natural height, towering over me?) and you were holding out a white dish with fresh green figs, sliced into quarters.

"From my family in Syria." You couldn't hide your pride as you said this, and you promised that they would taste to me like honey. But they were even sweeter. I would have filled myself with them if you had allowed it. Instead, you had a plan.

You brought me an apron, bowed your head slightly and said, "May I cook with you?"

I don't know how long we were in the kitchen; it might have been hours, but it didn't feel like it. "We will make tarts and a galette," you said. "Because you must see how pastry should be. And —" here you smiled, "— because it is very much fun."

Every moment of what followed I remember, Adnan, but these things stand out in my mind:

You said we would roast cherry tomatoes first, and so you washed two kilograms' worth and upended them into a large metal bowl. And then you passed this bowl to me. You poured olive oil over the tomatoes and asked me to tumble them in the oil to coat them. I asked if you had a large spoon and you shook your head.

"No, no," you said. "The tomatoes are delicate. You must please use your hands."

Was this a trick? Because Adnan, I think it was. I think you knew what this would feel like to me. You knew, because when I sunk my hands into the tiny tomatoes and began to move them around, coating them with oil, when I realized that this task you had given me would be the most sensuous thing I had ever experienced, your eyes smiled at me. And you said, "Take your time. This is something to do very slowly, and very well."

It was the tomatoes that seduced me, Adnan.

Then we made the pastry. I had watched Lesley bake things in the kitchen, and my mother, but somehow this was different. You had me work bits of butter into the flour, and then your hands joined mine in the bowl, and we worked together, burrowing through this soft, white earth. Then you rolled the pastry, and allowed me to cut it. Everything took a long time, and it all went by too quickly. By the time you began to heat up the oven, my dark clothes were spattered with flour despite the apron.

We made — or you made and insisted it was "we" — tarts with roasted cherry tomatoes and onions and ricotta cheese. And two apple, fig and rhubarb galettes. You called this the "food of many centuries, and many lands." And I teased you for talking like a documentary. Then you rolled out some of the leftover pastry and asked me to set my hand on it, and you took a small knife and traced the shape of my hand very slowly, around my thumb, between my fingers. Then you painted my pastry hand with egg white, and sprinkled it with cinnamon and sugar.

All of these you slid into the oven. And you switched on the light inside so I could watch. It was thrilling to see these simple, perfect things that we had made turn golden, start to bubble, become what they were meant to be. It was like watching ideas form, and marvellous to see how confident you were that everything would turn out as you intended.

Then we ate, Adnan. We sat on stools at the corner of the large steel table. Outside, the sun was going down, the outbuildings and leafless trees along the lane behind your kitchen were turning into hulks of shadow. You poured us wine, and I bit into our first tart. It crumbled between my hand and my mouth and for a moment I was caught up with not looking clumsy and ridiculous to you, which probably made it worse. It was almost as if I had never eaten before. But in a way, that was fitting, because it was true for the taste too. All these things, Adnan — apple and rhubarb, tomato and onion, cheese, pastry — I had eaten in other places, at other times. And yet, just then, in your kitchen, all those flavours and textures seemed foreign to me. It was as if whatever memories I'd had of eating those things had been wiped clean and replaced with this one experience. As if food was as new to me as you were.

And after we had feasted for a while you said, with a small, shy grin, “May I have your hand?” It was on the plate beside me, my pastry hand, golden brown and glittery with sugar, and as I picked it up for you I was overtaken by an idea. I knew what it would mean, and a part of me was outraged at the risk I was about to take. But I hated that part of me, and I was thrilled to stand up to it, after so many years.

I laid my pastry hand atop my own, aligned my thumb and fingers, and offered it to you, these two hands as one. This was a risk for you as well as for me, and there was a moment when you looked the question at me, and I hoped you would see the answer. Though I could hardly believe it myself.

You did, of course. You opened your mouth, closed it around two of my fingers, and gently bit down. I felt your teeth against my skin. Your tongue. And I closed my eyes again. But not because I was afraid.

Adnan, you stood up then and drew me toward you. I felt you press me against you, my body to your chest, my face against the skin of your neck. I felt the contrasting rhythms of our hearts. I can confess to you now that it was the first time in my life a man had held me that way. Maybe you knew. I can only guess what it felt like to hold in your arms this dark, trembling bird.

What comes to me next is lying back against your bed. A trick of teleportation, I suspect, more than memory. I remember your cheek against mine, your mouth. Your large fingers, with traces of flour still in the crevices, beginning to unbutton my blouse. And I remember the sudden fear — not of what you would do, but of what you would see. Somehow I had managed to avoid thinking about that, perhaps because for me the possibility of intimacy with anyone was so remote. I'd never had to think of it before. But just then, as you began to reveal me, my skin went cold, because I knew there was something ahead you could not foresee, and I had to warn you.

My shame made me woozy as I closed my hand around your fingers. I nearly fainted, I think. "I'm scarred," I said. You looked confused. You told me it was okay, that you would not rush me. You must have thought I'd said I was scared. I was. But I said, "No, Adnan. I have scars. I have scars on my skin."

You looked from my face to your hand, closed in mine, and I released you. But you didn't move, poor man, you were frozen. And so I said, "Let me."

My pounding heart made things difficult, my fingers barely worked, but I undid the buttons of my blouse with as little fumbling as I could manage and unhooked my bra. And then quickly, because I knew if I gave it a second's thought I would fail, I pulled them both away. And you could see.

You could see the confusion of white, raised lines over my chest, my breasts, my nipples. Amid the chaos of damage you could see the outlines of a heart, and an arrow, and the frenzy that came after these. The lines snaking into the sleeves of my arms, down my belly, disappearing under my waistband toward my thighs. Here and there you could see words. Fuck, and Happy, and Cunt. You couldn't see everything that had been done to me, but enough.

"I'm sorry," I said, but I wasn't sure that you heard me. You were overcome. I said it again, and you touched my mouth with your fingers, and I shut my eyes because I couldn't bear to see you crying about this thing, this fact about me that I couldn't change. Your tears fell onto my chest and I turned away. Shame and heartache are exhausting, Adnan. I wanted to curl up and go to sleep.

And so we did that for a while, lay snug against each other on your bed, which was a novelty in itself. I think I did sleep for a time. Outside, the sun set completely, and the room got very dark. Then I lay with my eyes open in the darkness and listened to you breathe, and thought back on the day and what led to it, all the things I've mentioned here. You couldn't see, but for part of that time in the darkness I was smiling. I was thinking of my thumb sticking to your hand, of riding in your van, of the tragedy of tomato and onion and ricotta sliding down my chin.

Other images came to me too, lying there, which had nothing to do with you. They came because they always do. They're a part of me, these scars in my head, and they'll last as long as any other. But then I had a moment of awe. I realized that now I had something else to think of when I looked down, or when I saw myself in the mirror, another image to apply to these remnants on my skin. I could think of you crying.

And though that was painful too, and not what I would have chosen, it was better than what I'd had before.

When I turned over to face you on the bed beside me, my eyes had adjusted enough in the dark to see that you were awake, and looking at me. I knew you were waiting for me to tell you something. To explain what I'd shown you, or maybe simply to say that I wanted to leave. I didn't want to do either of those things. I wanted to give you something. So I took your hand and kissed it, and laid it against my breast. I moved your hand over my skin so that you could feel it and know that I wanted you to. And then I asked you to be the first man to make love to me. And you did.

And it was lovely, Adnan. It was what I'd hoped it would be.

It's becoming harder to write this. And I want to be sure to send it while I can. Because it would be so unfair of me to leave you with nothing. I have written all this down so that you have proof that it happened, so that you can look back on it, and know that it mattered to me.

As for why I've done what I've done, you'll want an explanation. I wish I could give you one that you could understand. You see, I felt something with you that seemed so special, Adnan. It seemed a kind of magical thing that could be true only for us. And I was trying to figure out if it was. I was trying to prove it. Because I so wanted it to be, Adnan. I think for a long time I've been hoping for something. I've been desperate for it. Not magic, no, that's silly of course, but something just as powerful. Something big and rare and true. That might have been enough then, you see? It might have been.

But I proved the wrong thing, Adnan. Stupid me. I proved that it's not rare. I proved it can be faked. It's just chemicals, Adnan. It doesn't mean anything. Most of my life my ridiculous brain has tricked me into being afraid for no reason, terrified of threats that don't exist. Now it's tricked me into being in love.

I'm glad we made love, Adnan. And I'm glad I love you. It's such a nice feeling. But I know now that it won't change anything for me. It won't make anything different. It won't make me different. And I'm really so very tired of being who I am.

Hope

ZB Transcript 26

MARCIE, YOU EVER THINK, while you were typing all this out, what an asshole I am? Like what a complete moron? 'Cause if you did, I dunno why you didn't tell me. You should've fired me an email. "Hey asshole, why are you doing this?" Might've done some good, you know? Maybe got my attention anyway.

I dunno I'm just ...

Last night I was at Em's parents' place for dinner, like I told you. Had a really nice time actually. Wasn't like Ray or Joyce said much to me, you know. But at least when they looked at me they didn't shoot nails from their eyes. So that was a real positive change.

Em was warm to me all night. Real warm. Rubbing my leg or my shoulder every chance she got. I'd almost forgot what that felt like, that touching, you know? Having a hand on you, just for a second. You don't do that really, when you're just dating. It's only when you're connected to somebody. That's why it's special. I dunno ... that's what I think, anyway.

To be honest, the whole night, it felt like we were married again. Felt like we were back seven or eight years ago. I mean, our kid was a bit older but otherwise it was just like then. But better actually. Like it was fresh somehow, the feeling we had. Laughing. Relief as much as anything, probably, but ... it was good.

I didn't want to push it, though, so I only stayed for dinner.

And when I was leaving she walked me out to the car and we talked for a minute.

It was a bit chilly and she didn't have a coat on, so I didn't want to drag it out for her, but she wanted to. She thanked me for being there with her, at the school, during the whole thing with Pebs. Said she didn't know what she would've done without me. And, uh, she told me ... the last little while she'd gotten used to seeing me around, and she liked it.

I said, "Yeah, sorta feels like we're Fred and Wilma again." 'Cause that's what we used to call ourselves, when we first got married. She used to make these big roasts for dinner. I think back then it was all she knew how to cook. Somebody said we ate like the Flintstones and we just got joking about it and it stuck. It was kinda this thing we shared.

I mean, we were trying to ... I guess it was mostly me. 'Cause, you know, I didn't really have a goddamn clue what married people were supposed to be like to each other, you know? Fucking Flintstones, that's all I really had to go by. Fred would get into some stupid shit but Wilma'd always forgive him. And they loved each other. Nobody hurt anybody. They had fights but they made up and life went on.

So, yeah ... anyway, it was just a dumb comment and I was gonna kiss her goodnight, and then she said this funny thing.

"I thought something else was going to happen," she said. "But now I don't know."

She was kinda looking off when she said it, like out somewhere. I asked her what she meant, and she just shook her head and told me she had to figure it out on her own. And, Marcie, I got this idea then, I dunno where it came from but ... I got this weird feeling that she was talking about another guy. And then I remembered this thing Pebbles said to me, one of the times I was driving her to school.

She said, "I wish she'd pick you."

At the time, it didn't kick in what that meant. But now I'm thinking it's like me or some other guy. 'Cause "pick" means having a choice, right?

Anyway, I didn't get into it with Em. She was rubbing her arms 'cause she was cold, so I just gave her a kiss and said good night. Told her I'd see her in the morning when I picked up Pebbles for school.

But then this morning I got there late. We didn't really have time to talk. Pebs ran out to the car when I got there so Em and I, we just waved. Which ... I mean, I can't say that was an accident.

See, the thing is, Marcie, I can't ... I should be enjoying this, right? I should be pumping my fist and whooping it up like an idiot. I mean, this is what I wanted! I came here to make Em love me again and she does, Marcie! She fucking does! She told me herself yesterday. So that's it, I'm a winner! Right? That's the deal, isn't it? Right?

But it's like I can't ... you know how when you're running sometimes you can't get a good breath? You can't fill your lungs up? It's like there's something in the way. Right in the middle. No matter what you do, you can't get that air all the way in.

It's like that. I can't ... I can't get the feeling all the way in. The feeling like yeah, this is right. This is it. This is everything I wanted. I can't get it ... I can't ... I should be happy, Marcie. I should really just be happy and relieved and instead I'm sitting here feeling like fucking Darth Vader or something.

'Cause I scammed her, Marcie. That's the truth. The whole thing, it's just a big cheat. And I knew that. It's not like a big fucking surprise to me, but I figured, you know, end justifies the means, right? As long as she ends up feeling how I want her to feel, however she gets there doesn't matter.

But, I dunno. I think maybe it does.

I wanted to talk to Hope about it but she still isn't answering. And the more she doesn't answer the more I think she really did have something to do with that whole Pebbles thing yesterday and that ... fuck, that really pisses me off, if she did. Because what Em went through with that ... and me. It's just not right. And I know she didn't tell me about it because she knows I would've said no. No fucking way I'm putting her through that. But it happened anyway. And it happened because of me. So it's Hope's fault but it's my fault too.

And every time Em kisses me now I gotta think about that. I gotta think about what I did.

Anyway ... right now I gotta go talk to fucking Lino. I told him to meet me at the Steakhouse downstairs. And I'm gonna do what I said. I'm gonna put this thing on the table and record every word out of his mouth and get him to admit that he fucking screwed me. And Pebbles too.

And then what, I dunno. We'll see.

ZEP: "... OKAY. Not bad food."

Lino: "Good chairs. I like the solid chairs."

Zep: "Uh huh."

Lino: "So ... what's that?"

Zep: "That? That's a recorder."

Lino: "Recorder? What do you mean?"

Zep: "For dictation. Marcie set it up for me. See here? I just hit this and talk how long I want. And then I hit this here, send, and it goes right to her email. I've been using it a couple of weeks. Does a good job."

Lino: "So ... it's on now?"

Zep: "Yeah."

Lino: "Why?"

Zep: "'Cause I'm gonna record you. I wanna hear the whole story, you know, what happened with our guy, Hempleman."

Lino: "Why you wanna record it, though?"

Zep: "I dunno. Just seemed like a good idea."

Lino: "Yeah, that doesn't sound ... I don't want to do that."

Zep: "I don't care."

Lino: "Yeah, but ... I have to agree to it."

Zep: "Nah, not really. I'm just gonna do it. So ... you know. Let's talk."

[Silence.]

Woman: "Hi there, can I get your drink orders?"

Lino: "I dunno. I dunno if I'm staying."

Zep: "Sure you are. He'll have a Budweiser. You still like Budweiser? Okay, he'll have that, and I'll have a tomato juice."

Lino: "You're not even drinking?"

Zep: "No. I promised somebody, so that's it. I say something and I stick to it."

Lino: "Okay ... right."

Zep: "That's just me."

Lino: "Right. I see."

Woman: "One Budweiser, and a tomato juice."

Zep: "Right. And put it on here, okay?"

Lino: "No, wait a minute."

Zep: "No, no." [Crosstalk] "... seriously. And ... Miss? Yeah, you can take these back, we won't be eating. Thanks."

[Silence]

Zep: "Well, so far this is pretty fucking boring. You gonna start telling me a story or what? ... Stop looking at the thing and just talk."

Lino: "What are you even doing here anyway?"

Zep: "That's a good question. That's a really good question. You can answer it too. I'm here 'cause my daughter's here, obviously. And I'm doing some charity work, with the Bisons."

Lino: "Yeah, I heard that."

Zep. "What about you?"

Lino: "I dunno, I'm just —"

Zep: "Wait. What do you mean, you heard that about the Bisons?"

Lino: "I dunno. People are talking about it, I guess. I just heard it."

[Silence]

Lino: "What's the problem?"

Zep: "What do you mean?"

Lino: "You're looking at me like there's a problem."

Zep: "I'm just ... Anyway. Let's talk about Hempleman."

Lino: "What about him?"

Zep: "Well, let's see. He wanted to give me money, a lot of money, which I needed. Which you were helping me get. He was all hot to trot, and then nothing, for days. And I can't get ahold of you. You drop off the map, basically. And so finally I call him, and he tells me he's out. And he's out because of you. Because you talked him out of it. 'Bad investment,' you said. That's what he told me. So my question to you, my friend, my close friend, is ... what the fuck?"

[Silence]

Zep: "That sums it up, right? Pretty much? You were helping me, and then you screwed me. And you screwed my daughter."

Lino: "I didn't screw your daughter."

Zep: "You screwed her future."

Lino: "You keep saying me. It wasn't me."

Zep: "It *was* you."

Lino: "Not originally. It was *you* originally. Right? You're the one who spent her money."

[Silence]

Woman: "Here you go. Budweiser here, right? And tomato juice. And here's your card."

Zep: "Thanks."

Woman: "If you need anything else, let me know, okay?"

[Silence]

Zep: "What I want to know is, you didn't have a problem helping me before. So what changed? Why, after getting this guy all excited, why did you turn around and talk him out of it? Like, what the fuck is that?"

Lino: "... I guess, basically, I found out why you were here."

Zep: "Why am I here?"

Lino: "You're trying to get Emily back."

Zep: "Who the fuck told you that?"

Lino: "She did. Well ... she told me you were here, showing up all the time, so I figured it out."

[Silence]

Zep: "You were talking to my wife?"

Lino: "Your ex-wife? Yes. I talk to her."

[Silence]

Zep: "See, I'm waiting here, 'cause I'm thinking maybe there's more you want to tell me."

Lino: "... We've been talking for a while."

Zep: "How so?"

Lino: "... Seeing each other, sort of."

Zep: "Really?"

Lino: "Yeah. She's a good lady."

Zep: "Yes, she is."

Lino: "Yeah, so, we've known each other a long time."

Zep: "'Cause she was my wife and you were my friend."

Lino: "Yeah, whatever the reason, whatever the reason, it's a fact. We've known each other. Period. And I've always liked her. And I've always thought she deserved somebody ... somebody who really loved her. Who'd be good to — oh, sit down."

Zep: "You want me to kick your ass here or outside? It doesn't matter to me."

Lino: "You're such a fucking asshole. You're not going to kick my ass. You're not twelve. Right? Just sit down like a fucking grownup."

Woman: "Gentlemen? Excuse me, I have to ask you to keep it down and stop using foul language, please. Or you'll have to leave. Okay? ... Thank you very much."

[Silence.]

Zep: "They don't like people swearing here."

[Silence]

Zep: "So what does any of this have to do with Hempleman?"

Lino: "Well, first I thought it was worth doing if it meant getting some money to replace what you took from Pebbles. Even though I didn't think the body wash idea was going to fly."

Zep: "You didn't?"

Lino: "No, it's stupid. There's way too much competition. But I thought, you know, if we could figure out a way to get some of Pebbles' money back, it's all to the good. But then Emily said you were hanging around, trying to get back in her life, and then I realized if you could get money for Pebbles, that might help you."

Zep: "It would too."

Lino: "Sure it would. So that meant I couldn't let it happen."

Zep: "Why the fuck not?"

Lino: "... Zep, see ... I really do think of you as a friend."

Zep: "Hah!"

Lino: "No, I do. But you're not good for her. I never thought you were good for her. You're an angry guy. You're always thinking about yourself. Always. You never paid any real attention to her. You never saw how unhappy she was."

Zep: "Unhappy."

Lino: "Zep, she was unhappy for years. For *years*."

Zep: "She told you?"

Lino: "She never told me anything. I saw it in her face. I saw it in her eyes. Every time we were all together, I could tell. Maybe you didn't see it."

Zep: "I didn't —"

Lino: "Yeah, I know. I tried to tell you."

Zep: "When?"

Lino: "A few times."

Zep: "I don't remember."

Lino: "Well, whatever. I did."

[Silence]

Zep: "So you talked Hempleman out of it to hurt my chances with Emily."

Lino: "I know it sounds like a dick move —"

Zep: "Just a bit."

Lino: "I was only looking out for Emily."

Zep: "Yourself. Looking out for yourself."

Lino: "I guess."

Zep: "So, what, like ... you love her?"

[Phone ringing]

Lino: "Yeah. For a long time."

Zep: "What about her?"

Lino: "We'll see, man. We'll see how it goes."

[Phone ringing]

Zep: "I dunno, you might be in for a surprise."

Lino: "What do you mean?"

Zep: "What's 416 ... Toronto?"

[Phone ringing]

Lino: "Yeah, I think so. What do you mean, though?"

Zep: "Hello?"

[Silence]

Zep: "Who's this, Lesley? ... Yeah? ... No I haven't. I tried to get a hold of her a couple of times yesterday, and this morning too, and there ... Okay, so ... What email? ... Who's Adnan? ... So it ... right ... Okay, yeah ... Yeah I'll go. I'll go right now ... No, I'm like downstairs. It'll take me two minutes. Yeah, I'll go. I'm going right now. Bye ... I gotta go."

Lino: "What's going on?"

Zep: "I gotta go."

Lino: "Wait, what about your thing?"

Zep: "Oh yeah."

[Unintelligible. Sounds of rustling fabric]

Lino: (muffled) "What's happening?"

Zep: "I dunno."

Lino: "Okay, we'll talk later, I" [too faint]

[Sounds of rustling, movement]

Zep: "Excuse me ... Excuse me ... Look out, please. Look out. *Please*! ... Fuck ..."

[Sounds of rustling, footsteps]

Zep: "Hi, sorry hi, can I have a key card for room 609 please?"

Man: "Sir, I'm with a cust—"

Zep: "Please, it's an emergency. I need a key to room 609 now."

Man: "Your name?"

Zep: "Zep Baker. Just give me a key."

Man: "That room is registered to Hope Riopelle."

Zep: "I know. I'm paying for the room. Give me a key."

Man: "I can't do that —"

Zep: "*Give me a fucking key*!"

Man: "Sir, without permission from —"

Zep: "Fuck you! Never mind. Never mind."

[Sounds of rustling]

Zep: “Excuse me! Hold that please hold that! ... Thanks. Six please. ... Jesus, push the ...”

[Elevator sounds]

[Silence]

Zep: “Come on come on come on.”

Woman: “Some people are always in a hurry.”

[Silence]

[Elevator sounds]

Woman: “This is us, Margaret. Excuse us please ...”

[Elevator sounds]

Zep: “*Fuck*!”

[Elevator sounds]

[Unintelligible]

[Rustling sounds]

[Sound of banging]

Zep: “Hope! Hope! Are you in there?”

[Banging]

Zep: “Hope! Answer the door! Lesley called me and she’s worried. *Hope*!”

[Banging]

Zep: “Hey! Hey, you! Let me into this room.”

[Unintelligible]

Zep: “You’ve got a key, you’ve got a master key. Let me into this room! Now! It’s a fucking emergency!”

[Unintelligible]

Zep: “Fine, I’ll break it down.”

[Rustling sounds]

[Sounds of impact, exertion]

Zep: “Fuck. I can’t —”

[Sounds of impact]

Zep: “*Let me into the fucking room! Now*!”

[Sounds of screaming]

Zep: "Where is it? Where's your fucking key? Give it to me ... Is this it? Is this it? ... Fuck ... *Hope*! Jesus Christ how do you, how do you ... wrong ... okay. Hope! Hope! Where — oh, fuck. Hope! Jesus fuck. Oh shit no fuck fuck fuck ... *Call 911! Call 911*! Please now *please*!

"Oh God oh God Hope. Oh Jesus, what'd they do to you? What'd they do to you? Jesus Jesus Jesus come on Hope come on. I gotta ..."

[Unidentified sounds]

[Rustling, thumping sounds]

"I'm sorry, I gotta ... here so ... here ... I gotta do this ... come on come on come on."

[Unidentified sounds]

"Come on, Hope. Here ... we gotta ... we gotta move. Here ... *fuck* ... okay ... Help! Help us! Help ..."

[Sound of door closing]

[Voices but too faint to make out]

[Silence]

ZB Transcript 27

OKAY, SO ...

Jeez I'm out of practice here. I don't know how to get going.

Uh, so ... it's May ... seventh? Yeah, May seventh. Thursday. Uh ... I haven't been able to do any recordings since last Friday 'cause the police had my thing. My recorder. I guess it was in Hope's room, which ... I dunno, it must've fallen out when I was trying to put my jacket on her.

That was ...

Anyway, they searched the room and took everything that didn't belong to the hotel. So I had to fill out some forms to get it back. Had to prove it was mine first, which was easy 'cause my voice was on it. They were interested in that last recording too, once they knew it was on there, so that took a couple of extra days.

That's a lot on the fucking recorder though so I dunno, maybe just skip all that, Marcie. I'm just talking bullshit here; this is all useless. I dunno what the hell I'm doing.

I should really be talking about Hope ... Um ...

So she's ... you know, she's not good. I mean, she's alive, but she's still in the ICU. The doctors are saying she's lucky. The only reason she survived — I mean, she took enough drugs to do the job, and they probably would have eventually — but her temperature was way low, lying in that freezing bathtub, and her heart slowed down or something. That gave her a bit more time. I'm not family so I'm not getting all the details. Her mother is here. She's kinda suspicious of me, though. I guess that makes sense. Lesley's here too — they drove down together.

And the guy Hope wrote — uh, Adnan. He's here. Big fucking guy, taller than I am. It was a good thing he figured out to call Lesley when he got that email or else, you know ... fuck. They said she'd been in the water for over fourteen hours.

They weren't going to let him see her when he first got here. Adnan. I guess Hope's mom'd never met him so she wasn't ... but the thing, the thing is, it turns out Hope was pregnant, and she ... she lost the baby. They told me that much pretty early. I guess maybe they thought I was the father. And so ... yeah.

But I was talking to Lesley and she said it was Adnan's. The baby. And then he got here and nobody was telling him. Lesley didn't want to say anything because she said she'd promised Hope. She said Hope should tell him. I think she was kind of holding on to that, like the idea that Hope'd live, right?

But, so, nobody was telling Adnan. And he didn't know who the fuck I was then so it couldn't be me telling him. I mean ... it was better coming from a doctor, right? So I tried to tell these people, like, this guy's the father. Give him the news! Jesus Christ, he deserves to know, right? And let him into the fucking room!

Anyway. It took a while but I finally got somebody to listen to me. Adnan was pretty messed up when they told him everything. That was hard, seeing that. 'Cause he had no clue. He didn't know she was pregnant. It all came at him at once. He didn't know.

I got him out of the hospital for a couple of hours. This was Monday, I think. Yeah, Monday. He'd been here for two days, not sleeping. He looked like shit. So I said let's go for a walk. Nothing was changing with Hope. He didn't want to go but the nurse told him he wasn't gonna miss anything. So I said come on, let's take a fucking walk. I would've said a beer but I didn't know if the guy was Muslim so I figured maybe I shouldn't chance it.

Anyway, I got him outside at least. By then I'd already made him understand I wasn't like a rival or anything. I wasn't some guy who was after Hope. We're friends and we were here working together, that's all. He was clear on that. I hadn't really gone into what we were working on because I figured that's ... you know, that's a trickier conversation. And it didn't really matter. He had enough to think about.

We didn't say much for a while. There's a park a couple of blocks from the hospital so we headed over there. It was kinda cloudy, but it was warm enough.

There were some tennis courts but nobody was playing so we walked past that ... got into this treed area. The leaves are starting to come now. You know, that nice pale green. Something about being around trees here in the spring, I dunno ... we don't get much of it in Tampa. It's nice.

I asked the guy what he did and he said he was a chef. A caterer. Said that's how he met Hope. "I cooked for a party and she was there," he said. He said she looked lonely. Kind of keeping to herself. "So I make her something special, and she smiled." He sort of brightened up a little when he said that. "So I think, 'Good job, Adnan. Do it again.'" He said his whole goal that night was to make her smile.

I asked if he'd known her a long time. He shook his head. He said they'd spent an afternoon and evening together, that was all. I was kind of surprised. But he shrugged. He was quiet. He said, "I think I have always known her."

Then he asked the question I should've expected ... I guess I did expect it. You know, what were she and I doing here together? And somewhere in the back of my mind I'd been trying to figure a way to say it so it wouldn't ... you know, so I wouldn't sound like a nut job or something.

I told him about Emily, about how we'd been married and that I still love her and I've been trying to get back with her. And I said Hope was helping me. I left it at that and waited for a minute, to see if that would do it. I hoped it would. But you could see it rolling around in his head. And he looked at me.

"How?" he said. "What were you doing?"

And I didn't ... for a second I just stood there.

I mean, I'm looking at this guy, and there's ... I dunno, Marcie, there's something about him. He's a big, simple guy. He's real, or something I can't ... I dunno how to say it. After one day with a girl, he's there with her at a hospital. And she might die, and he's lost a kid and ... and he's the guy she wrote her letter to, her last letter, right? Her last letter. Whatever she needed to say, he was the guy she wanted to say it to.

One day ... and now it's everything. For both of them.

Then I look at me and Emily, and all the years, right? All the years, and all the chances I had to, I dunno, to connect with her like that. To make something ... I don't even know what, but something *more*, right? Just something more than it was. Whatever it needed to be to last. To be worthwhile or just, you know ... just good. Just, fucking, good.

I mean, it could've been that, I think. It could've.

But, so, what was I doing all that time? That's what I keep thinking about. These guys had one day. We had years. And I know Em was trying, so what the fuck was I doing?

And then so ... after I've used up all my chances. Now I'm here trying to just, like, make it happen. Snap my fingers. Trying to pull a fast one, basically, right? I'm playing a trick on her, is what I'm doing. Like that's supposed to be good and and and, you know, *real*. Like that's something to be proud of, like that's true, right. It's supposed to be true. That's the thing they say, right? Fucking true love. I never knew what that meant. *True* love. What the hell is that? Just a goddamn greeting card. *True* love.

But now here I am, and ... I'm proving it. I'm *proving* there's a difference. I'm the fucking poster boy of love that isn't true. I'm the opposite guy. I'm the *lying* love guy. I mean ...

Fuck, I was looking at Adnan standing there, waiting for an answer — What were Hope and I doing here? — and all I wanted to do was throw up.

So ... anyway ... I had to tell him something. I said I had this problem I needed to solve — how to make my ex-wife love me again. And since Hope was the smartest person I knew, I figured she'd know how.

Adnan took that in for a minute. Man, his eyes were ... I dunno. He looked beat up or something. He shook his head. "Hope is very wonderful, very smart," he said. "But I do not think she understands love."

We walked back to the hospital and checked on her. I gave Adnan my hotel key in case he wanted to go take a shower or something.

Lesley was in the ICU with Hope's mom. She came out when she saw me. She seems to like me for some reason. Or maybe she's that way with everybody, I shouldn't take any credit. I mean, she's the kind of person I probably would've never spent two seconds talking to before. She has a real hippie vibe going, if you know what I mean. Kinda this big, momma type of person, right? Like she's made out of thick, warm blankets. Just being around her you feel calm in a way, which ... I dunno, that might drive me crazy after a while, but ...

Anyway, she was nice to me from the minute she got here, which helped balance out all the side-eye everybody else was giving me. When she came out of the room she asked how I was doing. Like that mattered, right? Like who the fuck cares how I'm doing, I'm not lying in a bed with tubes, right? Like I'm fine so, whatever.

She asked how things were with Emily. She already knew a bit about what Hope and I'd been doing. I mean, I hadn't said much, but she knew enough.

I kinda shook my head.

"Have you seen her in the last few days?" she said.

I kind of laughed, 'cause, I dunno. I dunno why I laughed. She was looking at me. I was on edge or something. The whole thing with Adnan. Hope's in the ICU, it was just like, fuck. And she's looking at me. And waiting, right? Just waiting. Everybody's fucking waiting for me to speak all of a sudden. And I'm just shaking my head like an idiot.

After a minute she says, "What's going on, Zep? What are you feeling?" And she's kinda, like, zeroed in on me or something. So, I dunno, I laughed again. I said, you know, "I feel like a fucking criminal, if you want to know the truth."

She didn't say anything. Just stood there for a bit and then gave my arm a rub and went back into the room. So ...

SORRY, MARCIE, I SAW THE doc coming and I thought he had some news but it was nothing. This one doc, he walks around here like he's got cameras following him around or something. Guy pisses me off. Anyway. After that little thing with Lesley I got in my car and drove over to Emily's work. It was after lunch, so I figured she'd be there.

They told me to wait outside for her, so I stood in the parking lot for a few minutes. And then she came out with a bit of steam. You know, wondering where the hell I'd been since Friday, why

I'd totally disappeared, hadn't been picking up Pebbles. I said there'd been an emergency and I'd been spending a lot of time at the hospital.

She said, "I know that's a lie, Zep. You aren't doing any charity work at the hospitals."

I asked her how she knew that, and she said somebody'd looked into it and told her. Lino, I said, and she admitted it. So I asked her. I asked her straight out if she was seeing him.

"I was," she said. "Then you landed on my doorstep."

That made me grin. I said, "Like yesterday's news."

And then she wanted to know what was going on. This whole two weeks. Why was I really here?

I took this big breath and I said, "For you."

And then I told her basically the whole thing. Not everything, I mean ... I couldn't tell her about what happened in the car, and I don't even know for sure what happened with Pebbles at the school. But I said I'd been trying to get into her brain again. Trying to get her to think about me, and start having feelings for me, maybe even love me, like she used to.

"Why, Zep?" she said. "Why haven't you just moved on?"

And the thing is, Marcie, I didn't even know the answer to that until I opened my mouth. I had no idea why, except that I'd missed her. So much, you know?

But what I said was that I'd realized something. I said I'd failed at everything I'd ever done — baseball, business, whatever it was, I'd never done anything close to what I wanted to do. But it was okay, none of that bothered me, because I knew I'd tried.

I said the only thing that really got to me, the only thing that pressed on me and wouldn't let me sleep, was losing her. Because I knew, when it came to her, I hadn't tried hard enough.

But I knew I'd gone about this whole thing all wrong.

So ...

That was it, basically. She said, "What happens now?"

I said as soon as I could I'd be going back to Tampa. I told her I was gonna sell the house. Some of the value's come back on it finally, so whatever money I get, I'll put it into an education fund for Pebbles. And I'll keep adding to it until I've replaced what I took.

She said, "What about us? Now that you're in my brain again."

I told her if she thought Lino was the right guy for her, even though he's an asshole, then she should be with him. She should be with whoever was gonna do what it took to make things work. And I said, you know, the guy was willing to trash a good friendship for her, so that's probably a point in his favour.

I said the main thing was, she deserved somebody who wasn't going to screw her around and play games with her feelings, and probably that ruled me out. And if it did, then I could accept that. I told her I had more love for her now, and I felt closer to her than I ever did before, 'cause for a while at least, I'd thought about what she was feeling. Not just me. So even if nothing else happened for us, I was glad about that.

Then I kissed her and said goodbye. And I've been at the hospital pretty much ever since.

So I guess that's it for now, Marcie. See you soon.

Think positive thoughts about Hope if you can.

Uh, say hi to Ramone for me.

Okay.

I'll just shut up now.

Tuesday, May 19

LESLEY HAS LEFT ME ALONE for the afternoon. She brought me tea and said she was going out, without saying where. It's a trial run, of sorts. I earn the time I'm allowed to myself. Time with my thoughts, my intrusions and my intentions. If I can last an hour, I'm given two. In that, it's very much like life itself. Surviving one day means having to live another.

I try not to think about it too much. For now, not thinking too much about anything is as high as my goals reach. But at least I can put a checkmark beside "having goals." It's a beginning.

Tonight, Adnan will come over, and he will cook dinner for the three of us. It will involve saffron; that's all he's saying. But I like saffron, so that's something to look forward to. Having things to look forward to: checkmark.

Adnan is not going to Montreal, at least not now. He told me this a week ago in the hospital, on one of the rare occasions when my mother allowed us to be alone. I had been conscious for four days. There had been meetings, assessments. It was clear I would not immediately expire, certainly not thanks to this latest event, and people were starting to pose "what now?" questions. These were questions about continuing treatment, ongoing support, living arrangements. My mother initially proposed that I move back with her. I said, using essentially these words, that I would rather die. And so, other options were entertained. Adnan's decision to stay in Toronto to help watch over me was ultimately a condition of my release.

He doesn't seem to mind, although I don't press too deeply. For now, I would rather just assume that he is content with his decision. I would rather take his happiness, on this matter, for granted.

On another matter, on the loss of our child, the almost-life I'd never had the courage to mention, he insists he has forgiven me. Or, to be more precise, he insists there is nothing to forgive. I don't think that's at all true, but I don't know quite how to argue my case. Or whether I'm even entitled to one. I don't know how to insist he should mourn the loss of someone to love, when he hadn't known that someone existed. I don't know how to ask for company in this grief, when it is a grief I myself had intended to avoid.

It was the morning of May 8th when I opened my eyes. I think I had approached consciousness once or twice before that and retreated. But when I finally came to the surface and realized what it meant, it wasn't a disappointment. It wasn't a relief, either. In deciding to leave where I was, I hadn't thought about where I would be. When I came to I simply thought, all right. This, now.

Every solution begins in a neutral state.

A few days later, with all the decisions decided and the arrangements made, we went home as a convoy, my mother in her car, me in the van beside a stoic Adnan. Lesley went with Zep, who was planning to return his car and begin his trip to Tampa almost immediately. I had asked her, though, to see if she could make him delay his departure for a little while. And so, during the drive, she said something to him about the value of constancy amid a delicate transition. That gave us a few extra days.

I didn't see him for more than a few hours on any of those days, but it felt good, somehow, knowing he was still in the city. And when he came over to the apartment, I enjoyed watching Lesley adjust to him. At the hospital he'd kept himself to the background. I would see him standing in the hall, or sitting in a chair beneath a window, an almost bashful presence. Here and now, he was becoming more the Zep I'd known, filling the room. Lesley would look at me and rattle her head.

He was anxious, I knew, to return to Tampa. He talked about putting his house up for sale, and wanting to make plans for

Pebbles' summer vacation. Somewhere in Europe, he thought. Maybe he'd show her Germany. He hadn't been there since his honeymoon.

On his last day, we took a walk together, ostensibly for coffee, but more to get out of Lesley's hair. And it seemed right, somehow, to be just the two of us again. It was warm, and we found a place that had set up its patio with tables and chairs to take advantage of the sun. There was a table free, and so I claimed it while he went inside and ordered.

It took me a minute to realize that I was surrounded by couples at three of the tables, and another minute to gather in the strange, new fact that I had no curiosity about any of them. When the most tentative of these twosomes got up to leave, a man and woman a little younger than me, I watched but wasn't pulled to follow.

Zep noticed me looking, though, as he sat down. "Phase two, you think?"

"Definitely phase two," I said.

He smirked. "They got no idea what's coming."

In the hospital, it seemed that almost every conversation had had to do with me and the state of my well-being, and in any case, Zep and I had rarely found ourselves alone. So we'd talked hardly at all about what we had done together, about the status of his relationship with Emily, or how he felt now, about any of it. Somehow it seemed unnecessary. He had an air of resolution about him that told me most of what I needed to know.

It was on one of those mornings in my green-tiled room, as Zep offered to get someone a sandwich or sat with Lesley playing cards, that I finally realized something about him. I understood that of all the people I knew who had loved someone, he had done so most openly. Everything about Zep was brazen and unvarnished, unconcerned with appearance or accepted practice, and this was true of the way he loved. Whether or not it had always been so, it was when I knew him. He accepted his need to love and be loved, admitted it out loud, and was willing to do anything for it. He was like Dickens' hungry boy, risking shame and rebuke, holding out his bowl and saying, "Please, sir, I want some more."

When it came to love and how he pursued it, Zep may have been rash or wrongheaded — well that is almost certainly true — but at least he tried something. At least he was fearless. And just when I should have been looking for such an example, someone to show me that it was safe, or at least worthwhile, to step out of the shadows without concern for the consequences, to lift up my face and let the full possibility of love fall on me, I didn't need to look. He came to me.

The young couple was gone. Zep was unwrapping a pair of scones for us. I pried up the plastic tab of my coffee and asked if I would ever see him again.

The sun was hitting his eyes. He squinted at me and grinned.

ACKNOWLEDGEMENTS

I am grateful to Alison Fleming, Professor Emerita at the University of Toronto and a researcher in behavioural neurobiology and genetics, for vetting the essentials of the neuroscience used in this book (if not their unorthodox application). Thanks as well to clinical researcher Daeria Lawson and research assistant Aya Dudin for taking the time to show me around the vivarium.

Many thanks to the friends who read early drafts of the manuscript and provided wise and encouraging feedback, including Angie Abdou, Amanda Leduc, Joe Kertes, Janet Somerville, and Julie Wilson.

I am ever grateful for the funding support of the Canada Council for the Arts and the Ontario Arts Council.